The Wish-List Wife

"I'm matchmaking you, not dating you!" Haley flung out.

"So even though our kiss was scorching, you won't ever date me because you don't trust your judgment?" Adam asked with a degree of disbelief.

"Exactly!" she proclaimed, glad that he finally understood.

"I could modify the wish list," Adam offered.

"The list stands," insisted Haley, hands on hips. "I've memorized it and I'm going to find you someone who meets *all* the criteria."

"But not you."

"I don't meet *any* of the criteria."

"So you want me to forget all about the possibility of us and move on to other women."

"Absolutely. There is no *us.*"

The smile was back. He shifted forward, looking her deep in the eye. His touch launched a buzz that sang up her arm, swirling into a desire that zapped her strength.

He cocked his head, his lips parted. "I dare you to kiss me…and *then* say that."

For more, turn to page 9

Mad About Mindy…and Mandy

"Kiss me again," Mindy heard herself whisper.

Benton's mouth sank onto hers, and she kissed him with all the passion that had likely been hibernating inside her for years.

This was wrong. Her behavior had been intended to appall him, not entice him. But right and wrong seemed distant ideas at the moment.

He broke the kiss and stared at her. "Let's get out of here. Go to my place."

Abort! Abort! Every alarm in her head went off, screaming at her, urging her to do something to keep this situation from getting any more out of control.

Mindy pushed away from him, but he gently curled a hand around the back of her neck, halting her retreat.

"Benton, I…"

When she hesitated, he tenderly grazed his fingertips over her collarbone. "Yeah, honey?"

She swallowed, determined to try again. "I… Let's go back to your place."

For more, turn to page 197

HARLEQUIN DUETS

ISBN 0-373-44164-9

Copyright in the collection:
Copyright © 2003 by Harlequin Books S.A.

The publisher acknowledges the copyright holders of the individual works as follows:

THE WISH-LIST WIFE
Copyright © 2003 by Barbara Dunlop

MAD ABOUT MINDY...AND MANDY
Copyright © 2003 by Toni Herzog

The Wish-List Wife

Barbara Dunlop

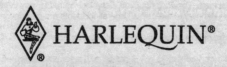

HARLEQUIN®

TORONTO • NEW YORK • LONDON
AMSTERDAM • PARIS • SYDNEY • HAMBURG
STOCKHOLM • ATHENS • TOKYO • MILAN • MADRID
PRAGUE • WARSAW • BUDAPEST • AUCKLAND

Dear Reader,

I always thought I'd make a terrific matchmaker. I love weddings, first dates, first kisses—and they don't even have to be mine. There are few things in life more satisfying than introducing two people and knowing from the sparkle in their eyes that it's the start of something big.

I happen to think single people are just biding their time until that perfect match comes along. Oh, I have some single friends who insist they're happy that way. But just between you and me, I know they're in denial. So I'm keeping my eyes open anyway.

I hope you enjoy meeting Haley, my tenacious matchmaker in *The Wish-List Wife*. She insisted she was perfectly happy being single. But I knew she was in denial.

I'd love to hear from you at bdunlop@yknet.ca or through my Web site at www.barbaradunlop.com.

Best wishes,

Barbara Dunlop

Books by Barbara Dunlop

HARLEQUIN DUETS
54—THE MOUNTIE STEALS A WIFE
90—A GROOM IN HER STOCKING

HARLEQUIN TEMPTATION
848—FOREVER JAKE
901—NEXT TO NOTHING!

For Jane Porter Gaskins
I never could have done it without you.
But didn't you say there'd be beer?

1

"I'VE DECIDED TO BECOME a lesbian." Haley Roberts hooked her glue-sticky thumbs into the belt loops of her worn blue jeans and took a step back from her kitchen wall. There she could get a good look at the seam of her new wallpaper.

"Excuse me?" Her older sister Laura looked up from the sink where she was scrubbing dried glue off her hands.

"A lesbian," Haley repeated, tilting her head sideways and considering the matchup of a cloverleaf and stem. She'd given this a lot of thought. Getting men out of her life completely would solve so many problems.

"That's ridiculous." Laura shut off the water and shook the excess droplets from her hands. A cool, summer night breeze gusted in through the kitchen window, dissipating the smell of glue.

The seam was almost invisible, Haley decided. She rubbed her palms together and the rubbery adhesive balled up into little gray cylinders.

"It's not ridiculous," she said, rattling her way

into the hardware store bag for the next roll. She was through with men. She'd just moved into a brand-new house in a brand-new town. It was time for a fresh start.

"Being a lesbian is a perfectly valid lifestyle choice these days," she asserted.

"Sure it is," Laura agreed. "For actual lesbians."

"What *is* a lesbian?" Haley brandished the vinyl roll in her sister's direction for emphasis. "If not a woman thoroughly sick and tired of relationships with men?"

She reached up and ripped the cellophane off with a flourish. She'd chosen a beautiful wildflower pattern. Very cheerful, *very* feminine.

"Anyone would be tired of men after Tony and Raymond," said Laura, referring to Haley's last two loser boyfriends. "You simply need to develop better taste."

"I have great taste," said Haley. "I matched you up with Kyle, remember?" She set aside the wallpaper roll and picked up her measuring tape from the scatter of tools on the kitchen table. "And you are but one of my success stories."

Haley's lifelong obsession with romantic relationships had been a boon for her friends and family. It was only her own romantic life that went south with such regularity. But, a romantic life couldn't go south if it didn't exist.

"True enough," Laura admitted, nodding her honey-blond head.

"But when it comes to me." Haley set her jaw with determination and resolve. "I'm a jinx. And it's mentally unhealthy to keep looking for something that doesn't exist." There was no man in her life now, and she'd decided there never would be.

No more looking for Mr. Right.

No more matchmaking.

No more obsession.

"He exists, Haley." Laura's voice softened. "You just haven't found him yet."

"Oh, I've found plenty of *hims*," Haley corrected. After all, man-hunting was practically a full-time hobby for well-bred Nelson girls. "And they all start out nice enough, but after a while their true nature shines through."

Tony was involved in a cleaning product pyramid scheme—he wanted Haley to become a "distributor" and attend inspirational conferences with him in Florida. And, Raymond—well, Raymond had a relationship with his domineering mother that still sent chills up Haley's spine. The really scary part was that she'd tried so desperately to make each of the relationships work.

"So, you're telling me you're going to have relationships with women instead?" Laura folded her arms, leaned back against the countertop and arched a shapely eyebrow. Even in the midst of wallpapering, her makeup and short hairstyle looked perfect.

"Why not? Women are nice. I like women. I hug them all the time."

Laura's mouth tightened in the beginnings of a grin. "And you're going to start kissing them now?"

"Sure." Haley shrugged.

"On the mouth?"

Haley repressed a small shudder as she stepped up to the wall. "Okay, so there are a couple of flaws in my plan."

Laura made a condescending sound behind her.

"I don't have to be *in* a relationship," said Haley.

After noting the measurement for the final wallpaper panel, she reeled in the metal tape with a snap then turned and picked up her pencil from the countertop. Crouching down, she sent the paper sprawling across the linoleum floor. "There are plenty of lesbians who aren't actually in relationships."

"So…what…you'll be a nonpracticing lesbian?" Lauren stepped forward to anchor the wallpaper roll while Haley measured.

"Right."

"Can't wait to tell Mom."

Haley ignored that, continuing with her own train of thought. "Then, when a man says, 'wanna come upstairs and see my etchings?' I'll simply say, 'no, thank you, I'm a lesbian.'" Nipping new relationships in the bud would save a whole lot of time.

Laura burst out laughing. Then she quickly stifled the sound, glancing in the direction of the staircase that led to where Haley's daughter, Belinda, and Laura's two daughters were asleep upstairs. "What if they offer to cure you?"

"They won't. I wouldn't be worth their trouble." Haley frowned at her paint-spattered T-shirt. The messy sister, she was hardly what anyone would call a hot babe. And, as a professional potter, she looked like this all the time.

"I've decided I will no longer let men impact on either me or Belinda," she continued.

Since her husband's death five years earlier, Haley had worked hard to provide stability in her daughter's life. But Belinda was nine years old now. Old enough to understand about dating. Old enough to know that when mommy went out with a strange man he might someday become part of their lives.

A steady parade of loser boyfriends were definitely not in Belinda's best interest.

"Now that you've moved to Hillard, I could have Kyle introduce you to some nice men," Laura offered. Her husband owned a construction company in Hillard, Vermont, so he had plenty of men on his payroll.

"Men are off my list," said Haley with conviction, drawing a straight line along the length of the wallpaper.

"Whatever you say." Laura shook her head. "Just try to snap out of it before September."

FIREFIGHTER ADAM HOLLANDER let his fist slowly come to rest against his thigh as his much modified wish list started to blur before his eyes. He'd spent an exhausting night shift battling a blaze at the old Halsteaders' barn, and he was having a hard time concentrating. The warm sun beat down on his shoulders and bare legs, and he felt as though he was sinking into the thick padding of the patio lounger beneath him.

"Daddy?" His nine-year-old daughter, Nicole, called from where she was skipping under the backyard lawn sprinkler.

"Yes, sweetheart?" Adam blinked, bringing himself back. He needed to decide whether or not to add the phrase "not too beautiful" to his *New Wife Wish List.*

"Can I invite her over?"

It wasn't that he necessarily cared about a woman's physical appearance, but his ex-wife had been drop-dead gorgeous, in a brittle, angry sort of way. And he was staying well away from anyone with anything in common with his ex. "Invite who over?" he asked Nicole.

"The new girl next door." Nicole paused beside him, smacking her cold, wet hand against his sun-warmed thigh.

Adam gasped and nearly leaped out of his chair.

Nicole leaned toward his ear. Chilly droplets of water fell from her long, blond hair onto his arm and his T-shirt. "She's peeking though the fence."

"Sure," breathed Adam. "Go ahead." He rubbed the spot where Nicole had raised goose bumps. The new neighbors had moved in two days ago, but he hadn't had a chance to meet them yet.

As Nicole jogged across the lawn, Adam went back to the list. He scratched out "not too beautiful." Instead he added, "beautiful to me." That worked. He was going for inner beauty this time.

After another minute's consideration, he erased "me" and added "Nicole." Whoever became his new wife had to be beautiful to Nicole. At nine years old, his daughter needed a mother.

He'd deluded himself for the past few years, thinking he could raise her on his own. But lately, she'd started asking questions that he didn't know how to answer. He'd seen her covetous looks at her friends' mothers during school events—none more poignant than the parent-daughter tea last week.

Sure, being politically correct, they no longer

called it the mother-daughter tea. But nobody was fooled.

His little girl deserved a mother who would attend teas, who would get her French braids to lie straight and who would sew matching outfits that brought a smile to her young face.

Cooking, sewing, patience, intelligence, a good sense of humor. Adam fully intended to find the perfect mother for Nicole.

She was his number one priority. And her happiness was what counted.

His gaze wandered to his daughter, now chatting with the new girl next door. They were the same height, and looked to be about the same age. He'd have to make a point of heading over to meet the girl's parents sometime today.

But not right now. He let the list rest against his chest. The sun was too warm, and he was far too comfortable.

His eyes drifted shut as the two young voices faded into the background.

"HE'S STILL BREATHING," said an unfamiliar child's voice, which sounded far away.

"I could sprinkle him," said Nicole.

"Might not be a bad idea," said an older voice, a woman's voice.

Adam forced his eyes open. He did not like the mischief in that woman's voice—not one little bit.

"Oh," said the woman. "I guess there's no need to sprinkle him. He's awake." She sounded disappointed.

Adam swung his body into a sitting position, planting his bare feet in the grass on either side of the lounger. He blinked at the bright sunshine.

"Daddy, this is Belinda's mom," said Nicole excitedly.

"Haley Roberts." The woman held out her hand at the same time Adam's eyes focused. "We just moved in next door."

Her auburn hair was drawn back in a perky ponytail, showing off high cheekbones and lightly freckled skin. Her tank top clung to nicely rounded breasts, and miles of tanned leg curved down from her cutoff jeans.

The thought that he'd like to wake up this way every morning skittered through his mind before he could stop it. He scrambled to his feet and shook her hand. "Adam Hollander."

She was maybe five foot six, and her gorgeous blue eyes sparkled as she smiled up at him. "Nice to meet you." Her voice sounded bedroom husky. But maybe that was just because he was barely awake.

He raked a hand through his short hair and gestured to the other lounger. "Please sit down. Can I offer you some..." The liquid in the pitcher on his picnic table was dark purple grape punch. "I could make some iced tea," he quickly amended.

"That's all right. I love purple punch." She flopped down on the second lounger and curled her legs beneath her.

Nicole and Belinda dashed toward the sprinkler, shrieking with delight as the cold water hit their skin.

"How old is your daughter?" he asked, his back to Haley as he filled the plastic glasses.

"Nine. She'll join Mrs. Livingston's grade four class on Monday. Yours?"

"Same age." He smiled. "Same class, too." It would be nice for Nicole to have a friend right next door.

"That's great. I know there's only a couple of weeks left, but I hoped she might meet some other children at school before summer gets started."

"Does Belinda have brothers or sisters?"

"Just Belinda. Though she has two cousins over on Maple Street."

He turned back to face her, a glass of punch in each hand. "That's ni—" His hands involuntarily convulsed around the glasses.

She was picking up his wish list.

"You dropped this on the…" Haley frowned, then squinted. "What *is* it?"

His first instinct was to snatch the list from her hands. In fact, he nearly caused a punch disaster before catching himself, quickly realizing it was too late. The title of the list gave everything away.

Taking a deep breath, he deliberately placed the two plastic glasses on the small table between the loungers. He had a choice here. He could demand the list back, or he could act as though he didn't care that she was reading his private desires.

After a split-second debate, he decided his best bet was to feign indifference. As casually as possible, he sat down and lifted his glass.

"Like it says, I'm looking for a wife." He tried to sound matter-of-fact as he took a swig—like he chatted with strangers about his love life every day of the week. Inwardly he cringed, waiting for her reaction.

"Oh," she said brightly. "I'm a lesbian."

Adam choked. Then he coughed, gasping for air. He could have cheerfully lived the rest of his life without knowing what it felt like to inhale grape punch.

"I see," he wheezed. "Thank you so much for sharing that."

"No problem." She ran her fingertip down the list. "So, what do you mean by *honest?*"

What do you mean by lesbian? "What do you mean, what do I mean?"

She crossed her legs and lifted her glass of punch, still holding his list hostage. "Do you mean honest as in 'I don't know who ate the last cookie,' or honest as in 'Who, me, embezzle three hundred thousand?' ''

''You'd lie about the last cookie?'' asked Adam.

''In a heartbeat.'' She grinned.

''I want both,'' he said, leaning back, cautiously sipping the grape punch a second time. He hoped she didn't say anything else outrageous. His lungs couldn't take it.

Haley nodded solemnly and continued perusing the list. ''Does she *have* to be a good cook?''

''I don't want a bad one. She'll be cooking for Nicole.''

''True,'' said Haley, glancing toward the two girls, who were happily ducking their faces in the spray. ''Belinda manages on my cooking, but then she was weaned on it.''

Adam looked from Haley to Belinda and back again. He was dying to ask how a lesbian ended up with a daughter, but he was a little afraid of the answer. Belinda was obviously Haley's natural child. The auburn hair and identical smiles were a dead giveaway.

''Mentally *stable?*'' asked Haley, referring to list item number five.

''Of course,'' Adam replied. ''I sure don't want somebody mentally *un*stable.''

''I just think some things would be self-evident.'' She flipped the paper over, checking out the back. It was blank.

Adam wasn't taking any chances this time. He'd married Nicole's mother based on emotion and hormones—big mistake. In fact, he was considering adding ''heterosexual'' to the list after Haley left. It seemed nothing in this world was self-evident anymore.

''I'm good at this,'' said Haley.

''Good at what?''

''This.'' She shook the list.

''Finding women?''

''Matchmaking.''

Adam's stomach clenched. *Please, God, no.* ''I don't think that's a very good—''

''Seriously. Now that I know what you want, I can prescreen and save you lots of time.'' She beamed, looking frighteningly excited at the prospect.

He reached out and whisked the list out of her hand. ''You're very generous. But, please don't. I can—''

''There are all kinds of pitfalls.''

''Pitfalls?'' He tried not to hug the list too close to his chest. No way in the world was this woman helping him find a wife. Haley was the antithesis of what he wanted. She was way too pretty, an admitted bad cook, her sanity was in doubt and she was sexual-orientation challenged.

She took a quick sip of the purple punch. ''Say,

for example, you ask a woman on a date. Maybe you can tell right off that she's not *the one*. But maybe she likes you." Haley paused, pasting him with a comically dire look. "I mean *really* likes you. Think Glenn Close and Michael Douglas. Think stalker."

Think lunatic. "That was a movie."

"You don't think it happens in real life?"

"Not in Hillard, Vermont."

"It happens in the best neighborhoods."

"I'm not going to date a stalker."

"That's the thing about stalkers." Her voice took on a conspiratorial tone. "They look just like you and me."

More you than me. He smiled indulgently. "Explain to me how *you'll* recognize them."

"That's the beauty of it. I won't be dating them, so they won't stalk me."

"What if they're lesbians?"

She frowned. "Hmm." She lifted a thumb to her mouth and bit down on the nail. "Hadn't thought of that."

Adam quickly jotted down the word "heterosexual" on the bottom of his page. Then he added an exclamation mark next to the phrase "mentally stable."

2

OKAY, SO SHE'D PROMISED to give it up. But if ever there was a man in need of matchmaking, it was her new neighbor Adam Hollander. And if ever there was a man she needed safely match-*made,* it was her new neighbor Adam Hollander.

It was bad enough that three days ago his skimpy shorts and worn T-shirt had made her question the sanity of becoming a lesbian—before the decision was even twenty-four hours old. But he'd also inspired blatantly heterosexual dreams. She'd woken up in a tangle of sweaty sheets three nights running.

Haley didn't need a neon sign. Before she got seriously interested in him, and was tempted to give men-kind another shot, she was going to find Adam a nice woman and put him safely out of her reach.

She handed her sister Laura a tall glass of pineapple juice and crushed ice. They'd crammed two chairs onto the small balcony outside Haley's second-floor bedroom. It kept them above the mosquitoes and caught the slight breeze wafting up from the river.

Belinda and her cousins, Ali and Caitlin, were turning cartwheels on the back lawn, and Adam's lawnmower droned next door.

Haley eased down on the lawn chair across from Laura, their knees brushing together in the small space.

"So, you're saying you want me to invite Joanne MacIntosh to Belinda's birthday barbecue?" Laura frowned as she picked up the thread of their conversation, resting the chilled glass on the plastic arm of her lawn chair and balancing it lightly with her fingertips.

"That's right." Haley nodded. All she needed was Laura's cooperation and a moderate amount of sunshine on Saturday afternoon, and her matchmaking scheme was off to the races. "I had a chance to talk to Joanne when she joined my pottery class last night, and I think she'd be a perfect match for my new neighbor."

"You're matching Joanne up with your neighbor?" Laura's eyes narrowed.

"Right."

The volume of the mower increased as Adam rounded the corner of his house. He was barechested, a sheen of sweat covering his tanned skin.

Beads of condensation tickled Haley's fingertips where she ran them along the smooth glass. She forced her gaze back to Laura. "He's looking to get married."

"That guy over there?" Laura's glance slid sideways to Adam and her eyebrows arched.

"Right," said Haley.

"The man pushing the lawnmower?"

"That's him."

"The one with the linebacker shoulders and the Chippendale butt?" Laura arranged her features in a look that clearly questioned Haley's sanity.

Haley kept her eyes front, refusing to check out the validity of Laura's butt statement. Though her teeth were starting to ache with the effort. "Exactly."

"And you don't want him for yourself?"

"Of course not." Haley struggled to make the words sound normal. It was a little hard to manage with her teeth still clenched.

Laura reached out and cupped her palm over Haley's forehead. "You feeling all right?"

"I told you I was giving up men."

"Oh, pooh," said Laura with a wave of her hand. "No need to waste a guy like that over some fleeting, misguided notion about the male species."

Haley's hands tightened. Giving up men wasn't a fleeting, misguided notion. It was a well-considered lifestyle choice. "Just because there's an eligible male in the vicinity doesn't mean one of us has to make a play for him."

"Us?" Laura sat back. "Who said anything about *us?* I'm married."

"I know. So are Sandra, Kathy, Melanie and Linda." Haley rattled off the names of her oldest sister and their three female cousins.

"Uh-huh," Laura agreed. "And that leaves you a clear field. This one could be your keeper."

"I don't want a keeper. I'm not looking for a keeper."

"That's just plain contrary," said Laura. "He's practically fallen into your lap."

"You sound like Mom."

"So?"

Haley set her juice glass on the top of the railing and leaned forward. "Don't you find it a little weird that every female member of our family was married before their twentieth birthday?"

"What's weird about that?" asked Laura.

"All of us. We graduated from high school, and we got married. Half of us had husbands picked out before our junior prom." In truth, it was their mothers who'd picked out the husbands.

"Coincidence," said Laura with another little wave of her hand, but her eyes narrowed like they did when she was working on the Sunday crossword puzzle.

"You think?" asked Haley. She lifted her glass

and took a slow sip of the tart pineapple juice, letting Laura ponder the rash of early weddings for a moment.

Haley hoped it would start her sister thinking along the lines that Haley had been considering for the past few weeks—ever since she saw that PBS special on subliminal familial pressure. Their family was a classic case.

The sound of the lawnmower died, and the girls' voices rose from the lawn below.

"Do you remember my mock wedding with Stephen?" asked Haley.

"I remember the real one better," said Laura.

"We were what, maybe twelve years old?"

"So?"

Haley shrugged and touched the rim of her glass with her index finger, avoiding Laura's eyes. "I just think it was strange to put so much focus on marriage at such a young age. Why didn't we play executive suite or university student or television star?"

"Kids dress up and play wedding all the time."

"But most mothers don't sew a ten-foot wedding veil and bake a three-tiered, rosebud cake." Haley traced circles around the smooth, wet rim of her glass.

"It was a great cake," said Laura.

Haley nodded. She could still recall the French vanilla puff pastry and butter-cream icing. It was a masterpiece. It was also totally inappropriate for twelve-year-olds playing dress-up. Haley was beginning to wonder if that event had helped set in motion her eventual real marriage to Stephen.

It wasn't as though they were passionately in love when they graduated high school. It was more that they couldn't think of any good reason *not* to get married.

Haley took a deep breath. "I'm beginning to think our family is unnaturally obsessed with marriage."

There was silence as a gusty wind stirred the maple trees.

"I don't think there's anything unnatural about my marriage," Laura ventured.

"Oh, not your marriage," Haley rushed on.

"Then whose?"

"Nobody's in particular. It's just… Let's say I'm bucking the trend."

"By matchmaking your neighbor?" Laura unexpectedly grinned. "That sounds like a *real* big change from past family practice. Are you going to sew him a veil and bake him a cake, too?"

"I'm bucking the trend by not making a play for the neighbor myself," Haley clarified. She'd give up matchmaking, too.

Soon.

Once Adam was out of the way.

"Even though you secretly want to?" Laura

leaned forward and finished on a note of triumph, a twinkle in her eyes.

Haley shrugged, pretending Laura wasn't right. It wasn't like it was a real attraction. She was simply experiencing a sort of Pavlovian response: see man, chase man, marry man. Years of psychological indoctrination would take a while to erase.

"There's no denying he's good-looking," she admitted. "But so what? That doesn't mean I'm automatically interested."

"So, you seriously want me to bring Joanne to the barbecue?" asked Laura.

"You bet." Haley cleared her throat to get rid of the hollow sound. "I've already invited Adam and his daughter, Nicole. I think Joanne will be perfect for him."

WASN'T THIS JUST PERFECT?

Adam didn't think he could ask for a better character combination in a meddling neighbor. Haley was not only mentally unstable, but she didn't understand the meaning of the word "no."

The birthday barbecue was in full swing as he reached out to shake Joanne MacIntosh's hand. Her no-nonsense grip was firm, her smile was friendly, but the assessing glimmer in her eyes was unnerving.

He felt like a pound of ground chuck in Rosenthal's display window. *What* had Haley said to this woman?

"Joanne grows fresh vegetables in her greenhouse," Haley offered, beaming at Adam as if she expected him to drop down on one knee here and now.

"And she's a marvelous cook." Haley slipped in the third wish-list criterion disguised as an introduction. Or, maybe it was the fourth. He'd lost count.

Joanne heartily pumped his arm. He'd describe her as stocky, but it certainly seemed to be all muscle. Haley opened her mouth again.

"Nice to meet you," Adam interrupted, afraid of what else Haley might say.

If she brought up the woman's mental stability, he swore he was going to clap his hand over her mouth and drag her into the house.

"Would you care for a crab puff?" asked Joanne, retrieving a tray decorated with parsley and lemon slices, obviously ready to back up Haley's claim with concrete evidence.

"Can I have a rain check on that?" Adam mustered a smile and took a judicious step backward. Joanne was probably a perfectly nice woman, but everything inside him told him to run for his life. This was *not* how he'd pictured meeting a potential wife—like some kind of bug under a female microscope.

His gaze slid to Haley's bright, satisfied smile, and he briefly wondered how many years he could get for strangling her. He didn't suppose the insanity defense would hold water when it was the victim who was insane.

Joanne's attention shifted to the four girls playing under Haley's maple. "And which one is your darling daughter?"

Oh, no. Adam was definitely not letting his *darling daughter* get dragged into this.

He latched on to Haley's upper arm, bending his head close to her ear. "I need to speak to you," he ground out in a stiff undertone. "Over there. By the cooler."

Her eyes narrowed in confusion. "Now? Are you sure you wouldn't like—"

"Right now."

"What? You want a beer?"

Though alcohol was probably a great idea, what he really wanted was a way out of this mess. If he and Nicole were going to stay for the rest of the party, he needed to find out exactly what was going on and do some serious damage control.

He tossed a polite "excuse us" over his shoulder to Joanne, all but dragging Haley toward the patio.

"Are you out of your mind?" he growled as soon as they were out of earshot.

"What do you mean?" Her ponytail bopped

from side to side as she hustled along beside him. In her faded cutoffs and tank top, she looked so sweet and innocuous that it was hard to believe she was Machiavelli in drag.

"*What* is Joanne doing here?" he clarified. As if he didn't already know.

"She's a great cook," said Haley. "You should have tried the crab puffs."

Adam grunted, not quite trusting himself to speak. They came to an abrupt halt beside the fence. They were still in full view of the other guests, but this was as good as it was going to get.

"And she knows how to dance," said Haley. "I asked her about that at pottery class."

"I told you I didn't want your help." He'd never experienced a blood pressure problem before, but he had a feeling one was about to start.

"This is a golden opportunity." Haley made a shooing motion with her hands. "Don't waste time talking to me. Go talk to Joanne."

He glared at her through narrowing eyes. "I am not going to date Joanne."

"Why on earth not? She meets your criteria. I had a great talk with her."

"I can find my own dates."

Haley sighed and shifted her hands to her hips. "Don't be so obstinate."

"*Obstinate? Me* obstinate?" This from a woman who latched on to an idea like a steel bear trap and shoved it down the throat of innocent by-standers.

"Yes, obstinate," said Haley. "She's here. You're here. Go for it."

"I am not obstinate."

Haley released a long-suffering sigh. "You want a wife candidate. I found you one."

Adam could feel his blood pulse against his temples. "I told you to stay out of it. You ignored my wishes. You've put me in a terribly awkward position."

"She's a really nice woman."

Like that made it okay. "Just butt out."

"No offense, Adam. But how many dates have you found for yourself so far?"

Adam blinked incredulously. Did she not recognize his annoyance? Did she have a death wish?

"See?" She made an open palm gesture with both hands. "You really can't afford to turn your nose up at Joanne, can you?"

Adam took a step closer, dipping his head forward. "Read my lips."

Her gaze dropped to his mouth. Finally she listened to *something*.

His tone was clipped and precise. "My romantic life is *not* now, and won't ever be any of your business."

Her lips parted and she sucked in a little puff of air. Then her eyes widened and blinked up at him, cobalt blue and sparkling like diamonds in the afternoon sunshine. "I was only trying to help." She sounded genuinely bewildered.

Oh, great. Now he felt like an ogre. He relaxed his tense muscles. His tone softened. "I know."

"And she's a really good dancer," said Haley, obviously a master of the emotional recovery.

Adam prayed for patience.

"I meant to ask you," her brow furrowed. "Why do you want a wife who knows how to dance?"

"Because I'm tired of poaching on other guy's wives at the firefighters' ball." The honest answer jumped out, surprising him. In fact, it sounded kind of stupid now that he said it out loud. While he was writing the wish list, it seemed to make sense.

Haley nodded. "Never did learn to dance," she confessed. "Well, except for that bouncy shuffle thing you do in high school when you really don't know what you're doing."

Interesting, but totally irrelevant. Kind of like Haley herself. Still, he couldn't help forming a mental picture of her in a high school gym, dressed in satin and sequins, shoes kicked off, gyrating to a scratchy amateur band.

He shook his head to clear it of the image. He had a serious problem here—figuring out how to dissuade Joanne without ruining the party. Fantasizing about Haley in a high school gym was not going to help—no matter how good she looked.

"Just give Joanne a chance," she suggested.

Adam stared into her hopeful eyes. For some reason her open, sincere expression evaporated his anger.

Not that he was going to let her innocent beauty sway him on this. Not on your life. His message to Joanne needed to be quick and clear.

"I know you'll like her," Haley said. Her lips parted in anticipation and suddenly looked kissable.

Uh-oh.

Adam cocked his head sideways. Or maybe not so *uh-oh* after all. He felt a plan click into place. Sure, it was the plan of the unprepared and desperate. But it was the best one he had. "Does Joanne know you're a lesbian?"

"What?"

"Joanne. Does she know you're a lesbian?" Heck, what better way to throw a curveball into this grand scheme? It would serve Haley darn well right…

"No." She looked puzzled.

"Good." He wrapped his arms around her waist, mentally damning the torpedoes. "You got me into this," he muttered. "You can get me out."

Her eyes went wide as he bent forward, and her

mouth tried to form a word. He strongly suspected that word might be ''no,'' but he didn't much care.

It wasn't going to be a real kiss, just a brief meeting of the lips, just long enough to convince Joanne that he was taken and there wasn't any point in pursuing him as marriage material. It wouldn't take much. He was certain Joanne was still watching them.

His lips brushed Haley's.

They paused.

They clung.

They parted.

A robin chirped in the trees and a gust of wind swirled the scent of freshly mowed grass. The children's laughter rose and fell from the other side of the yard.

His mind cataloged the irrelevant details as he brushed against Haley. A shaft of pure white heat ricocheted through his nervous system. Now *that* was relevant.

Maybe he harbored some latent lesbian fantasy. Or maybe it was just a male ego thing all wrapped up with a forbidden fruit syndrome. All he knew for sure was that this was the first time since Nicole's mother that he'd heard bells ringing.

He deepened the kiss. One of his hands crept up her spine, seeking the tanned skin above her scooped neckline.

This was not good. In fact, this was very, very

bad. A misguided hormonal reaction to Haley was the last thing he needed in his life.

She made an inarticulate sound of distress deep in her throat. It occurred to him that he might be the first man she'd ever *really* kissed.

Damn shame, that.

His fingertips convulsed against her. Of its own volition, his body pressed closer.

He was only playacting, he reminded himself. Okay, so he was going for an award-winning performance. He slanted his mouth over hers, settling in for a better angle. Her lips were soft and warm and sweet. They molded to his own.

He had to stop kissing her.

He really…

Truly…

Had to…

Like *now,* a small voice interrupted.

But she was kissing him back. No. That couldn't be. She wasn't kissing him back. It was just his fevered imagination.

The same small voice pointed out that they'd probably convinced Joanne they were an item by now. Heck, they could probably step up to the podium and start thanking their friends and family.

So, stop already!

He forced himself to pull back. She looked dazed and vulnerable and gorgeous.

He forced himself to let her go.

His pulse was pounding and his lungs worked double time. He could feel sweat popping out between his shoulder blades.

Her cheeks were flushed, her lips slightly swollen, and those big blue eyes blinked up at him.

It had to be done, he assured himself. Kissing her was his ticket out of the Joanne debacle.

"Why?" Her sweet breath fanned his face. "What were you…?"

"I'm not interested in Joanne," he said. "This way nobody gets hurt."

"But she's perfect."

Maybe she was. But it didn't matter. Adam was finding his own dates. On this, he was firm.

"Leave it alone," he warned Haley in an undertone. Leave *her* alone, he silently warned himself.

"But you need to find someone," she insisted. "Fast. How will you do it without me?" There was an edge of panic to her voice.

"Your faith in me is overwhelming." He looked past her shoulder and focused on the fence, forcing his body to relax and his muscles to unclench.

It was just a quick kiss, he assured himself. Nothing to get excited about. She was pretty, that's all. Anybody would agree she was pretty.

And now he was free. Another couple of pecks on the cheek during the course of the barbecue, maybe an arm around her shoulder, a whispered secret, and they'd officially be a couple.

"So…" There was a distinct thread of laughter in Laura's voice that made Haley cringe. "How's the matchmaking coming along?"

Haley sighed. "You saw?"

"Hard to miss," said Laura. "For a second there, I thought you were going to haul him upstairs."

"What about the girls?" Haley was more than a little embarrassed by Adam's blatant, public display—fake though it was.

"They were busy with the swing. I don't think the two of you broadened their education."

Thank goodness.

"Mommy, mommy, watch!" Laura's youngest daughter, Caitlin, called to Laura from the maple tree.

The previous owners of the house had built a platform five feet off the ground and tied a rope swing in the tree.

They watched while Caitlin swung out, spun around, and arced back. She shrieked in delight on the backswing as her older sister Ali grabbed her around the waist and pulled her back on the platform.

"He just decided Joanne wasn't the right woman." Haley felt like she needed to give her sister some kind of an explanation. "I was the decoy."

"That doesn't explain why you kissed him back," said Laura.

"I didn't kiss him back." Haley felt her face heat. Okay, so she'd puckered just a little. It was a conditioned response. After all those years of romantic indoctrination at her mother's knee, she couldn't be expected to reform overnight.

It was barely a pucker. In fact, it was more of a purse—caused by surprise, not arousal. Definitely not arousal. A purse didn't even count.

"Liar," whispered Laura, the thread of laughter still in her voice.

Haley sighed and shook her head. "It's nothing. He's just faking it so that Joanne won't get hurt."

"Joanne's fine. I told her you and Adam had had a fight, but it looked to me like you'd made up."

"Gee, thanks."

"I thought the story was quite inspired. Particularly on short notice. She decided to leave."

"Oh, no."

"It's fine."

"I feel so rude."

"I thought you didn't kiss him back."

"I didn't."

"Then you have nothing to feel rude about. She

was very good-humored about it. She thinks you and Adam make a cute couple.''

Haley felt her jaw go slack.

''Hang on tight,'' Laura called.

Belinda soared out on the swing. Although she wasn't very high off the ground, Haley held her breath until Ali pulled her back onto the platform.

''Great party.'' Adam's voice startled Haley.

His big hand on her bare shoulder startled her even more. Her nerves leaped beneath his callused fingertips. Conditioned response, she assured herself. It didn't mean a thing.

''Hey, Laura,'' he said. ''Nice kids you've got there.''

''Thanks,'' Laura smiled. ''I gave birth to them myself.''

Adam chuckled. ''It shows…''

Startled by the apparent insult, Haley stared incredulously up at him.

''…they have your beauty,'' he finished smoothly, with a wink to Laura.

Laura laughed. ''Glad to hear my stomach crunches weren't a complete waste of time.''

Laura worked hard at the gym and consequently had the toned figure of an athletic twenty-year-old. Haley quickly realized Adam never would have made the joke if it hadn't been completely preposterous.

She touched her hand to her own abdomen.

She'd never had to worry about her weight, but there was a slight rounding beneath her shorts that hadn't been there before Belinda. Maybe she should think about doing a few crunches herself.

Not that she cared what men thought—especially not Adam. But Laura did look drop-dead gorgeous in her bikini, where Haley had switched to sensible one-pieces a few years back.

"You, too," Adam whispered to Haley, covering her hand with his own.

"What?" She tried to ignore the way his fingers overlapped her smaller hand, gently brushing the soft denim beneath her navel. It wasn't erotic. It was just…

Nothing. It was nothing.

"Belinda has your beauty." His voice was husky. "And you're still—"

"Adam, stop," she hissed under her breath, pushing his hand away from her stomach. This was going way too far. "Look. Nicole is going to swing now."

Nicole looked decidedly nervous up on the platform. When Adam glanced up at her, his hand tensed on Haley's shoulder. Haley knew she should step away from him and the silly responses he evoked, but her feet were glued to the grass.

Ali placed the rope in Nicole's hand, and showed her how to stand on the knot. With a final word of encouragement, she gave Nicole a gentle push.

Haley could feel Adam's tension. She willed Nicole to hold on tight as she swung full out, higher and higher off the ground. Suddenly, at the apex of the arc, a smile burst out on Nicole's face.

The tension left Adam's hand, and it left Haley, too.

"Well done, kiddo," Adam whispered under his breath.

"Wasn't she great?" asked Haley, turning to check out his fatherly pride.

"Amazing," Adam agreed.

Then, before she could move, he leaned down and gave her another kiss.

She was sure it was meant to be a quick peck, just for show. He probably didn't realize Joanne had left. But somehow his lips didn't bounce back quickly enough. His thumb tightened against her shoulder, and she felt her lips part.

She tried not to pucker, really she did. But, her eyes were closing, her lips were clinging, and a rush of sexual desire was chugging its way along her extremities.

Laura cleared her throat.

"Haley, *honey!* Who *is* your new young man?"

The sound of her mother's voice froze the pucker right out of Haley's lips. She gasped against Adam's mouth, and her heart dropped straight to her toes.

3

"MOM?" HALEY FELT HER eyes go wide as she turned to face her parents. "Dad? What are you doing here?" Panic flooded her system and she quickly put some space between her and Adam.

"You know how your mother is." Haley's father pulled Laura into a brief hug and kissed the top of her head. "Woke me up at six this morning and said we weren't going to miss Belinda's birthday."

"Grandma, Grandma!" Belinda, Ali and Caitlin dropped out of the tree and came running across the yard.

"Oh, my little darlings." Grandma spread her arms wide.

Adam leaned down to mutter in Haley's ear. "Do they know?"

"Who? Know what?" Haley's mind raced. Her parents had driven clear across the state just in time to catch her faking a kiss in the arms of a good-looking fireman. Could her luck get any worse?

"That you're a lesbian," Adam whispered.

"No!" Haley shuddered. The kiss alone was going to take at least an hour to explain. Maybe she shouldn't have been so quick to tell all her friends and family to stop by her new house anytime.

"Great." Adam draped one arm loosely around her shoulders and reached out to shake her father's hand. "Adam Hollander. You have a wonderful daughter."

Haley's heart screeched to a stop.

"Warren Nelson. Haley hasn't mentioned you."

Oh, no. She was going to start hyperventilating.

"I'm her new neighbor." Adam gave Haley's shoulder an obvious squeeze. "Just met a few days ago. But we hit it off right away."

"How *won…der…ful.*" Haley's mother moved forward, taking Adam's hand in both of hers.

Was he out of his mind?

Playacting for Joanne was one thing. But, her parents…her *mother.* Ellen Nelson was mentally measuring Adam for a tux right now.

"Mom, Dad. I don't want you to misunderstand. Adam and I are just—"

He kissed her.

Up and kissed her again, right there in front of her mom and everyone. Didn't he understand? Joanne was no longer the problem here. She'd been relegated to a minor detail.

"Go get the ice-cream cake before it melts, Warren," said her mother, patting her father on the arm. "We picked it up on the way," she added to everyone else.

"Yippee," called Belinda, leaping in the air and doing a half twirl. "Ice-cream cake."

"I baked a cake," said Haley, trying not to feel miffed on top of everything else.

There was a moment of silence.

"This way everyone will have a choice," said her mother diplomatically.

Oh, sure. Like anyone was going to take her lopsided devil's food and lumpy icing over cookie crumble and a layer of fudge.

Haley sighed. She'd woken up this morning with a new determination to hone her mothering skills. She'd decided that a good mother would bake a homemade birthday cake.

"I'll eat your cake," Adam offered.

She gave him a brief incredulous look and muttered, "If you're not careful, you'll be eating my cake for the rest of your natural life."

"Huh?"

"Can I open my presents now, Mom?" asked Belinda, bouncing up and down on the spot.

"Oh, honey. I thought we'd wait until—"

"Sure you can, sweetheart," said Grandma, ruffling Belinda's hair. "This is the perfect time to open presents."

Haley slid a glance to Laura. Laura just shrugged and smiled. There was no point in trying to organize anything with their mother around. She might be kindhearted, but she was also a steel-spined dictator.

"Ali, you get the plates. Belinda, a big knife. Oh, and I think we're going to need a bowl of hot water." Her mother turned to Haley. "Maybe spoons would be better than forks for ice cream. Do you think spoons?"

Haley opened her mouth to answer.

Her mother nodded decisively. "Spoons it is. Caitlin, get us some spoons."

"Grandma, this is my friend Nicole," said Belinda, drawing Nicole forward. "Adam's her dad."

"How wonderful." Haley's mother bent down to smile at Nicole. "Nice to meet you, Nicole. I want you to call me Grandma."

Nicole grinned, but Haley cringed. She could feel herself spinning deeper and deeper into disaster.

"Oh, good," said her mother. "There's the cake. Not that end of the table, Warren. Put it in the middle where we can get pictures." Ellen marched over to the picnic table.

Everyone else dispersed to their assigned jobs, but Haley hung back to confront Adam.

"Why did you *do* that?" She crossed her arms,

not even attempting to keep the anxiety and frustration from her voice.

"Do what?"

"Let my parents think we were a couple?"

"Haley." He gave her a disbelieving look. "I was *kissing* you when they walked in."

"So?" They could have explained a kiss away. But now they were in serious and complicated trouble.

"So I'm not in the habit of kissing women unless I'm having a relationship with them."

Haley blinked incredulously up at him. Kissing her without benefit of a relationship seemed to be his full-time occupation this afternoon.

He sighed. "Okay, so maybe it was different with you. But would you rather they think I was a cad and you had loose morals?"

She clenched her hands by her sides. "Quite frankly, I'd rather they think *anything* other than that you're my boyfriend."

"Why? I'm gainfully employed and I have all my teeth."

Haley refused an answering smile. "In my family, we take boyfriends very seriously."

Adam shrugged. "So, we'll break up."

Haley snapped her fingers. "Just like that?" He was so naive.

"They live six hours away, right?"

Haley nodded.

"Next time they call, tell them it didn't work out and we're just friends." Adam started moving toward the picnic table.

Haley blew out a sigh before following. It wouldn't be that simple. Somehow, deep down inside, she knew it wouldn't be that simple. "This is scary, Adam."

"You're getting way too worked up." Once again he draped his arm around her shoulders, pulling her against his hard body. "Relax."

Relax? A wanna-be lesbian, with a marriage-rabid mother, who was being hugged by a great looking, great feeling, great smelling fireman who had kissed her three times in the past hour?

Not likely.

"Get a picture, Warren." Ellen placed the two cakes side by side on the picnic table and began plugging in candles.

Haley's lopsided rectangle looked even flatter next to the mountain of whipped cream and chocolate shavings.

"Maybe you should try a mix next time," Adam suggested in an undertone.

"That was a mix," said Haley.

"Oh." He was silent for a couple of steps.

"I have talents," said Haley.

"I'm sure you do."

"They just don't happen to include cooking."

"Cooking's overrated these days, anyway."

"It's on your list."

"True."

"Smile, girls," called Ellen, wrapping her arms around the small covey of children standing behind the cakes and a sea of flickering birthday candles.

Haley and Adam came to a halt next to Laura and her husband, Kyle. While Warren snapped pictures of the children, Belinda blew out the candles.

"Don't they all look cute?" Laura asked.

Haley couldn't help smiling at Belinda's wide grin and shining eyes. Okay, so an ice-cream cake wasn't such a terrible idea after all.

"It's a good thing we brought the RV," said Ellen, plucking out the pink and yellow candle stubs. "Hand me the knife, Belinda."

"The RV?" asked Haley, a sinking feeling sliding through her stomach.

"I can easily call Bernice and have her water the plants."

"Why?" Haley's voice had risen an octave. She didn't even want to *think* about why her parents would need their plants watered.

"It'll give you kids a chance to get out together," Ellen beamed at Haley and Adam. "We can watch the girls for you."

Laura turned her head to look at Haley, grinning

the way only a big sister can grin. "What a splendid idea, Mom."

"Do you have an outlet at the front of the house?" asked Ellen.

Haley whimpered.

"Go look for an outlet, Warren." Ellen dipped the knife in the hot water and sliced a wide row off one end of the ice-cream cake. "Dad will get us all fixed up."

"I'm the birthday girl, so I get a corner piece," sang Belinda.

"Belinda, don't be rude." Haley's voice was probably sharper than it needed to be, but she was under a bit of stress here.

"Of course you can have a corner piece," said Ellen. "Let's see, four girls, four corner pieces. Exactly right."

Haley closed her eyes.

"It'll be okay," Adam whispered.

No, it wouldn't be okay. Her parents were moving into her driveway so that she could date her sexy neighbor. Her mother would probably insist on staying in Hillard at least until the engagement party. Her parents were retired. Heck, as long as Bernice was willing to water the plants...

Ellen finished passing out corner pieces of ice-cream cake. "How about you, Kyle? Adam? Ice-cream cake or chocolate?"

"Ice—"

Laura elbowed Kyle in the ribs.

"Both," he said on a gasp. "A piece of each, please."

"I saw that," Haley whispered to her sister.

"He wanted both," said Laura complacently. "A wife knows these things."

"Sometimes before her husband," added Kyle.

"Chocolate for me," said Adam.

"That's not necessary," said Haley. Charity cake eaters almost made it worse.

"I like chocolate. So sue me."

"It's Saturday," said Ellen. "Why don't the four of you go dancing after dinner?"

"Dancing?" Haley couldn't keep the incredulity out of her voice. Her dancing skills were right up there with her cake-baking skills.

"How would you girls all like to sleep in the motor home with me and Grandpa?"

"Mom, you can't—"

"There's plenty of room." Ellen smiled.

"Can we, Mom?" asked Ali.

"Can we, can we?" echoed Caitlin.

"I'm the birthday girl, so I get the bunk."

"Belinda!" Haley was mortified by her daughter's selfish demands.

"Shh," whispered Adam. "She's just excited."

"I don't know about you, honey." Kyle wrapped one arm around Laura and shuffled a few dance steps on the lawn. "But I'm not about to turn down free baby-sitting."

"We could go to Angelo's," suggested Laura.

"Wait!" Haley called.

"You're right," Adam put in. "The Edge has a better dance floor."

Haley glared at Adam.

"Play along," he whispered in her ear. "Maybe you and I can have a fight there. A big fight. Then we'll break up later tonight." There was a grin in his voice.

"Nicole can have first choice of beds," said Belinda, a wobble in her voice.

Glancing at her daughter's damp, shining eyes, Haley felt like a heel.

She pushed forward to give Belinda a hug. "I'm sure you can all agree on beds," she said softly. Then she pulled back and looked down, smoothing Belinda's hair. "But you need to pick fairly, okay?"

"Okay, Mom." Belinda sniffed.

Somewhere down inside Haley realized she'd just agreed to go dancing with Adam.

ADAM DIDN'T LEAVE NICOLE with new baby-sitters very often, but she'd been so happy and comfortable with Haley's parents that he'd felt no qualms at all. When they arrived at The Edge, the dimly lit dance floor was already filled with sway-ing couples.

"Do you think we could order a drink first?" asked Haley as Adam pulled out her chair.

"Sure," he said, signaling a waiter.

"Let's get a bottle of chardonnay," said Laura, already bouncing to the beat of the music, the slight breeze from her movements flickering the candle flame in the middle of the table. "It's been so long since we've done this. Haley should get new boyfriends more often."

Kyle chuckled, draping an arm around his wife.

Both Laura and Haley had changed into form-fitting, little black dresses. Adam would have loved an excuse to drape his arm around Haley's bare shoulders, but he figured he'd better not press his luck. Haley was already strung tighter than a pressure-charged hose.

"He's not my boyfriend," she pointed out through tightly pursed lips.

Adam glanced from Kyle to Laura. "You guys know we're just friends, right?"

He and Kyle had met last fall when Kyle's com-pany did some renovation work on the fire hall.

"Uh-huh." Kyle nodded smiling. "But just friends have a way of becoming just husbands real fast in this family."

Haley shook her head with a fatalistic sigh. "I tried to warn him."

The waiter appeared and Kyle ordered a bottle of wine.

Laura clucked her cheek. "We're not that bad."

Haley arched her eyebrows, and Kyle sat back in his seat with a wry grin.

"What?" said Laura, glancing back and forth between her husband and her sister, obviously trying to interpret their expressions.

"Your mother—" said Kyle.

"Not that *bad?*" asked Haley simultaneously.

Laura's shoulders tensed.

Adam quickly jumped in to change the subject. "I have a feeling Haley and I are going to have a terrible fight tonight." He paused. "Okay, not that terrible. We'll probably part as friends."

Laura appeared to relax. She caught Haley with a secretive gaze. "You know, you don't have to—"

"Here's the wine," Haley chimed in.

Adam would have loved to hear what Laura had planned to say.

"Just be careful," Kyle warned in a dire undertone as the waiter poured the chardonnay.

Adam shook his head. "Don't you start, too. Haley's stressed out enough for all of us."

"Just don't say I didn't warn you," said Kyle.

"Warn him about what?" asked Laura, smiling a thank-you at the waiter as she picked up her glass.

"Mom and the wedding fixation," said Haley.

"It's not a fixation," said Laura.

Kyle leaned forward and stared pointedly at Adam. "I consider you a friend, so it's only fair to warn you that one minute Laura and I were necking after the senior prom." He snapped his fingers. "The next we were married."

"You mean you *had* to get married?" Adam quickly caught himself. "I'm sorry. None of my business."

"He's joking," said Laura, smacking Kyle's arm.

"Just watch your step," Kyle warned Adam.

"Why are you going on about this?" Laura's eyes narrowed, blue-black in the candlelight. She sat up straight and turned to her husband.

"You must admit, our relationship was a whirlwind," said Kyle.

"She wasn't pregnant," Haley whispered to Adam.

Adam cringed inwardly. "That was a thoughtless thing to say."

"It wasn't a whirlwind," said Laura. "We dated for four years."

"In high school," said Kyle.

"So?"

Adam didn't like the darkening expression on Laura's face. He tapped his hand on the tabletop in time to the music. "Anybody want to dance?"

"Dating in high school isn't quite the same thing as dating when you're an adult," said Kyle.

"And you've dated lots of adults?" asked Laura, sarcasm creeping into her tone.

"The music's really good," said Adam.

"Don't be ridiculous," said Kyle. Then he muttered, "It's not like I ever had the chance."

Adam leaned over to Haley. "Should we uh…"

Haley shrugged helplessly.

"If you wanted to date adults," said Laura, her voice rising, "you probably shouldn't have asked me to marry you."

"Laura," said Adam, scrambling for a way to intervene. "Would you like to—"

"I don't actually recall the asking part," said Kyle.

Laura's mouth worked for a second, but no sound came out.

"Your engagement party was so nice," Haley put in smoothly. "All those balloons, and the little white bells."

"Tell me all about it," Adam quickly suggested.

"What do you mean, you don't recall asking?" Laura's face had paled a shade.

Kyle lifted his wineglass and shook his head. "I'm not saying I regret anything."

"Well, thank you so very much." Laura folded her arms across her chest.

"Can we drop this?" asked Kyle.

"No, we can't drop this. You just told me you didn't want to marry me."

"I did not."

"Why did you marry me if you didn't want to?" Laura's chest rose and fell with deep breathing.

Adam leaned over to Haley. "Maybe you and I should take a turn around the dance floor?"

"I can't dance," she whispered back.

"I don't really think that matters right now—"

Kyle deliberately placed his glass back on the table. "Once your mother had the hall rented I felt a little silly asking questions."

Adam stood up. He reached out to take Haley's hand, not really caring if she could dance or not.

"It was the same with Haley and Stephen," said Kyle. "Right, Haley?"

Haley squirmed.

Laura arched a brow in her sister's direction.

"Who's Stephen?" asked Adam.

"Haley's husband," said Kyle.

"Haley has a husband?" For some reason the breath felt like it had been sucked right out of Adam's lungs.

"I'm a widow," said Haley.

A widow? How was a lesbian a widow?

"What about it?" asked Laura. "Did Stephen propose?"

Haley paused. Her thumbnail went to her mouth.

How could a woman forget a marriage proposal?

"See?" said Kyle.

"Haley?" asked Laura.

"He… Well… Everyone already knew…"

Kyle slapped the tabletop. "You mean your mother already knew." He shot a warning glance at Adam. "You have no idea what you've gotten yourself into."

Laura's expression darkened further.

"It wasn't a bad thing," Haley quickly put in. "It was more that there was no reason to say the actual words. We loved each other," she said.

"Right," said Kyle, glancing worriedly at Laura's stiffening posture. "Just like us." He tried to put an arm around her, but she shrugged it off.

"Did you love Stephen?" she asked Haley.

"Of course," said Haley.

"I mean were you madly, passionately in love with your husband?"

Adam sat down. He wanted to hear the answer to that one, too.

"That's not a fair question," said Haley.

Laura turned to glare at Kyle. "Is it a fair question for you?"

"Sweetheart, why are you—"

"Wrong answer, Kyle." Laura shot up out of

her chair, grabbed her evening purse and headed for the door.

Kyle swore under his breath as he scraped his chair backward. Then he followed his wife outside.

Haley blinked at Adam for several seconds before taking a deep swallow of her wine.

"Well…" she finally said.

"That was…" His voice trailed away.

"My mother's legacy," she said. "I did try to warn you, you'd be trapped."

"Is there a preacher hiding behind the bar?"

"No. But there might be one in the living room when we get home."

Adam couldn't help chuckling. "I'll take my chances." He leaned back in his chair. The bottle of wine was nearly full, and they'd arrived in Kyle's car—which was likely gone now. "What now?" Adam asked.

"Near as I can figure," she said. "We find you a wife. Get my parents out of the driveway. Convince my mother we've broken up before she rents a hall. And patch up my sister's marriage."

And, after all that, maybe Adam should take some time to figure out why he'd kissed his meddling, widow, lesbian neighbor three times running—and why he wanted to do it again right now.

4

HALEY WATCHED ADAM ROCK forward in his chair, sliding it back from the table across the wooden floor.

"Come on," he said, cocking his head toward the dance floor. "I'll teach you how to dance."

"Exactly which one of our problems will that solve?" she asked.

"Who cares? It'll be fun." He held out his hand.

There was no way in the world Haley was going to get out there on the dance floor and make a fool of herself. "We should be out finding you a wife."

"How about if we check out the other couples. If one of them seems to be fighting, we can switch partners."

And step on a *stranger's* toes? Haley glanced over at the dance floor. "Not a chance—"

Adam grinned and snagged her hand, gently pulling her into a standing position. "Gotcha. You're saying we should stick together out there."

"What about Laura?" Haley glanced toward the

exit, worried about her sister and feeling responsible for the fight.

"I think Laura is Kyle's problem right now."

"But I should—"

"Believe me, if I were Kyle, I'd want some time alone with my wife."

"You think?"

"They're either still fighting, or making up. Either way, three's a crowd."

He had a point. "But what about finding you a wife?" Judging by the close clinches on the dance floor, they weren't going to find any unattached women out there.

"I think I've had enough matchmaking for one day."

"Already? How can I help you if you're going to be a wimp about this?"

"A *wimp?*"

"Show a little stamina. We have not yet begun to matchmake."

"You want stamina?"

"Yeah." She tipped her head defiantly.

He glanced meaningfully at the dance floor. "I'll give you stamina."

"I'm serious, Adam. You know we are not going to find a new woman out on the dance floor."

"I won't need to find a woman. I'll have you."

"I'm not a woman."

He grinned. "You're not?"

''You know what I mean.''

He chuckled. ''Well, you fulfil all of my current requirements in a dance partner.''

''But not in a wife,'' she scoffed, cringing as she realized how that sounded. She didn't care about meeting the criteria on his list. Not in the least.

''Well, I can teach you to dance.'' He turned and pulled her toward the dance floor. ''But I don't know what we're going to do about your sexual orientation.''

''Don't forget about my cooking.'' They weaved in and out amongst the tables.

''And the fact that you failed the honesty test.''

''I did?''

''You'd steal the last cookie,'' he tossed over his shoulder.

He had a point there.

''So, it's hopeless,'' she said. Thank goodness.

''It's hopeless,'' he agreed.

''Right.'' Haley swallowed. There was no need to take it personally. Adam was entitled to want any kind of woman in the world. So, it wasn't her? Big deal. She didn't want him, either.

Once on the dance floor, he smoothly turned to face her. ''Left hand on my shoulder,'' he instructed.

She stared up into his hazel eyes, and a warm hum of attraction buzzed through her body.

If she wanted to keep her lesbian status, dancing with this man was definitely *not* a good idea.

He wanted a wife. She wanted her equilibrium back. Dancing would get each of them exactly nowhere.

"We could go bowling," she suggested, moving her focus determinedly on his chin. It was a strong chin, a sexy chin, but thank goodness it didn't hold a candle to his eyes. "I bet lots of nice motherly types go bowling on Saturday night."

He lifted her left hand, placed it on his solid shoulder and held it there for a moment. "Like this," he said.

Haley tried to ignore the buzz of hormonal electricity that pulsed into her palm. For goodness sake, it was only his suit jacket. It wasn't like she was touching actual skin or anything.

"Bowling," she repeated, attempting to engage his attention. "The kind of woman you want won't be at a dance club, she'll be at a bowling alley."

"Now, I know this is going to be a hard concept for you to grasp." He gently tipped her chin up so that she was forced to look him in the eyes again. Then he placed an arm around her waist and clasped her other hand. "But *I* get to lead."

"Or roller skating," she suggested a little desperately, the majority of her brain cells debating whether his eyes were more green than hazel. It was hard to tell with the dim lighting on the dance floor. "Is there a place to go roller skating in Hillard?"

He pulled her closer to his body. "This is a waltz." His deep voice was low, close to her ear, husky, sensual. She swallowed against a dry throat.

"Three four time." He rocked his body back and forth to the rhythm, brushing gently against her. "That's one two three, one two three. Feel that?"

And how. "Swimming?" she asked, breathlessly. "Very popular family activity, swimming."

"Haley?"

"Yeah?"

"Shut up and dance."

"I do know how to swim," she said, stumbling as he moved and she didn't.

"So do I." He put pressure against her spine, trying to steer her in the right direction. "Swimming's a very important life skill."

"Is it on the list?"

He chuckled softly, knowingly in her ear.

"I just meant…well, if it's on the list, and you meet somebody at the pool, well, you'll already know…"

"One two three," he whispered, pulling her into the steps.

"Fine," she sighed. "One two three." She attempted to follow his movements.

"You've got it." He shifted so that their feet were slightly offset, her leg was between his, and his between hers. His body was rock solid, his hand on her back purposefully guided her through the beat.

Haley's legs felt stiff as she tried to follow the music. Between her lack of experience and her escalating sexual arousal, it was hard to keep the rhythm.

She missed a beat. Then she clipped the side of his foot and nearly fell off her heel.

He pulled her tight against him, keeping her upright. "Relax," he whispered. "You're a natural."

"Right." She couldn't help but laugh at that.

"Don't listen to the music. Feel the beat." He tapped out the one two threes on her back. "Trust me. Follow me. Let yourself go."

Haley took a deep breath and tried to let the tension drain out of her body. They could find him a wife tomorrow. Maybe she should be learning to dance anyway. After all, she was thirty. How much longer could she reasonably expect to avoid dancing?

"That's it. Just relax. Feel when I go right."

She followed.

"Feel when I go left."

She followed again.

"It's on the beat," he whispered, hand pressing

tighter into the small of her back. "Always on the beat."

As if by magic, their movements started to match. Her body settled itself against his, and she could feel his heat, his breathing, his heartbeat.

She closed her eyes.

"Forward and back," he said.

"Left and right," he said.

In and out, her mind added.

Her imagination screeched to a halt. Her body stiffened, and her eyes popped open.

"Don't," he crooned, rubbing circles on her back, fingertips grazing her bare skin at the top of her low-backed dress. "We're just dancing. You're allowed to like it. People do it all the time."

Haley tried to relax again, but the sexual arousal coursing through her system was a force to be reckoned with. It might be just dancing to Adam, but it was turning into a whole lot more for Haley.

Her brain acknowledged the fact that she'd given up men, but somehow the message got lost on the way to her hormones. Far from realizing Adam was out of bounds, her body was revving up for what it assumed would be a cataclysmic ending to this date.

Haley stopped, stepped back and shook her head. "I'm sorry. This isn't working."

He stared down at her. "But you were doing great. You were really into it."

That was the problem. She was into it. She was into him. "It's hopeless. I'm hopeless. Can we please go bowling?"

"Bowling." His tone made bowling sound like a medieval torture.

"Lots of nice women go bowling," she said almost desperately. *And the lights are bright, and you can't dance close, and everybody looks like a geek in rented bowling shoes.*

Watching Adam knock down pins under fluorescent lights had to be way safer than snuggling up to him on a dim dance floor and feeling his heartbeat right down to her toes.

"Fine," he muttered, turning to head back to their table. "Whenever I'm out with a gorgeous woman who's dressed to kill, I know bowling's the first activity on my mind."

Haley's hormones heard the word gorgeous and gave a happy little shimmy. Her brain shut them down straight away. He meant gorgeous in a generic, "you're a warm, female body that I'm on a date with" sort of way. It didn't mean a thing.

ADAM WATCHED HALEY LINE her ball up with the white-and-red bowling pins at the far end of the lane. She looked ridiculous in her little cocktail dress.

Okay, she looked stunning in her cocktail dress—except for the red and navy rented shoes. It was the bowling alley that looked ridiculous around her.

Balls rattled, pins crashed and casually dressed patrons called to one another as they trekked back and forth from the snack bar.

Haley was hunched over, lining up the ball, striding to the head of the lane, swinging her arm back... This was the part he liked best: where she bent over to release the ball, and her dress stretched tight across her cute little tush. This time, he was also treated to a fleeting glimpse of the tops of her stockings.

The ball hit the polished floor with a *thunk,* and then rambled down the lane, veering off to the left...teetering...holding...*whump,* into the gutter again.

Haley turned around with a philosophical sigh. "Your turn."

"You got two that round," he offered as the pins reset.

"I think I'm starting to catch on." She glanced around at the other bowlers and did a couple of mock practice throws.

"Are you always this, uh—" He coughed.

"Bad?" she asked. "I don't know. I've never played before."

"I thought we were here because you liked

bowling?'' Adam stood up and selected one of the purple, marbled balls in the rack.

''I do, so far.''

''Why were you so determined to come if you'd never even tried it before?''

''To find you a woman.''

''Haley...''

''What about those two down there.'' She pointed down the long series of lanes.

''I'm not even going to look.'' He moved to the arrow marker, squaring his shoulders, lining up.

''Seriously. Lane five.''

''Out of the way, please.''

''The lady with the red hair. She looks nice.''

Despite himself, Adam glanced down to lane five. ''She's pregnant.''

''Don't be silly.''

''Sure she is. Look at her.''

''That's just a little potbelly. You're not getting an eighteen-year-old you know.''

He glared at Haley. ''I'm not interested in eighteen-year-olds. But I don't necessarily want a wife with a potbelly, either.''

''That wasn't on your list.''

''I'm adding it.''

Haley's hand went to her abdomen. ''Oh.''

Adam sighed, relaxed his muscles and rested the ball against his stomach. ''You do *not* have a potbelly.''

She glanced down at the front of her dress. "It hasn't been the same since Belinda was born."

"Oh, for goodness sake. You're—" He stopped himself. "Pretty. Thin and pretty. Now get out of my way."

He lined the ball up again. He'd been about to say sexy. He'd been about to say gorgeous. He'd been about to say *hot*.

But he doubted Haley would be pleased to know she was considered hot by a man.

He strode toward the foul line, drew back, aimed the ball at the head pin, slightly to the left like he'd learned in high school, released and watched it thunder down the lane.

There was something satisfying about having all ten pins crash down in a cascade. He hadn't bowled in years, but he could understand the appeal. He grinned and turned back to Haley.

She was gone.

Ladies' room?

Drink?

Candy bar?

Maybe she was upset because he was beating her so badly. He swallowed a twinge of guilt. Maybe he should have messed up a few frames.

He glanced around.

Lane five. Oh, no. Disaster in progress on lane five.

Haley was talking to the pregnant redhead.

Worse, she was laughing with the pregnant redhead.

The pregnant redhead was picking up her sweater.

The redhead's friend was picking up her purse.

They were coming over.

Adam stifled a low wail. Maybe he could make a run for it.

Haley smiled and waved happily to him. Two young boys ran by with candy bars clutched in their fists. Adam took an unconscious step toward the exit. Surely he could at least outrun the pregnant one.

Trouble was, there was no way he'd abandon Haley. Which meant he had to stand still, watching fatalistically as they grew closer.

"Adam, this is Tina."

The redhead smiled. "Nice to meet you. My teammate is Rosie."

The other woman, shorter, slightly plump, also looking to be in her late twenties, dropped her purse on the plastic bench. Thank goodness Rosie, at least, was wearing a wedding ring.

Haley reset the electronic scoreboard. "You guys go ahead and start." She motioned to Tina, who was putting down her sweater and pushing up the sleeves on her shirt.

Adam turned away from the newcomers, advancing on Haley, gritting his teeth. "Do you have an *off* switch?"

She laughed, lowering her voice. "Don't be silly. She's nice. And she can cook."

"She's *pregnant*."

Haley made a dismissive motion with her hand. "She might not be model thin, but she's honest."

Adam didn't care about model thin. He didn't really even care about potbellies. "How can you tell she's honest?"

"I told her I'd found a dollar on the floor and asked if it was hers. She said no."

"Oh, well, in that case," he muttered. "Bring on the preacher."

"That's the spirit."

"That was sarcasm."

"I know. I'm ignoring it. Now be nice." Haley moved so she could watch while Tina lined up, threw the ball in a straight, rocket line and knocked down seven pins.

"How can I get you to stop?" Adam persisted. "Threats? Money? Chocolate?"

"Chocolate?" Haley turned back toward him, her eyes lighting up. "I'd love a Snickers."

"Will Tina be gone when I get back?"

"Of course not."

"Then, forget it."

"Spoilsport."

Tina quickly cleaned up the other three pins for a spare, and it was Haley's turn.

"Haley says you're a fireman," Tina said, opening conversationally as she stepped back from the lane.

"That's right," Adam nodded. "Over on the south side."

She shifted her attention to Haley. "You know, your girlfriend's form's all wrong."

"Her first time bowling," said Adam, declining to correct Tina on the term *girlfriend*. Haley was his protection against all comers for now. Though he was betting Tina had either a husband or a steady boyfriend. Because she was definitely pregnant.

"Square your hips," Tina called to Haley.

Haley turned to look.

Tina demonstrated with her hands. "And make sure you follow through after you release the ball."

Haley nodded, eyes narrowing, looking cutely determined as she turned and lifted the bowling ball to her chest.

"Interesting outfit," said Tina, eyebrows lifting.

"We were dancing earlier," Adam explained. He'd hung up his suit jacket, removed his tie and rolled up his shirt sleeves. Aside from his formal pants, he blended fairly well with the rest of the bowling crowd.

But there was no hiding Haley's cocktail dress, fancy hairdo and classy jewelry.

Once again she drew back and sent the ball plodding down the lane. Though it *was* going in a straight line this time. After a lengthy journey, during which both Haley and Adam held their breath, the ball took out the middle pins, leaving a wide hole with three pins on either side. Turning, she grinned and punched her fist in the air with joy.

"Not bad," said Adam.

"I really think I'm catching on," said Haley, all but skipping over to pick up another ball.

She knocked down two more pins before her turn ended.

Tina and Rosie were formidable players, easily beating Adam and Haley. But Haley did manage a spare in the last frame and nearly jumped with joy.

Her excitement was deflated somewhat when Tina announced, with a pat on her belly, that she and "Jr." had to get home to bed.

Adam couldn't resist shooting Haley an "I told you so" look as the two women headed for the exit.

"She knew how to dance and everything," said Haley with a sigh, dropping down on the plastic bench and untying the rental shoes.

Adam took a spot beside her and started on his own shoes. "Can't win 'em all." Thank goodness.

Haley glanced around at the emptying bowling alley. "I guess that's it for tonight."

"We are *definitely* done here." He rose to his feet. He was tempted to clarify that they were, in fact, done matchmaking forever. But, she'd just call him a wimp again. And he didn't suppose protesting would do him any good in any case.

Haley dangled her black sandals in one hand, frowning at them. "I think my feet are swollen. I can't get these things back on."

"Get your purse," said Adam. "I can carry you to the parking lot." He wanted to get out of here before Haley spotted any more wife candidates.

"I'd feel silly."

"There's nobody left to see you."

Haley scanned the big room. There were a few stragglers left in the lounge, and a couple of games still going on at the far end. But the alley was essentially deserted.

"Okay." She stood up. "I guess it's better than blisters."

"Oh, please. Do stop," Adam protested, shrugging into his jacket and pocketing his tie. "I get so flustered when women tell me I'm better than blisters."

5

"I CAN WALK ON THE GRASS," Haley pointed out as Adam carried her up her driveway after the taxi dropped them off.

"It's not like you're heavy," said Adam. His strong arms shifted her easily, and she felt a now familiar tingle running through her body. Her hip was pressed against his hard stomach, and one of his hands was wrapped around her thigh.

"I'd still rather walk," she protested. Adam's arms were definitely not a safe place for her psyche.

"Whatever you want." He stepped sideways onto the lawn and lowered her to the soft ground.

Her stocking-clad feet sunk into the cool, thick grass. A slight breeze rustled the maple leaves, shifting the dappled light from a low, summer moon. Wisps of Haley's hair tickled her cheek.

"Thanks," she said, daring to look Adam in the eye. They were a clear, moon-green. She swore that, chameleonlike, they changed with their surroundings.

"Thanks for an interesting evening." He brushed a stray wisp of hair from her cheek. "Hope everything turns out okay with Laura and Kyle."

"I'm sure it'll be fine." She forced herself to ignore the seeming intimacy of the touch. Another minute, two tops, and she'd be back in the house, safe from her unruly attraction. "After twelve happy years, the exact wording of the marriage proposal has got to be a moot point."

Adam chuckled low. She shivered, deciding she'd better get the heck out of here. She took a step toward the porch.

The motor home door squeaked open.

Her mother stepped down onto the lawn and smiled sleepily. "Hi, kids," she whispered, tightening the belt on her blue terry robe. "Have a good time?"

"It was great," said Adam, his smile lingering.

"I was just saying good-night," said Haley, with another step toward safety.

Her mother drew up beside her. "I put out a bottle of wine in case you two wanted a nightcap."

Oh, no.

"It's on the dining-room table." She leaned closer to Haley and whispered. "I polished the spots off the crystal, and lit some of those white candles."

Haley stifled a groan. "It's late," she said aloud, glancing at her watch.

"Haley." Her mother moved even closer, grasping her upper arm, and whispering in her ear. "Don't be a fool. He ate *two* pieces of your cake."

"So I should *sleep* with him?" Haley whispered back, incredulous. For a second she wondered if her mother had laid out a couple of condoms as well.

"Don't be melodramatic." Her mother backed away and patted her arm.

"I'd love a glass of wine," Adam put in, a mischievous glow in his eyes.

Perfect.

"Perfect," said her mother. "You two kids go on in and relax. The girls have been asleep for hours. See you in the morning," she sang, with a wave.

Adam headed for the front door. Haley guessed it was too much to hope that he'd just been humoring her mother and planned to cut over the low hedge to his own house. He was probably getting a kick out of her embarrassment.

"I can't believe this," she muttered as she opened the front door.

"She thinks I'm your boyfriend," said Adam, following her in. "She's just trying to be nice."

"Don't you know when you're being set up? She's got a big, fat son-in-law target painted on your forehead.'' Haley dropped her purse and shoes on a chair in the foyer.

''Wow.'' Adam stared through the doorway into the living room.

''Wow,'' Haley echoed with a sinking stomach. She'd been joking about sleeping with Adam. But she guessed her mother had graduated from ten-foot wedding veils and rosebud cakes, and was orchestrating early honeymoons now.

Maybe she thought Haley was running out of time.

The lights were low. Warm candlelight bounced off the closed curtains and made the crystal wine-glasses sparkle. A vase of fresh flowers sat on the pressed, white tablecloth on the dining-room table.

But what really caught Haley's attention was the fact that the big room was spotless. It had been vacuumed, dusted and waxed to within an inch of its life. There wasn't a single toy to be seen any-where—not a shred of evidence that the girls had been playing in here just this morning.

Classical music played softly in the background. The fact that Haley didn't actually own any clas-sical music was testament to how much trouble her mother had gone to in only a few hours.

''I guess we'd better drink some of the wine,'' said Adam.

''I hate it when she does this,'' said Haley, striding across the room to the table. She was with

Adam on the wine. A shot of alcohol sounded like a great idea at this point.

"She does this often?" Adam followed, gently lifting the wine bottle from her hand.

"Well, not this *exact* thing," Haley admitted. She left him to deal with the corkscrew and flopped down on the couch, curling her legs up beneath her. She had to admit, her mother had never set up a seduction scene for any of her previous boyfriends. "But she does try to manipulate my life on a regular basis."

"She's your mother. It's her job." He popped the cork out of the wine bottle. "Just play along."

Sure. Fine. "As long as *we* both know there's nothing romantic going on here." They could break up later. Maybe tomorrow.

Adam poured two glasses of merlot and crossed to the couch and Haley. He folded his big body onto the other end, handing her a glass.

"Nothing romantic going on here at all." His husky tone gave her a split second's pause.

"Good." She nodded decisively, accepting the glass. "Because I have nothing that you want."

"Exactly." He took a sip.

"And I'm not interested in you, either."

"Obviously."

"Oh…my…goodness…" A hollow feeling settled in the pit of Haley's stomach. She set her glass down. There were candles flickering in the master bedroom.

"What?" Adam craned his neck to follow the direction of her gaze.

She could just barely see the bedroom doorway at the top of the stairs, but the candlelight bouncing off the opposite wall was unmistakable.

She rose. Morbid curiosity drawing her up the stairs. "She's probably drawn a bath." Haley stifled a hysterical laugh. "Maybe set out a basket of condoms."

Adam stood up, and followed. "She wouldn't…"

Haley's hand rose to her mouth. "No. I suppose not condoms. She's probably hoping I'll get pregnant."

"What kind of a mother would…"

"I did try to warn you."

"But this is…" They stood side by side, slowly pushing the bedroom door fully open. Haley had the bizarre feeling they were in the middle of a horror movie.

Attack of the Giant Condoms. No, *Attack of the Marriage-Crazed Mother.*

As the door panel connected with the wall-stopper, Haley groaned out loud. Her bed was turned down, a slinky nightgown draped across the foot, and another half-dozen candles flickered in the darkness, perfuming the air.

They both stood in silence.

"At least I know where you get it from," Adam finally said.

"Get what?"

"Never mind."

Haley couldn't help herself. She started to laugh. She ventured forward and picked up the unfamiliar nightgown, holding it against her body, swaying back and forth. It was spaghetti-strapped, dark purple, and came to midthigh. "If this doesn't score me a husband, I don't know what will."

"I can see I'm going to have to add slinky lingerie to my list."

"Good idea. Maybe my mother could help you."

"Find slinky lingerie?"

"No. Finish the list." Haley dropped the nightgown back on the bed. "Wait a minute." She bent over the bedside table and cupped her hand behind the candle flame, blowing until it went out. "That won't work."

She made her way around the room, blowing out another, and another. "She'd pare your list down to one item." Haley blew out the last three candles in rapid succession. "Haley Roberts."

"And Haley Roberts isn't available." Adam's voice was right behind her.

Haley straightened. Her sheer curtains billowed as a sudden gust of warm wind burst through the half-open window. The rising moon shone across her polished dresser.

He gently touched her bare shoulder. "Right?"

"Right," she breathed. She was definitely not available.

"It would sure make things simpler."

"What would?"

He didn't mean her. He couldn't mean her. The arousal that had been humming all evening started to convulse through her body in insistent waves.

"Having a single name on the list, instead of all those qualifications." His breath was hot on the back of her neck.

She let out a nervous laugh, banishing the confusing feeling of disappointment. "Of course it would. That's why I've been trying to..."

His callused fingertips brushed the curve of her shoulder.

Did he have no idea what he was doing? Any other woman would take that as a romantic gesture.

"That's why I've been trying to help you." She turned to face him, intending to get this mood back on an even keel. "If you'll quit fighting me, I'll find a single name."

But not Haley Roberts. Never Haley Roberts. She was *through* with men. She was *not* giving in to her mother's brainwashing and manipulation.

"Haley?" He ran his palm along her shoulder and up the curve of her neck.

She met his dark eyes and her throat went dry. "Yes?" She rasped. There was no mistaking the meaning behind that touch. Her eyes fluttered closed as she suddenly stopped fighting.

"I'm sorry…"

She took a deep breath and inhaled his scent—rich, musky, masculine. Though her mind screamed for order, her hormones screamed for release. Her head slowly tipped sideways, counterpoint to his.

"I never—" his wine-sweet breath puffed against her cheek as he bent closer "—meant…" His lips touched hers.

It was a gentle, questioning, almost reverent touch, but it ignited a series of explosions along her nervous system.

He backed off and paused for a heartbeat.

Haley's breath froze in her lungs. She waited, eyes closed. Her hormones longed for another kiss, while her mind prayed he'd just leave.

His hand tightened around the back of her neck, sliding up into her hair. His other arm wound around her waist, drawing her against his steel-hard body.

She softened, twined around him. It was like the dance, only better than the dance.

His lips sought hers again, open this time,

malleable, moist, questing. She opened for him, letting her arms go around his big body, reveling in the feel, smell and taste of him.

The kiss lasted seconds, then minutes, then longer.

Adam finally pulled away with a gasp. "I thought you said you were a lesbian?"

Haley opened her eyes, blinking through the haze of passion and astonishment. "I am," she said. "I'm just not very good at it yet."

I'M NOT VERY GOOD AT IT YET.

Haley's words from Saturday night echoed through Adam's brain as he hung his sooty helmet on a hook at the fire station. He unzipped the front of his turn-out jacket and shrugged out of it.

Why the heck had she lied to him?

"Nice work, Hollander." Patrick Wright clapped him on the back, a thread of laughter in his voice as he headed down the line of firefighters' lockers.

"I'll start the paperwork on your commendation right away," the chief called as he headed for his glassed-in office in the corner of the fire hall.

"Yeah, yeah." Adam shook his head, and waved off their weak jokes. It was obviously going to be a long time before he lived this fire down.

The tree house down by the river had been relatively easy to extinguish. But a plump tabby had been caught in the next tree, smoke panicking the poor animal. Adam had climbed the ladder to get it.

The rescue was too trite for words.

He stepped out of his fireproof boots, swiping the back of his hand against his sweaty forehead. His thirty pounds of protective gear were mandatory and necessary, but dastardly hot in the summer months.

"Hey, Adam."

Adam braced himself for another joke. But it was Kyle who'd strolled in the front door, stepping his way around hoses and equipment as the crew carried on with the cleanup.

"Get a call out?" he asked.

Adam nodded, easing down on the bench to lace up his runners. The big bay doors were open and the summer breeze wafted through. It felt good to strip down to lighter clothes.

"Everything go okay?" Kyle took a seat a few feet down the white painted bench.

"Hollander's the hero of the hour," called Patrick.

Kyle raised his eyebrows questioningly.

"Saved a cat stuck in a tree," said Adam fatalistically.

Kyle grinned.

"Don't say a word."

"Wouldn't dream of it."

"It was a cute cat."

"I'm sure it was."

"Little girl was thrilled to get it back."

"You'll probably make the front page."

"You got that right," said Adam. "A reporter from the *Times* got a picture." As luck would have it, Hillard was having a slow news day.

"Congratulations. I'm sure Ellen will clip the article and frame it."

"Oh, perfect." His heroic deed captured for posterity.

Kyle settled back and folded his arms across his chest. "I can see I've got some competition as her favorite son-in-law," he arranged his features in a mock frown.

"Haley and I aren't getting married," Adam felt compelled to point out yet again. He stood up and crossed the hall to engine number one.

Even if he *was* interested in Haley's lying, deceiving ways—which he wasn't—she obviously didn't think much of him. Telling a whopper like being a lesbian.

And for what?

Entertainment?

To keep him at arm's length?

He briefly considered asking Kyle. But there was no tactful way to broach the subject. At least none that Adam could think of.

"You keep telling me you're not getting married.'' Kyle's tone was skeptical as he followed Adam across the fire hall. ''But, so far I see no signs of you two breaking up. And Ellen's got that 'going to the chapel' light in her eyes again.''

''How'd everything turn out with Laura on Saturday night?'' Adam figured a new topic of conversation was his best defensive maneuver. A topic that put Kyle in the hot seat rather than Adam.

He opened the trap door on the fire engine and began restowing a clean hose in the cross lay.

''All's well on the home front,'' said Kyle.

''Just like that?'' Adam glanced at Kyle in surprise. Whenever he'd fought with his former wife, which had been pretty often, she'd pout for weeks.

''Are you kidding? There was nothing 'just like that' about it. I took her to the Ashbury Inn, rented a suite with a hot tub and proposed all over again.''

''You're a very smart man.'' Adam nodded his admiration as he automatically packed the hose into an accordion load.

''I'm a very experienced man,'' said Kyle. ''Cave big and cave early.''

''Words to live by.''

''Sorry about stranding you and Haley.''

Adam shrugged. ''No problem. We took a cab to the bowling alley.''

Then they'd taken one home. But he didn't want to think about that part. Her kisses in the bedroom had very nearly fried his brain. Not to mention certain other parts of his body.

"You went *bowling?*" asked Kyle.

Adam shrugged. "Haley had it in her head she wanted to bowl."

He wasn't adding anything about matchmaking. Hillard was a small town. If the construction worker community got wind of his wish list, the cat rescue would pale in comparison.

"Whatever turns her on," said Kyle, stepping back out of the way.

"Speaking of which…" Adam tucked in the nozzle and latched the trap door. It wasn't exactly the perfect opening. But it was the best he could hope for on short notice.

"Speaking of bowling?" asked Kyle.

"Speaking of turning Haley on," answered Adam.

Kyle's eyes lit up. "So there *is* something going on between you two."

"Not like *that.*" Well, kind of like that. Only, not like that.

Oh, hell. Adam didn't know.

"Like what, then?"

Asking Kyle for information seemed like the lesser of two evils. Curiosity was going to kill him soon anyway.

Adam took a deep breath. "What's all this about Haley being a lesbian?"

Kyle's eyebrows shot up in obvious shock. "Haley's a lesbian?"

Oops. "Actually I think—"

"And Laura didn't tell me?"

"I think she lied about it."

"Laura?"

"Haley."

Kyle's brow furrowed in confusion. "She told you she *wasn't* a lesbian?"

"No." Adam gave his head at little shake, wondering how he'd could realistically bail on this conversation before things got any worse. "She told me she *was*."

"Why?"

"*That's* what I'm trying to figure out."

"So, ask her."

Right. And get his ego tromped into the dust when she told him it was because she was singularly unattracted to him. He didn't think so.

"You want to keep dating her?" asked Kyle.

"I'm not dating her now. Besides, she's not my type." He had to keep remembering that the woman scored a big, fat zero on his wish list.

If Kyle didn't know anything about the lesbian lie, fine. Aside from idle curiosity, the point was meaningless anyway, since Adam had no intention of pursuing a relationship with Haley.

"Sounds more like you're not *her* type," Kyle chuckled.

Adam folded his arms across his chest. "All right. I can see my day's not going to improve until I get rid of you. So, what are you doing here?"

"I'm here on behalf of the school funfair committee," said Kyle. "We're hoping you'll bring the fire engine again this year."

"No problem." Last year's end of school funfair had been extremely successful. The kids had a great time, and the money raised had been used to upgrade the playground equipment.

Adam was happy to help out. Although he was definitely planning to avoid the dunk tank this year.

"I'll just have to clear it with the chief," he said to Kyle.

"Great."

"You want help with anything else?"

Kyle shook his head. "My crew is already working on the new obstacle course. And we've finished the repairs to the dunk tank."

"Glad to hear that," said Adam dryly.

"Hey. You volunteered."

"Nobody told me about the ice cubes."

For twenty-five cents a cube, people were encouraged to drop ice into the water before their favorite dunking victim climbed into the chair.

"Can I help it if the women of this town wanted

to see you get cold?'' asked Kyle. ''I think you single-handedly paid for the new slide.''

''Next time just tell me how much the equipment costs. I'll write a check.''

Kyle chuckled and started for the door. ''I meant what I said.''

''About what?''

''Ask her.''

''I don't think so.''

Kyle turned to face Adam, walking backward toward the door. ''Trust me. I have more experience in these things. Besides, I'm as curious as you are.''

''Then ask Laura.'' Maybe Laura could clue them both in.

''And make it easy for you?'' Kyle shook his head. ''I don't think so.''

''I thought you considered me a friend.''

''I do. So, it's my duty to help you see the light.''

''What light?''

Kyle shot him a knowing grin. ''Think about it, Adam. If it didn't matter, you'd go ahead and ask.''

Adam shook his head in denial.

No, he wouldn't. Not a chance.

6

————

"TAKE A CHANCE," said Laura.

Haley shook her head as she finished washing the clay from her hands in the big tub in her laundry room. She had five pots in the kiln. It was a good beginning to her latest contract with the South Bay Art Gallery.

She shut off the taps, shook her hands dry and grabbed the towel hanging above the sink. "Don't you see? This is exactly what I was afraid of."

"He's a nice guy," said Laura, glancing toward the door that led to the kitchen, lowering her voice. "You said yourself his kiss curled your toes."

And how. "Just because he's a better kisser doesn't mean it isn't the same thing all over again," Haley whispered, conscious of her mother and the girls through the doorway in the kitchen.

"Let's go out on the deck." Laura grabbed Haley by the arm and pulled her toward the back door.

"I'm not going to talk about this," Haley

warned, tossing the used towel on top of the washing machine.

"Of course you are. That's the only way you'll figure out what you want to do."

"I already know what I want to do."

Kiss Adam again, an unruly part of her brain suggested.

No. *No.* That wasn't it.

"You're confused." Laura pushed Haley down onto a wooden deck chair then took the chair opposite, crossing one bare leg over the other.

"I was confused about Tony and Raymond," said Haley, adjusting her tank top over the waistband of her cutoff jeans. The cool, outside air was refreshing after the heat of the pottery shop. "I'm perfectly lucid now."

"Who are Tony and Raymond?" The sound of Adam's voice sent an adrenaline shot through Haley's system.

"Adam." Laura grinned over Haley's shoulder. "Nice to see you again."

Haley shot her sister a frustrated look. Oh, sure, act all friendly and encouraging when Laura knew darn well Haley was trying to avoid him.

"Hey, Laura," he said. "How's it going?"

Haley refused to turn and look.

It might be rude, but if she looked at him, she'd remember the kiss. If she remembered the kiss, she'd blush. And then he'd think the kiss had mattered. And heaven only knew what Laura would think.

"I'm just fine," said Laura, rising from her chair. "But, I have to go home now."

"Laura—"

"See you at the meeting tomorrow night." Laura squeezed Haley's shoulder as she passed. So much for loyalty between sisters.

"You coming to the funfair planning meeting tomorrow night?" Laura asked Adam as she headed back across the deck.

"I'll be there. I'm bringing the fire engine again this year." The sound of his voice moving closer sent a split second shiver through Haley. Then she heard his footsteps on the short staircase, and her chest tightened around her rising heart rate.

Stop that.

"Oh, good. So, Kyle talked to you about it?" asked Laura, pausing with her hand on the knob.

Haley drew in a deep breath, then another, trying to stabilize her nervous system.

"Saw him down at the fire hall a few hours ago." Adam appeared in Haley's peripheral vision.

"See you both tomorrow, then." Laura disappeared back into the house.

"So…" Adam shifted into full view. His blue jeans were snug, and his worn T-shirt emphasized the breadth of his shoulders and the definition of his biceps. Memories of being held in his arms rushed back.

He folded his body into the chair Laura had vacated. "Who are Tony and Raymond?"

Haley tamped down her body's unruly response. He was just a man. Nothing special, nothing spectacular.

"Nobody important," she said briskly. She had no intention of rehashing her ex-boyfriends with Adam.

They were in the past. And they were none of his business.

"Are they a secret?" he asked.

"No." They were simply no longer relevant.

"Then why won't you tell me?"

"Why won't you leave me alone?"

He drew back, surprise flitting across his face, and she immediately wished she could call back the words.

He *had* been leaving her alone. She hadn't seen him in three days. It wasn't his fault that her hormones had run amuck.

She almost apologized, but then bit back the words. Maybe it was better like this. If he was annoyed with her, he'd stay away.

He watched her in silence as the afternoon wind whispered through the oak trees. Perfume from her flower garden swirled around them, and the muted sounds of her mother and the girls faded into the background.

"Why did you lie to me?" His raspy voice broke the silence.

Oh great. He'd just topped Tony and Raymond as awkward topics of conversation.

"What are you talking about?" she bluffed, hoping against hope he was referring to something other than her lesbian plan.

Not that he had a long list of her lies to choose from. But, in the cold light of day, that one was particularly embarrassing. What had made her think it would work?

Okay, so the answer was easy. She'd never imagined getting this close to a man. She never planned on follow-up conversations. Never mind follow-up kisses. Never mind battling follow-up yearnings night after night.

Adam leaned forward, placing his elbows on his knees. "You're no more a lesbian than I am."

"Well…" She tucked her hair behind her ears, squirming involuntarily against the wooden slats of the chair, glancing from the fence to the maple tree to the rope swing and back again.

"I could have been." At the sound of her defiantly petulant voice, the absurdity of the situation suddenly struck her.

Yeah, right. She could have been a lesbian.

Maybe if she'd tried harder?

Maybe if she hadn't fallen head over heels in lust with Adam?

She glanced back at him, suddenly finding it hard to keep a straight face.

Adam's lips curved into a slow grin. "I don't think so." He shook his head. "You kissed me like I was water and you were lost in the desert."

"Please," she scoffed, rolling her eyes. "Can we tamp down the ego just a little bit?"

"That's not ego. That's pure, unadulterated fact."

Haley declined to comment. He was right, but she wouldn't give him the satisfaction of agreeing. Besides, it was irrelevant now. Thirsty or not, she was staying well out of Adam's arms in the future.

"What I want to know," he continued, voice softening, "is why such an obviously sensual woman, with a Stephen, a Tony, and a Raymond in her past, lied to me about her sexual orientation?"

Haley hesitated for a moment, then she sighed in defeat. Time to resort to the truth.

Maybe the truth would work better anyway. She had perfectly valid reasons for staying out of romantic relationships. Once they both knew where she stood, she could get on with matching him up.

"Okay." Using spread fingers, she combed her hair back from her forehead. "Fine. You want my cards on the table?"

"Yeah." He leaned back, slid down in his chair and stretched his legs out in front of him until his runners were nearly touching her sandals. "That'd be nice."

"You're a nice guy," she said, stalling, mentally trying to compose an explanation that wouldn't make her bad luck with men sound too pathetic.

"Why, thank you."

"And I think you're going to make some woman a terrific husband." That was true enough. From what she'd seen, from what she knew.

"Thank you, again."

"But, what happened the other night…"

"You mean when I kissed you for the fourth and fifth times and you—"

"Right." She interrupted, clearing her throat. The last thing she needed was a blow-by-blow replay of the event. "*That.* It can't happen again."

"Why?" His eyes glowed in the long sunrays. "I kinda liked it."

It was her turn to lean forward. "Because *we're* finding *you* a *wife*." Maybe if she said it distinctly enough, the message would penetrate his brain.

Adam stared at her in silence, gaze softening, hazel eyes darkening to mocha with expectation, a small smile playing about his lips. "I know…"

She blinked.

Uh-oh.

There it was.

He might as well have shouted the question. Since their kiss had practically lit up the Hillard skyline, why didn't she put herself in the running?

"I failed your wish list," she reminded him.

"Who are Tony and Raymond?" he asked softly, unexpectedly.

"Old boyfriends." It was a sad state of affairs when talking about Tony and Raymond was her fallback position for getting out of an uncomfortable conversation.

"I see."

"No, you don't." He couldn't see, because she hadn't explained anything. She hadn't put her cards on the table yet.

Okay. She was going to do that right now. "Tony had a terrible sense of humor. He was loud and crude and sarcastic."

"So, why did you date him?"

"That's the million-dollar question, isn't it?"

"Why don't you give me a million-dollar answer."

"I dated him because he was a man. And my family was thrilled that I was getting over Stephen's death and getting on with my life. You've met my mother. In her eyes, the barometer of a woman's life is her current romantic relationship."

"That's ridiculous."

"I know that. Now. So I'm not doing it again. I've given up men."

"All men?"

"Yes."

"Why not just give up the losers?"

Haley felt her hands curl into fists. "Because I don't seem to have the ability to tell the difference. Raymond was worse than Tony, but I still tried to make it work. I'm not making that mistake again."

"You think I'm a loser?" Adam asked.

"What I think is irrelevant. I'm *matchmaking* you, not dating you."

Adam straightened in his chair and sighed. "So, even if our kiss rivaled the Fourth of July, you won't ever date me because you don't trust your judgment."

"Exactly." Now he was catching on. But she sure wished he'd stop mentioning their kiss. "I'm still willing to help you find the right woman."

"Matchmaker par excellence."

"It's a gift."

"I could modify the wish list."

"Why?"

"Because I think you and me are worth exploring."

Haley stood up. "Oh, no, you don't." She held up her hands in an effort to forestall that line of reasoning. "The list stands."

Adam stood up, facing her. "It's my list. I can do anything I want."

She leaned forward, staring hard into his eyes. "*I'm* the matchmaker. I've memorized the list, and I'm going to find you somebody who meets *every* criteria."

"But, not you."

"I don't meet *any* criteria."

"In other words, you want me to forget all about the possibility of us, and move on to other women."

"Absolutely. There is no *us.*"

The smile was back. He shifted forward, looking her deep in the eye, crowding her space while his fingertips found hers. The touch launched a buzz that radiated up her arm, swirling into desire that zapped her strength. She couldn't back away.

He cocked his head, and his lips parted. His minty breath fanned her face. "I dare you to kiss me…and *then* say that."

HALEY WOULD SAY IT to herself a thousand times if she had to. Men were not in the cards. Adam was not in the cards.

The fact that he was sitting next to her on a folding metal chair with his arm loosely around her shoulders, sending her hormones into a frenzy, had no bearing whatsoever on the situation. He was only playacting because her parents were attending the funfair planning meeting along with them.

Which reminded her, they'd have to hurry up and stage their breakup. Her mother had picked up a few bridal magazines this week, and she had a frightening gleam in her eyes.

It was time to end the charade, and Haley knew just how to do it.

She'd already volunteered to help the grade-four class make pottery for the funfair. So, while the principal stood at the front and outlined the other volunteer requirements, she took the opportunity to glance around the library. With a good fifty people attending, there had to be at least one woman in the crowd who was a match for Adam.

She started methodically checking along the rows, dismissing those women who were obviously in the wrong age group and those who had husbands by their sides. That left her with ten.

Whoops. Nope. Make that nine.

The blond woman near the front looked pregnant. And Haley had already made that mistake once.

She took a deep breath. She could do this. She'd put on a cheerful face, chat with each of them during coffee and cookies at the end of the meeting, and enthusiastically match him up with the most likely candidate. Then, she'd simply let nature take its course.

The sooner he was unavailable, the sooner her life could get back to normal.

ADAM POURED HIMSELF A CUP of coffee at the refreshment table. The meeting had lasted just over an hour. And now the adults were mingling and the children were racing up and down the halls, fueled by juice and chocolate chip cookies.

"Adam?" Haley's determined voice was behind him. "I'd like to introduce Kimberly Smith."

Adam sucked in a too-hot sip of coffee and cursed under his breath. Nursing a scalded tongue, he turned, bracing himself for what was sure to come next.

"Kimberly's the new kindergarten teacher," Haley cheerfully continued. "You might not have had a chance to meet her."

Adam nodded. "It's a pleasure." He transferred his cup and held out his hand to Kimberly.

She was a pretty woman. Slightly taller than Haley, thin, twenty-five or so, with long, blond hair. She had a friendly smile. Adam could easily see that she'd be popular with young children.

"Nice to meet you," Kimberly responded, briefly shaking his hand. "You're Nicole's father?"

He nodded.

"The fireman?"

"That's me."

She laughed. "My students are really excited

about seeing the fire truck up close. I'm having a hard time convincing them they won't be able to sound the siren.''

"I can probably let them ring the bell," Adam smiled in return.

"Oh, they'll love that."

"Kimberly was saying that she loves the theater," Haley put in eagerly.

Adam tried to think of a way to inconspicuously elbow her in the ribs.

Kimberly smiled, looking decidedly embarrassed by Haley's obvious hint.

"I noticed *Fiddler on the Roof* is playing down at the Guild Hall." Haley glanced expectantly from Adam to Kimberly and back again.

The woman was an absolute maniac.

"Are you busy on Friday night?" Adam dutifully asked Kimberly.

Haley had made her position abundantly clear. *Abundantly.* And he still needed a mother for Nicole.

He wasn't going to find one if he didn't bite the bullet and get out on a date or two. Kimberly seemed like a perfectly nice woman, even if Haley's methods were a little extreme.

Kimberly put up a hand. "You don't have to—"

"I want to," Adam interrupted sincerely. "I'll see if I can get tickets."

"Okay, then." She nodded. "Sure. Friday sounds good." She took a step back. "I should go check on my students."

"I'll call you," said Adam.

"Great." Kimberly melted into the crowd.

Adam watched her walk away, refusing to let himself second-guess his decision to ask her out. It was the right thing to do.

This infatuation with Haley would pass. It was only because she was an undeniably attractive woman, and he was a perfectly normal man. Plus, he had inside information on the way she kissed.

But, she couldn't have made her disinterest clearer if she'd used a neon sign. And it was passion not reason that was attracting him. It wasn't like he'd pictured anything long-term with her. He wanted long-term here. Not a temporary, sexy, mind-blowing fling.

Definitely not that. He raised the cup to his lips for another sip.

"Okay," said Haley, shoving the sleeves of her sweater up to her elbows and rubbing her hands together. "Let's talk logistics."

"Excuse me?" Adam glanced at her. Her expression made him *very* nervous.

"Your date. We've only got two days to plan it."

"You should be locked up."

"I don't want you to blow this."

"We're going to see a play. What's to plan?"

"What time does it start? Are you going for dinner? Drinks? Coffee? Before? After?"

"I don't know."

"Adam."

"What does it matter?"

"It matters a lot."

"Dinner, then. We'll do dinner."

Her eyes narrowed. "Dinner? Right off the bat?"

Adam threw up his free hand in a gesture of frustration.

"I mean," said Haley, "dinner right off the bat is pretty romantic. Where were you planning to take her?"

"Forget dinner, then. We'll do drinks."

"I didn't mean you should—"

"Haley."

"What?"

"We'll do drinks."

"Before or after?"

"What's the difference?"

She leaned back against a table, folding her arms across her chest. "Well, before the play, you have a deadline. You can chat a bit, get to know each other, but if you don't hit it off there's no huge silence to fill, and it doesn't look obvious if you have to break if off early to, say, get in line or get your seats."

She took a breath. "If you have drinks after the play, you're obligated to chat for at least an hour or so. It can be awkward if things aren't going well. Plus, there's that whole dropping off, do you kiss her, does she invite you in—"

"*Before* the play," said Adam. "We'll have drinks before the play."

"What if—"

"Why don't you just come along."

"Don't be silly."

"That way you can tell me where to sit, what to say, when to put my arm around her—"

"You're going to put your *arm* around her?"

"Maybe." Was that jealousy? Did he dare hope Haley wasn't as blasé as she pretended?

No. He didn't hope that. He wasn't going to hope that. He had to get her right out of his mind.

She frowned. "That might be a little juvenile. You know, in the back row of the theater, with the lights dim…"

Adam shook his head. "It *is* a date."

"Yes. Well." Haley shimmied up onto the table, crossing her blue jean legs.

Adam settled back on his heels, deciding he might as well play along. "Should I kiss her?"

"Maybe good-night." Haley didn't look at all sure about that answer. She caught his gaze and held it for a moment. "You should probably…go by…"

"*Mom,* Grandma says it's time to go home." Belinda skipped across the library, hopping up on the table next to Haley.

Haley quickly slid off, glancing around guiltily. "Don't sit up there, honey."

"But—"

"Tell Grandma we'll be right there."

"Go by what?" Adam asked, stopping Haley with a hand on her arm before she could follow Belinda.

"Her." Haley swallowed, gazing after Belinda, not meeting Adam's eyes. Her voice sounded suddenly hollow. "How she acts. What she says. Her body language."

Although Haley wasn't looking at him, Adam nodded. "Makes sense to me." The warmth of her arm made his fingertips tingle.

"I hope you have a good time," she said in a low voice.

"Thanks." He let go of her arm. "I hope so, too."

And he did. He really did.

ON FRIDAY NIGHT, HALEY tried valiantly to ignore the sound of Adam's car. But she heard it start. Then she heard it back down the driveway. Then she heard it pull away from the curb and fade to silence down the block on his way to pick up Kimberly.

Annoyed with herself, she headed for the kitchen, where her mother was baking cookies for the school funfair with Belinda and Nicole.

"I've never made cookies before," Nicole was saying. "We always buy them at the bakery."

Each of the girls were standing on a kitchen chair in front of the breakfast bar, colorful aprons tied around their waists, watching while Grandma measured shortening into a bowl.

"Then it's about time you learned," said Grandma. "Belinda, you read the recipe. And, Nicole, you can measure the sugar."

"It says you have to whip it with an electric mixer," said Belinda.

"How much sugar?" Nicole opened the stoneware canister and peeked inside.

"I thought I heard you and Adam leave," said Grandma, looking up at Haley.

"Not me. Just Adam. He's gone out on a date."

"Two cups," said Belinda. "Hi, Mom," she sang. "Grandma's teaching us how to make monster cookies."

"They have *four* kinds of candies in them," said Nicole with a wide grin.

"A date?" asked Grandma, regarding Haley with a frown, a furrow forming across her forehead.

"You fill up this one." Belinda handed Nicole a plastic measuring cup.

"Can we taste the candies?" asked Nicole.

"She'll let us try some while they're baking," Belinda whispered conspiratorially.

Haley shrugged in her mother's direction. "I never said Adam and I were dating exclusively." This seemed like a good opportunity to start letting her mother down gently. Not to mention proving to herself that she truly and sincerely wanted Adam to find a wife.

She was glad he was out on a date. Kimberly seemed like a very nice woman. This empty feeling in her stomach would go away soon.

"But…" Her mother glanced to where the girls were dumping sugar into the bowl.

"Was it up to the top line?" her mother asked Nicole.

Nicole nodded.

"Did you level it?"

"It was level," said Belinda. "Can I work the mixer."

"Sure," said Grandma, plugging in the electric hand mixer. "Remember to hold it straight up and down."

"I will," said Belinda. "You can have a turn, too," she said to Nicole, flipping the switch to low.

The humming of the mixer motor filled the room.

Haley's mother shifted closer to her.

"Are you sure that's wise?" she asked Haley.

"What's wise?'

"Letting Adam date other women?"

"I'm not *letting* him do anything." Well, in reality she was pretty much forcing him to do it. "Adam's old enough to make his own decisions."

"Did you two have a fight?"

"No." The word was out before it occurred to Haley that this was a perfect time to pretend they were fighting.

"It must be something," said her mother.

Belinda turned the mixer up another notch, and her mother glanced back at the girls to make sure all was well.

"Why don't you cook him a nice dinner?"

"Cooking? Me?" asked Haley. That sure wasn't the safest way to impress a man.

"Give Nicole a turn now," her mother called to Belinda. "I'll help you cook," she said to Haley.

Belinda transferred the mixer to Nicole's eager hands.

Haley sighed. "Mom, I'm not—"

"You can wear that silver dress. You know, the one you bought for Melanie's wedding."

"That one makes me look fat."

Adam wasn't going to like that dress. He'd said he didn't want a woman with a potbelly, and the silver dress clung to every little curve. Sure, she'd started doing sit-ups in the mornings, but her abs had a ways to go yet.

Wait a minute. *What* was she thinking? She wasn't out to impress Adam. She wasn't about to cook up a fancy dinner and dress to the nines for him.

"It doesn't make you look fat." Her mother put a hand on her shoulder. "Oh, honey, why do you say things like that? Your figure is absolutely lovely. And, you've always been so pretty."

"But I always had Laura standing right beside me in all the pictures." Super-model-look Laura was enough to give anyone a complex.

"So?"

"Mom. Haven't you noticed? Laura's gorgeous."

"Oh, pooh." Her mother waved a hand. "She keeps herself too thin. She's attractive enough. But not like you. You have Grandma Markwell's blue eyes. Those eyes stop traffic."

Haley drew back. "You think so?"

"I know so." Her mother gave her a quick squeeze. "The silver dress looks good on you. You should wear it."

The mixer went silent. "I think it's ready," said Belinda.

Nicole swiped her finger across the edge of the bowl and popped it into her mouth. "Mmm!"

"Next we add the flour," said Grandma, heading back to the breakfast bar. She turned back to Haley for a moment and smiled reassuringly. "We'll make him a nice lasagna."

7

—————

ADAM STARED AT THE PAN in Haley's hand, then he took in the clingy silver dress, her curled hair and her perfectly made-up face.

"Sorry." She rolled her eyes heavenward and brushed past him into the front foyer of his house.

"About what?" he asked, letting his gaze drop to her strappy sandals and shapely calves and linger there. He sure couldn't see anything to be sorry about. Unless it was his casual blue jeans and T-shirt.

"Mom got worried that Kimberly was my competition." She spun around and held up the lasagna. "She thinks the way to your heart is through your stomach."

Considering the lukewarm good-night kiss Adam had given Kimberly last night, and their agreement to develop a friendship rather than a romance, she was hardly competition for anyone.

"What's in the pan?" he asked.

"Lasagna."

"Did you really make it yourself?"

Haley paused and glanced at the foil covering. "I grated the cheese."

"Good enough." He lifted the pan out of her hand. "I've got a bottle of wine to go with it."

"Sounds great to me." Haley kicked off her sandals and followed him into the kitchen.

Adam turned the oven dial to three-fifty and set the timer. "I take it Nicole's over at your house for the duration?"

Haley grinned. "Tonight, they're baking lemon tarts and butterscotch squares. I think my mom is going to pay for the new computer lab single-handedly."

Adam popped the pan of lasagna into the oven and crossed to the small wine rack in his dining room. "So, what do we have to do tonight to keep Mom happy?" he called over his shoulder.

"It'd be nice if you proposed," said Haley.

"Don't have a ring." He selected a bottle of merlot, feeling relaxed and happy with Haley in his kitchen. It was a nice change from the tension of last night. He'd forgotten how stressful dating could be.

"Darn." Haley snapped her fingers. "That would have made her year."

"We could pop down to the Value-Mart after dinner and buy one. I think it's open till nine."

"Never work. My mother can spot a cubic zirconia at a hundred paces."

"Too bad."

Haley slid up onto one of the stools at the breakfast bar and crossed her legs. "Can't win 'em all. Oh well, sipping wine and eating lasagna for a couple of hours ought to do the trick for tonight."

"Works for me." He pulled a corkscrew out of the drawer. "I was planning on takeout later on. This is a whole lot better." The company was a whole lot better, too.

"Where are the glasses?" she stood up.

"Cupboard beside the microwave."

Haley headed across the kitchen. "I have to warn you, you should expect an inquisition next time you see Mom. She told me I was making a mistake by *letting* you date other women."

"She's right." He popped the cork. "I sure wouldn't want any girlfriend of mine dating other men."

"Well… Under normal circumstances, maybe."

"And, under normal circumstances, I wouldn't have given Kimberly or anyone else a second look. I'm a loyal guy."

"That's very admirable of you." The glasses clinked as she pulled them off the high shelf. "So… Since you and I are anything but normal, how *was* the date?"

"Hey, speak for yourself." Adam puffed out his chest. "I'm perfectly normal."

"You know what I mean."

''The play was good,'' he said, twisting the cork off the corkscrew. ''You should try to see it before it closes.''

Haley nodded. ''Maybe I will.'' She set the glasses down on the counter. ''Did Kimberly like it?''

''She said she did.''

''Did you put your arm around her?''

''And you're warning me about your *mother's* inquisition?''

Haley shrugged easily as she slipped back onto the stool. ''Hey, your matchmaker can't do her job if you're not straight with her.''

Adam poured wine into the two glasses, and handed one across the counter to Haley. ''Okay. I'll be straight with you.''

''Good.''

''What do you want to know?''

''Everything.''

''*Everything?*'' He lifted his eyebrows.

She drew back, her hand going to the stem of her wineglass. ''Well…I mean…'' After a silent moment, she leaned forward again, eyes wide and curious. ''*Is* there an everything?''

''You are *so* nosy.''

''I'm not nosy.'' She looked affronted. ''I'm simply trying to help.''

''I didn't put my arm around her.''

''Why not?''

"I was sitting there in the dark, in the middle of act three, thinking this was the time to make a move if I was going to make a move. But then I remembered what you said about it being adolescent." He shrugged. "And I didn't."

"I see." Haley took a sip of her wine. "And later?"

"That was the last act."

"You know what I mean."

He stood up to check on the lasagna. "Okay. I'll take it from the top. We went to The Edge for drinks."

"Did you dance?"

"No. I honestly never thought of it." Funny that he hadn't. "We didn't have that much time before the play started."

"Um-hmm."

"I had a scotch. She had a martini." He took a sip of his wine. "She was wearing a blue dress, with sort of a V neck."

At least he thought it was a V neck. He searched his memory for more details. But with Haley sitting right in front of him, Kimberly seemed to fade into the background. "I think she had a white sweater, and her hair was done up in a kind of twisty thing…"

"What did you talk about?"

"She told me about her kindergarten students."

Adam smiled. "She sends home *The Kindergarten News* every Friday afternoon."

He shook his head. "The kids each report a story from home. They tell her some of the most amazing things. My personal favorite was 'Jenny's mom and dad got a big surprise in the middle of the night when the bed broke.'"

Haley raised a hand to her mouth to stifle a laugh. "Oh, no."

"Oh, yeah."

"She printed that?"

"Uh-huh."

"Kindergarten teachers could probably get rich through blackmail." Haley lifted her wineglass again and stared contemplatively into the dark liquid. "Do you think you'll have more children?"

"With Kimberly?" That was definitely not happening.

"With anyone."

Adam shrugged, thinking seriously about the question. "I guess that depends."

"On?"

"A bunch of things. On how Nicole feels. On whether the person I marry wants more children." From a personal perspective, he could quite happily add a few more kids to his family.

"What about you?" he asked, watching her closely.

"You mean if I was to forsake my 'no men' vow?"

"Just for a minute, let's pretend you did."

"Then I'd definitely have another baby." She smiled, the thought seeming to make her happy.

"Yeah?"

"I miss babies. And I love toddlers. I'd even risk being a headline item in *The Kindergarten News.*"

"Only if we broke the bed." He chuckled before realizing he'd used the word "we."

Haley put her face into her hands and shook her head. "Wouldn't you just die?"

"I doubt the kindergarten kids caught on. And Jenny's parents probably weren't the only ones in the neighborhood having sex."

"True." She cleared her throat. "So, how did it end?"

"The bed incident?"

"No. The date."

"Oh. Right. Well, I told her a few stories about Nicole. We went to the play. And I took her home."

"That's it?"

"That's it."

"Did you kiss her good-night?"

Adam put down his glass. "See. I knew you were going to ask me that."

"Well, did you?" She raised her eyebrows.

How could he explain it? It had been a kiss, but not a kiss. It was more an answer to a question for both of them. Not a surprise, simply a confirmation of what they'd suspected all evening.

The timer buzzed for the lasagna, and he was given a reprieve.

"Plates?" asked Haley.

"Middle cupboard on the top shelf." He retrieved a couple of pot holders from a drawer and put the hot lasagna pan on the stovetop. "You want to eat in here or in the dining room?"

"Here's fine." She set the plates on the breakfast bar and started hunting for the cutlery.

"Far left," said Adam, liking the way she just plunged in to help. "Should we worry about the girls?"

"What do you think?"

He grinned. "That we could take off for a weekend in Vegas, and your mother wouldn't even break her stride."

"You got it."

"She's a very nice woman."

"She's also a very energetic woman."

"Did she bake you cookies and play games with you when you were a kid?"

"All the time. Whether it was a game of cards, a camping trip, or marrying one of us off, she always believed you just got to it and got it done."

"No easing into anything."

Haley shook her head and laughed. "Why waste time?" She began arranging the plates and the knives and forks. "What were your parents like?"

"Dad was a fireman."

"Just like you?"

"He'd say I was just like him. Only, he's retired now. They live in northern California. Mom was a nurse."

"Brothers and sisters?"

"Just me." He paused. "I was lonely growing up. Maybe that's part of the reason I want more for Nicole."

Haley glanced up, meeting his eyes.

Neither of them said anything for a still moment, but he knew they were both thinking about Belinda and Nicole's fast friendship. He was grateful for the way Haley's parents had taken Nicole under their wing. She'd been so proud of the cookies she baked last night.

A sudden shiver of emotion passed through him. "I kissed her," he said.

Haley nodded, and went back to arranging the cutlery. "I see." Her voice was small.

"But…" He struggled to put it in perspective, not knowing why he suddenly felt guilty. This was what Haley had wanted, after all.

But, there it was. He felt as though he had somehow betrayed Haley by kissing Kimberly. Even though it wasn't a real kiss. Even though it had meant nothing.

He set the pot holders down and walked around to the other side of the breakfast bar.

"You see…" He tried again, coming to a halt in front of her, taking the last fork out of her hand and setting it gently down on the countertop.

"The thing was…" He took a breath and looked deeply into her luminous blue eyes. Oh, man, she was so beautiful.

"You don't have to explain," she said.

He reached down tentatively to take her hand. Fingertips to fingertips, hers warm and smooth. They curled and brushed his palm.

"Yes, I do," he said softly. "You're my matchmaker. You need to know everything."

She smiled.

"And, so," he breathed, throwing caution and good sense to the wind, tipping his head forward. "Here we go. I did it like this."

He gave her a short, chaste, closed-mouth kiss on the lips. It was hard to bounce back. It was doubly hard not to lean in for a second taste. But, he managed.

"When…" His voice dropped to a whisper as he savored the white-hot rush of desire that coursed through his body at the mere brush of her lips. He stroked his palm across her flushed cheek, sliding a hand to the back of her neck, burying his fingers into her hairline. ''I really should have done it like this.''

He tipped his head forward again.

This time it was a proper kiss, a long-lasting, openmouthed, serious, satisfying kiss. A kiss that answered questions. A kiss that told a man everything he needed to know about himself.

And, she kissed him back. Tentatively at first, then hotly, passionately, enthusiastically. And it was all he could do to bring it to an end.

But he had a point to make here. At least, he'd had a point when he started. Right now his brain cells were consumed with one thought.

Haley.

''Because,'' he said, pulling back, mentally regrouping. He still held her hand, still cradled her head. ''That kind of a kiss would have told me she was the right woman.''

''Is she?'' Haley asked, an unfathomable look in her eyes.

Adam smiled and shook his head. ''No. That's why we never made it to a real kiss.''

When his lips had met Kimberly's last night, his desire had flat lined.

When his lips met Haley's, it shot to the moon.

''I see,'' she said.

''Do you?'' He let go of her hand, and snaked his arm around her waist, flattening her against his body. His other thumb stroked her soft cheek, and he inhaled her sweet, fanning breath. "I really don't think you do."

It wasn't the fact that he didn't want Kimberly that counted. It was the fact that he *did* want Haley.

Despite all of the very logical reasons not to, he definitely wanted Haley.

He slowly bent toward her once again, giving her plenty of time to pull away. She didn't, and her blue eyes turned opaque as he lost focus.

This time, when he kissed her, it was the culmination of an entire week's buildup. Days of longing to touch her, a whole evening of wishing he was with her instead of another woman, not a lifetime of looking for someone who was just the right fit.

Desire exploded within him. He deepened their kiss, thrilled when her tongue met his halfway. His hand tangled in her hair.

She moaned his name, and her arms twined around his neck. The feel of her lips sent ripples of need cascading through his system. The scent of roses wafted in through the window, mingling with the fresh scent of Haley.

He smoothed his hands down the sides of her sexy little dress, feeling her curves, reveling in her soft breasts, her firm hips, her shapely thighs. When he got to the hem, he hesitated. He desperately wanted to follow her stockings up, but he didn't know where this was leading.

Sure, she wanted to kiss him. And it was obvious there was some serious mutual chemistry between them, but he didn't want to take anything for granted.

Her fingertips started down his arms, they tightened on his biceps, stroking and kneading, sliding under his T-shirt sleeve, making their way to the bare skin of his shoulders.

Encouraged, he broke off their kiss to taste her neck. He left a wet trail along one shoulder, nudging the strap of her dress out of the way.

"Adam," she breathed in his ear.

"Yeah?" Despite his best intentions, one hand slid slowly up the back of her thigh. When he hit warm skin at top of her stocking, his heart pounded into overdrive.

He kissed her fully on the mouth again, putting every scrap of his need and passion into a kiss that went on and on. When it was either breathe or pass out, he finally drew back a fraction of an inch.

She touched her forehead to his. "I can't believe—"

He placed his index finger gently across her lips, worried that she'd call a halt, worried that her crazy vow would assert itself. "Believe," he said simply.

She hesitated for a split second, then he felt her nod.

The weight on his chest disappeared.

His hand slipped past her stocking top, seeking its way farther up her leg. Her eyes widened, and then they closed, her head falling back. He touched his lips to her neck, suckling the tender skin.

He cupped his hands beneath her bottom, pushing her short dress out of the way, pulling her tight as he kissed her. Then he lifted her right off the floor. Holding her against him, higher and higher, until the thin silk of her panties brushed the denim of his jeans, and her legs encircled his waist.

When her thigh muscles reflexively tightened, he groaned.

"Adam." Her voice was hot against his ear.

His thumbs caressed the tender skin between her stocking tops and her panties. His gaze roamed to the tanned skin revealed by her bunched dress. Her lacy white panties contrasted.

"Yeah?" It was almost more than he could do to form the word.

Her fingers burrowed in his hair, short breaths tickling his neck. "Don't...."

He grazed the white silk with his knuckles. "Stop?" he asked.

"Yes. No. Don't. Just don't..."

He brushed back the opposite direction.

"Ahhh...stop."

"I won't." He started with a kiss above her scooped neckline. Then he bent his head farther, nuzzling, testing, exploring. He opened his mouth and moistened the tip of one breast through the stretchy fabric. The action fed his desire to taste her bare skin.

Frustrated by the cloth barrier, he pushed down her neckline, freeing her arms, bunching the dress around her waist. He feasted his eyes and then his mouth on her pink nipples.

Her fingertips dug into his shoulder, and her breath came in small pants.

The breakfast bar was too high, so he took the few steps across the kitchen, lowering her onto the dining-room table. He stripped off his T-shirt in one quick motion. He needed to feel her skin to skin.

He wrapped his arms tightly around her bare back, pressing her close, absorbing her heat and softness, desperately wanting the moment to go on forever. But, his passion was insistent. His fingertips ached to explore every inch of her. He drew back, gazing at her perfection for a long moment.

She reached out and touched her palms to his chest. Then she leaned forward, following the gentle touch with kisses, leaving damp circles that made him moan. Her soft hair brushed against him, nearly driving him out of his mind.

He slipped a finger beneath her panties.

She moaned, ratcheting up his arousal as she wriggled against him.

"Upstairs?" he asked, kissing her eyelids.

"Right here," she replied, hands tightening on his shoulders.

"Right here," he agreed easily.

"Condom?" she asked.

"Bathroom," he answered.

She blinked, giving him a pained look. "Upstairs?"

"Two seconds," he replied. He sprinted down the hall and ripped open the cabinet.

"Not bad," she smiled, as he rushed back. She'd slipped off her dress and now sat naked on his maple table.

"I'd run through fire," he said as he drew her back into his arms. "No oxygen, no helmet, no hoses." He gently rubbed his hands up and down her bare back, kissing her mouth. Her warmth and softness sent fresh tremors of arousal shifting through him.

"You're overdressed," she teased, burying her face in his neck and doing amazing things with the tip of her tongue.

"I am," he agreed on a rasp.

"Lose the pants, cowboy."

"I'd have to let go of you."

"Two seconds," she said, reaching between them and popping the snap on his jeans.

He shuddered as her dainty hands slowly pushed down his fly, brushing, lingering. Two seconds was going to be the honest truth if she wasn't careful.

He shucked his pants and donned the condom.

''Ready?'' he asked, pausing, sucking in a heavy breath, staring closely into her blue eyes.

She nodded.

He cupped her bottom and pulled her close, gritting his teeth as he sank into her heat.

''So good,'' he gasped, stilling for a moment, unable to assimilate the intense sensations gripping his body.

''So good,'' she echoed, meeting his mouth.

The sound and smell and taste of her fogged his brain. His reality contracted to their rhythm as she gripped his shoulders and moaned his name.

8

HALEY FELT LIKE A RAG DOLL, laying on top of Adam's sweat-sheened body. He'd carried her to his bed at some point, that much she remembered. But most of the past two hours had been a haze of mind-bending passion.

Now, his arms were wrapped loosely around her waist, and he was drawing absent little circles on the small of her back with his fingertips.

There were warning bells going off inside her brain, and she was coherent enough to know that making love with Adam had been a serious mistake.

But, she was honestly too drained at the moment to put it into context. Maybe once she regained full consciousness, she'd be in a better position to get their relationship back on track.

With an effort, she raised her head to look at him.

His eyes were closed, and his breathing was deep. He was, hands down, the sexiest, most compelling man on the planet. As a test of her resolve, he was as tough as it got.

But, she was resolved, she reminded herself. Even now.

"This doesn't mean we won't find the right woman for you," she said.

He opened one eye and stared up at her. "Oh, good. I was getting a little worried about that."

"Just because Kimberly and Joanne didn't work out—"

Adam cut off the sentence by placing his index finger across her lips. "Do we have to talk about this now?"

"I suppose not," she muttered around his finger.

"It's not like we'll be doing any matchmaking tonight," he said.

Haley let her head drop back onto his shoulder, because she was too tired to hold it up any longer. "True enough," she agreed with a contented sigh. "Unless you want to go bowling later."

Her fingertips itched to feel their way across his broad chest one more time. But, she knew that would only compound her mistake, so she kept them still.

"I'll be lucky to make it as far as the lasagna," he said.

"If you don't eat any, my mom's going to be pretty upset."

"We could send her a Polaroid as a consolation prize."

Haley couldn't help laughing. "That would definitely do the trick."

Adam reached up to stroke her hair, whispering on a serious note. "You want to talk about us?"

She shook her head. There was nothing to talk about.

Her momentary libido meltdown notwithstanding, she knew deep down inside that she couldn't do a relationship. There was no point in pretending any different.

She'd simply built Adam into a bigger fantasy than any of the rest. She thought she'd fallen for him, but it was really the rose-colored glasses talking. It was only the brainwashing, the indoctrination, the deep down visceral feeling that she wasn't complete without a man that made him look so darn good. Made him feel so darn good. Made him taste like ambrosia.

It was all an illusion. She and Belinda could make it on their own. And Haley was going to prove it.

Just as soon as she could move again.

In fact, now that the curiosity factor was satisfied, she'd be stronger than before. It should be even easier to keep her friendship with Adam on an even keel. Now that she knew. There'd be no more wondering in the middle of the night.

Right?

Right.

She could focus on finding him a woman.

"Haley," he sighed, combing back her hair with his fingertips. "I really think we need to—"

"It's not like anything has to change." She drew away from him, pretending she wasn't trying to convince herself as much as him.

"Haley." He craned his neck so that he was looking her in the eyes. "You're laying naked in my arms, and we just made a serious dent in my condom supply."

He had a point. Oh, boy, did he have a point.

She forced just the right note of sarcasm into her voice. "And your point is?"

"Something has definitely changed."

She slid to one side of the bed and sat up. She didn't have the strength to argue with him right now. "Do you remember where I left my dress?"

Adam sat up, too. *"Haley."* He drew out the syllables of her name in a disapproving manner.

She shifted her feet to the floor. "Okay, so now I have more detailed information to work with. It should make my job even easier." She quickly stood up, forcing her mind away from the soft bed and tousled sheets. "The dining room, I think," she said determinedly.

"Make your job even *easier?*"

"Yeah."

Adam groaned and fell back on the bed, clamping his palms over his face.

"Want me to grab your jeans?" she asked.

"Why not," he mumbled.

"MOM SAID YOU AND ADAM had a big date on Saturday night." Laura grinned as she spread a plastic tablecloth over one of the craft tables in the grade four classroom.

"His date was with Kimberly," Haley corrected, grabbing one end of the cover, settling it on the table and smoothing out the folds.

"That was Friday. I'm talking about lasagna and wine at his place." Laura waggled her eyebrows.

"Oh, that…" Haley turned away to open up the top of her supply box.

Having her mother living in the driveway was definitely a mixed blessing. Belinda and Nicole were having the time of their lives, but Haley was definitely suffering from a lack of privacy.

Not that her mother knew any of the finer details of her dinner with Adam. As far as her mother knew, they'd eaten lasagna and sipped wine until the respectable hour of ten-thirty.

"Oh, *that*… What?" asked Laura.

Haley kept her head down, sorting through the jars of glazes. Mrs. Livingston would keep the class in the library for another ten minutes while

Haley set out the supplies. The children had thrown their pots yesterday, and would spend the rest of the afternoon applying the glaze.

"It was nothing," Haley finished.

Laura peered around to where she could see Haley's face. "Define nothing? I heard you made him dinner."

"Ha!" Haley straightened. "All I did was grate the cheese."

"Hey, for you, that's pretty good." Laura reached around Haley and pulled a second tablecloth out of Haley's supply box. "Now, tell me about the rest."

"Mom made the sauce and boiled the noodles."

"I'm not talking about *that* rest." Laura tossed the cloth over a second table, and Haley grabbed the other end.

"What *are* you talking about?" she bluffed, tightening the plastic at the corner, then heading back to the box for the jars of glaze.

"Don't play coy with me," Laura admonished.

Haley tipped her head in her sister's direction and blinked rapidly. "Who me? Coy?"

Laura picked up a handful of brushes and set them out. "I want details."

"Okay." Haley leaned across the table, lowering her voice to a conspiratorial level. She glanced over at the classroom door, then back at Laura. "I'll give you details."

"Yeah?" Laura grinned, her eyes lighting up.

"First," said Haley, "you make a layer of meat sauce."

"Give me a break."

"Then…you add a layer of noodles."

Laura drew back, making a disgusted sound in the back of her throat.

"Then… And, this is the really good part, you grate the cheese."

"You're hopeless." Laura turned back to the supply box for another handful of brushes.

"What were you expecting?" asked Haley. She set the dark glazes out on one table and the lighter colors on the other. The kids would probably distribute themselves evenly by color choice.

"Something steamy," said Laura. "Something exciting. Something that would prove to me you're not made of stone."

"Like, he kissed me? And I ripped off my clothes? And we made love on his dining-room table?"

"Yeah. That would do nicely."

"Okay," said Haley, rounding the end of the table and focusing on the correct placement of the glaze jars. "He kissed me. And I ripped off my clothes. And we made love on his dining-room table."

"Yeah, right."

Haley shrugged. "Believe me or don't."

"Wait," Laura squeaked. She grabbed Haley by the upper arm and stared deeply into her eyes. "You *didn't*."

Then, after a few seconds, her jaw dropped open. "You *did*."

Haley shrugged again. "It didn't mean anything." She had to keep telling herself that.

"That's ridiculous."

"I'm still going to match him up with somebody else." It was her duty. And it was her only route to salvation.

"That's even more ridiculous."

Haley broke from Laura's grip to get the last of the glaze jars. "Everything I said about me and relationships is still valid."

"It was never valid."

"Adam wants a wife. I want my freedom."

"Was he any good?"

"*What?*"

"I mean, let's strive for a little balance here. Your freedom, versus good sex. I've been free and I've had good sex."

"You've never been free," said Haley.

"Sure I was. The whole year I was nineteen."

"You were dating Kyle when you were nineteen."

"But, we weren't having good sex. Believe me when I tell you good sex is much better than freedom."

"Uh-hmm." Mrs. Livingston cleared her throat from the open doorway of the classroom.

Haley spun around to see several sets of grade-four eyes peeking out from behind Mrs. Livingston's skirt.

"Oh my goodness," she mumbled to Laura. "We're going to make the kindergarten news."

"What?" asked Laura.

"Never mind." Haley took a few steps forward and pasted a bright smile on her face. "Hi, kids. Everybody remember to bring their paint smock?"

She decided to assume Laura's voice had been too low for anyone but Mrs. Livingston to make out the words. The teacher moved to one side, and a wave of children headed for their desks.

"Your vases and pots are set out along the window," Haley called above the chatter. "Put on your smocks, find your project, and you can pick out a color of glaze."

"Row one students may go first," said Mrs. Livingston. She slid Haley a speculative smile as the students filed up to the wide window ledge.

Oh, perfect. Her sex life was going to be the talk of the school staff room.

"Ms. Roberts?" One of the girls stopped in front of Haley. She held a very nicely crafted vase.

"Yes?" Haley asked.

"Do we *have* to sell them at the craft fair?"

"Well…I…" Haley sure didn't want to make a

child part with a creation they wanted to keep. She glanced up at Mrs. Livingston for guidance.

The teacher smiled and took a couple of steps closer to them. "No, you don't, Alyssa." Then she raised her voice. "Class?"

The noise in the room slowly subsided. "Donating your pottery to the funfair is purely voluntary. Anyone who wants to take their project home instead, may do that."

A cheer went up from some of the students, and the talking immediately resumed.

"I'm afraid we may not get too many pottery projects at the craft sale," Mrs. Livingston said to Haley.

"Is that a problem?"

"Not at all. Fund-raising is a minor component of the funfair."

"They can have mine, Mom." Belinda whizzed past, painting smock half on.

"That's very generous of you," said Mrs. Livingston.

"Mine's ugly," said one of the boys, holding up a misshapen bowl. "Nobody'll pay any money for it."

Haley lifted the bowl from his hands. "Have you ever heard of D'Aniche?" she asked, raising her eyebrows in the boy's direction.

"Who?"

Haley inspected the bowl. "He makes very

modern, artistic pottery that looks very much like this. Want me to show you how he glazes it?''

"How?'' The boy looked unconvinced.

"Take it over to the far end, by the browns and blacks. I'll get a smock and show you.''

"Bet nobody buys his, either,'' said the boy.

"People pay hundreds of dollars for it,'' said Haley.

"Why?''

"Because they think it's beautiful.''

"You sure?''

"I'm positive.'' She handed him back his bowl.

Looking skeptical, but definitely curious, he headed for the far end of the craft table.

"Nice save,'' said Mrs. Livingston.

"Thanks,'' said Haley.

"She's right you know.'' Mrs. Livingston leaned a little closer to Haley.

"Who?''

"Laura. Good sex is a whole lot better than freedom.'' She winked and patted Haley on the shoulder.

"I HEAR YOU'RE HAVING SEX with my sister on the dining-room table.''

Startled, Adam drew back from Laura's probing smile. The afternoon of the funfair had arrived. Decked out in his sweltering firefighting gear, he was manning the engine display.

She was dressed more sensibly in shorts and a loose T-shirt. She crossed her arms and leaned sideways against engine number two. Students chattered in the background as they climbed all over it, their excitement level rising with each passing hour. Adam had promised them he'd reel out the hose at the end of the day and spray some water into the creek.

"What?" He finally asked Laura in amazement. He couldn't believe Haley had told anyone about them making love. But Laura obviously had some pretty detailed information.

A group of little girls trotted by. They wore balloon animal hats and carried huge balls of cotton candy.

Laura leaned closer to Adam. "I'm naturally concerned about my little sister's welfare." She paused. "So, let's have the details."

It was a nice try. But the twinkle in her eyes gave her away.

Adam crossed his arms over the chest of his yellow jacket. "I don't kiss and tell."

"Haley already told."

Adam's gaze wandered to where Haley was talking with Elsa Johnson beside the game booths set up along the gym wall. She'd been holed up in her pottery workshop for the past two days, using the excuse that she had to fire the students' pottery projects before the funfair started.

"So, what do you need me for?" he challenged.

A group of boys rang the bell up on top of the engine. It was cosmetic, of course, but a big hit with the kids. Even though he was competing with ring toss, balloon darts, a dunk tank and a giant blowup fun house, he'd had a good crowd all day.

"I want to know your intentions."

Adam snorted, nodding toward Haley and the newly divorced Elsa Johnson. "You're better off asking your rabid matchmaking sister what her intentions are."

Laura followed his gaze. "Elsa?"

Adam glanced at his watch. "I give her five minutes, and she'll be over her extolling the virtues of Elsa's peach pie."

He was having a hard time with the fact that Haley seemed as determined as ever to fix him up with another woman. Their evening of making love and sharing lasagna had been one of the best nights of his life. Maybe she could simply toss it aside and carry on as if nothing extraordinary had happened, but it had shifted something inside him that couldn't be put back.

"That doesn't answer my question," said Laura.

"I have a question for you," said Adam. "What's the story of Haley swearing off men?"

"Why do you want to know?" Her eyebrows

rose, and a little gleam came into her eye, making her look just like her mother and Haley.

The whole family was incurable.

Which wasn't necessarily a bad thing, if some of them were willing to help him.

"Why do you think I'd want to know?" He removed his heavy yellow helmet and set it on the bumper of the engine.

"I think you like my sister."

Adam was silent for a moment, debating the merits of his answer. He might as well go for broke here, he decided. If anybody could help him understand Haley, it was Laura.

"I more than like your sister," he admitted. "And she won't give me the time of day."

Laura's grin widened. "I *knew* it! I could tell from the first time you kissed her."

"Yeah. Well. I guess the big question is…" He looked over at Haley again. She was laughing with Elsa, and he knew it was only a matter of time before she tried to corner him into a date and he'd have to fight with her again. Because, he wasn't about to let himself get talked into going out with another woman.

"The big question is," he repeated, turning his attention back to Laura. "What the heck can I possibly do about it?"

"Well, I'm no expert in matchmaking."

Adam rolled his eyes at her ridiculous assertion.

He was beginning to think her entire family was genetically programmed for matchmaking.

"Not like my mom and Haley."

"Fine," he said. "I'll only pay you half rate."

Laura laughed.

"She told me about Tony and Raymond," he said.

"I'm beginning to think Stephen was worse for her."

"How so?"

Haley hadn't ever said much about Stephen.

"Looking back, I realize she loved him. And I suspect he loved her. It just wasn't with the kind of head-over-heels, madly-in-love passion that sees you through the bad times kind of love."

"How could anyone not be passionate about Haley?" Adam's gaze found her again. Even from this distance, she took his breath away.

"They were…settled," said Laura. "And she might actually think that's as good as it gets."

"Not hardly," said Adam. He knew that because of Haley. Why couldn't Haley see it, too?

"Of course not." Laura broke off, waving to Caitlin as the girl stuck her head out the driver's window of the fire engine. "And with Tony and Raymond. Well, I think what scared her with that, isn't so much that they were losers. It was because she tried really hard to make the relationships work. Looking back now, she must panic at the thought of having actually married one of them.''

"I know she doesn't trust her judgment."

"Exactly."

"Which means, no matter now perfect I am—"

"And, no matter how modest you are."

"Let me rephrase. No matter how she might feel about me, she thinks it's all an illusion."

"Agreed."

"Great. Doesn't give me much to work with, does it?"

"On the contrary, you have plenty to work with," said Laura.

"How so?"

"She made love with you."

"That's true."

"And, I assume it was…"

"I'm still not going to kiss and tell." But he knew their cataclysmic lovemaking had affected Haley. In the thick of things, she'd been just as astounded by their chemistry as he was—which was pretty darned astounded.

"Okay. Then I'll just assume the best. I know Haley, and she wouldn't make love with you unless she meant it."

Laura paused, obviously waiting to see if Adam would elaborate. But, he stayed silent.

"And," she finally continued, "you know, you

have one extremely formidable secret weapon at your disposal.''

"Which is?" he asked, glad to let the conversation move on. Haley might feel comfortable discussing their physical relationship with Laura, but he was keeping their private moments to himself.

Laura looked pointedly at the bake-sale table. "My mother."

"Ahh." Adam felt a slow, speculative smile form on his face. His spirits lifted for the first time in three days. "You mean…I could actually…"

Laura's voice turned serious. "You can. But, you'd better be sure you know what you want before unleashing her."

Was he sure? Adam's chest tightened as he scanned the schoolyard for Haley.

To his surprise, she was no longer talking to Elsa. She had Belinda and Nicole at the dunk tank, throwing tennis balls in an effort to douse the principal.

He watched her toss her auburn hair back under the bright sunshine while she laughed with their two daughters. Then he had a sudden vision of her vulnerable expression when her saggy chocolate cake was put up against the ice-cream cake. Then the brief look of pain that had flashed through her eyes when he told her he'd kissed Kimberly. Then, her slumberous blue eyes staring straight into his soul while they made love.

That was the vision that stayed. The one that told him they were made for each other. He'd wanted a mother for Nicole, never dreaming he'd find the perfect fit for himself along the way.

Was he sure?

Not a single doubt.

"I'm sure," he said to Laura.

"Till death do us part sure?" she asked.

"Absolutely."

9

PRINCIPAL RUSKIN HAD obviously just dried off from the funfair dunk tank. His wet hair was combed back, and he was wearing a dry set of sweats with the school logo across the chest. He put a bullhorn to his mouth and announced the start of the family obstacle race—the final event of the afternoon.

"Can we enter, Mom?" Belinda grabbed Haley's arm and bounced up and down beside her. "The prize is a chocolate cake!"

"I think Grandma made that cake," said Haley.

"So?"

"We can probably get one at home."

"But it tastes *better* if you win it."

Haley looked doubtfully at the obstacle course, which stretched across the baseball field. "Don't you need four on a team? There are only two of us, and I don't think Grandma and Grandpa want to crawl through the tunnel."

Laura and her family were already heading for the start/finish line.

"Nicole will go get her dad."

Haley squelched the little nervous reaction to the mention of Adam. She hadn't exactly been avoiding him since Saturday night. It was more that she'd been so busy with both the school projects and her own pottery.

She'd had a new order from her craft distributor in Chicago. And it was going to take her at least a month to fill it.

"Please, Mom?" said Belinda.

Haley glanced down at her daughter. What kind of a mother deprived her daughter of a race because of her own insecurity? "Okay. Sure."

So, she'd been naked with him. Fundamentally nothing had to change in their relationship. She'd still find him a new girlfriend just as soon as possible.

She'd tried with Elsa today. But, that hadn't worked out. Hard to put her finger on it, but something wasn't quite right about Elsa.

It must have been because in the few weeks since she'd met Adam, Haley had gotten to know him a little better, and she could sense right away that Elsa wasn't *the one*.

"Go get your dad," Belinda called to Nicole.

Nicole waved and took off running.

Haley watched the girl's progress across the parking lot toward her father. Adam had given the fire hose demonstration a short time ago, and was now locking up the engine.

He tossed his helmet into the front seat, then swiftly undid the zipper on his heavy jacket. Stripping it off, he revealed a plain white T-shirt.

Haley's mouth went dry as she suddenly remembered running her hands over his biceps, his chest, his rock-hard stomach.

Nicole came to a halt beside him, talking excitedly, gesturing toward the obstacle course.

Adam looked up. His eyes caught Haley's for a second, and then he gave them a smile and a wave.

"He's on his way," sang Belinda, as Adam started toward them.

Haley forced herself to swallow. She had to stop remembering him naked.

"You and Adam going in the race?" her mother stopped beside them.

"Yes!" Belinda shouted as Adam and Nicole drew closer. "We're going to win the cake."

"Looks like we're racing," Haley answered her mother, with a tentative smile in Adam's direction. Her chest tightened when he smiled back.

"How're you doing sweetheart?" He wrapped an arm around her shoulders, and placed a quick kiss on her temple. "I've missed you," he whispered in her ear.

Her pulse leaped, even as she reminded herself it was all for show. They were still pretending to be dating in front of her mother. Although, why Adam couldn't get it through his head that they were pretending to cool things off, not heat them up, was beyond her.

"Better get to the starting line," said her mother. "Good luck, girls." She gave Belinda and Nicole each a little hug.

"Through the tunnel," Principal Ruskin said through his bullhorn, "along the balance beam, over the climbing wall—kids on the left side, adults on the right."

Haley shaded her eyes and gazed at the huge purple and yellow soft wall they'd had set up for the course. The children's side was angled, but the adults had to scramble over the ten-foot vertical wall using only tiny hand and footholds. Thank goodness there was padding at the bottom in case anyone slipped.

She wished she'd thought to do free weights along with her morning stomach crunches. Her arms sure weren't in the best shape of her life.

"Shoot a basket at the far end, then sprint back to the finish," said the principal. "We'll run two timed races, eight teams together in each. Ribbons for first, second and third in each race. Fastest time overall wins the cake. Are the first teams ready?"

A cheer went up from the assembled racers.

Laura was up for her family team in the first race. Adam, Haley and the girls joined a line, set to race in the second heat.

The principal blew a whistle, and the first teams took off across the thick grass to a rousing cheer from the assembled crowd.

Laura dove through the padded tunnel, then leaped onto the balance beam like a gazelle. Haley took a second to be thankful that she wasn't running head-to-head against her sister.

"You want to go first for us?" Adam asked from where he stood directly behind her. She ignored the way his voice raised goose bumps on her warm skin.

"What do you girls think?" Haley looked at Belinda and Nicole.

"Mom, then Nicole then me," said Belinda, decisively.

"You want me last?" asked Adam.

"You're fastest," said Nicole, slipping her hand into his.

"Hear that?" Adam asked Haley, giving Nicole's hand an obvious squeeze and ruffling her hair. "My kid thinks I'm the fastest."

"I'm not sure about getting over that wall," said Haley doubtfully, as she watched Laura struggle with the hand- and footholds. The mother from another team was catching up to Laura.

"Go, Auntie Laura," Belinda shouted, her voice blending in with the other cheers from the teams and the sidelines.

"Go, Auntie Laura," Nicole echoed. "Maybe if they win they'll share the cake," she ventured in an excited voice, glancing to the big timing clock in the corner of the field.

"If not, Haley can bake one for us," said Adam.

Nicole and Belinda stopped cheering and looked doubtfully up at Haley.

Haley elbowed Adam in the ribs.

"Hey," he protested, bending over in an exaggerated attempt to protect himself. "I *liked* the last one."

"Sure you did," Haley muttered. She had to admit, he was a very good actor. Anybody watching him eat her cake at the barbecue would have believed he liked it.

"It'll taste way better if we win it," echoed Belinda as Laura tossed the basketball through the hoop at the far end of the obstacle course.

Laura turned to sprint back to the start/finish line and slap Caitlin's hand.

Adam leaned down to unlace his boots. "If we're going to be competitive, I'd better get rid of these."

As her turn to race grew closer, Haley stretched her shoulders and her arms, shaking her legs to warm them up. "I used to sprint in high school," she bragged. She might not be able to dive through tunnels like Laura, or jump up onto the balance beam, but she was pretty sure she could make it from the basketball hoop to the finish in good time.

"I used to climb mountains," said Adam.

"Really?" she asked.

He nodded.

"Any tips?"

"Don't lose your footing."

Haley rolled her eyes. "Gee. Thanks."

Caitlin made her way carefully across the balance beam, then sprinted for the kids' wall.

"Go, Caitlin," called Belinda. "Climb, climb, climb."

Adam put his arm around Haley and squeezed her shoulder. "You're going to be great."

He was *such* a good actor. Anybody looking in from outside would actually believe they had a romance going.

The way Haley instinctively leaned into him would probably help, too. She knew she wasn't supposed to like his touch, but she couldn't help herself. There was something comforting in the weight of his big hands, and his unique scent made her want to cuddle up to him and forget about the rest of the world.

"I'll be cheering for you," he mumbled low.

She loved the seductive sound of his voice, too.

Caitlin's hand clapped against Ali's, faded to the background, and Haley let herself remember making love to Adam. Maybe if she let her mind freely think about it now, the images wouldn't torture her again tonight.

Last night, along about 3:00 a.m., she'd found herself rationalizing making love with him again.

She'd stood by her bedroom window gazing out at the moonlight, across the yard to his bedroom window, wondering what would happen if she propositioned him, wondering what would happen if she showed up at his door in the middle of the night.

Would he turn her away?

Welcome her with open arms?

"Next teams to the starting line." Principal Ruskin's voice in bullhorn interrupted her thoughts.

"Second!" cried Belinda. "Ali and Caitlin got second."

"That's wonderful," said Haley, feeling a little guilty because her attention had wandered.

Adam gave Laura and her family a quick thumbs up.

"Go fast, Mom," said Belinda.

"I know you can do it." Adam patted Haley's shoulder as she put her left foot on the starting line.

"I'll cheer loud," said Nicole.

Haley crouched down, ready to start.

She was nervous. It was only a silly elementary school obstacle course. Nobody was expecting an Olympic performance. But, her sister's family was getting second-place ribbons. And she couldn't help feeling like she'd be letting the girls and Adam down if she didn't do well.

The whistle sounded, and Haley started to run.

She made it to the tunnel and scooted through.

At the balance beam, she had to use both hands to get up, but she didn't have any trouble making it to the end. As she jumped off onto the grass, she dared to glance to either side. It looked like she was in the lead approaching the climbing wall.

She raced to the adult wall and grabbed a hand-hold. The holds were bigger than they looked from the starting line, and she wasn't nearly as scared as she'd feared. She could hear the cheers of the crowd beside her and of the other competitors behind her.

She imagined Nicole and Belinda cheering madly, and she smiled as she hoisted herself higher and higher. Over the top, in first place, she dangled her legs down the other side, hung by her hands, and dropped to the padding below.

Only the basketball hoop was left.

She sprinted for it, and grabbed a ball out of the equipment box. She missed the first try, but made a basket on the second. Still in the lead, she ran her heart out for the finish line.

Nicole was waiting, hand outstretched.

Haley clapped her palm against Nicole's, and nearly fell into Adam's arms.

He held her tightly against his chest as she gasped for air.

"You came first," he told her.

She nodded, quickly turning her head to watch Nicole's progress.

So far, Nicole was holding onto the lead. But she looked shaky on the balance beam.

Haley held her breath as Nicole wobbled.

"Come on, sweetheart," Adam muttered.

Nicole slipped and fell to the ground, landing on her back.

Belinda groaned.

Haley could feel Adam's muscles tense.

But Nicole was up again in a second. She jumped back onto the balance beam and finished walking across.

Haley cheered, calling out Nicole's name, even though she knew Nicole would never make out a single voice in the roar of the crowd.

Nicole lost the lead as a grade-seven boy passed her. Then another team got ahead of her when she missed two basketball throws.

But she ran hard in the final sprint, and slapped Belinda on the hand.

"You did great, sweetheart." Adam swung her into his arms and gave her a big kiss on the cheek.

"I fell off," she panted.

"But you got right back on," said Haley. "We're so proud of you."

"Look at Belinda," gasped Nicole.

"She's tied for second," said Adam.

"Oh, shoot, no," Haley groaned as another older boy passed Belinda.

The boy made it over the wall in about three

steps, while Belinda had to struggle, using both her hands and her feet.

"Third again," said Nicole dejectedly.

"She's doing her best," said Adam. "Look. She made the hoop in one try."

Sure enough, Belinda was already on her way back.

Adam put Nicole down and stood ready at the starting line.

"Just do your best," said Nicole, patting him on the arm.

"I will." He grinned and winked at Haley. "I've got a craving for chocolate cake."

Haley's chest contracted, as Belinda smacked his hand. Adam took off like a shot. Even though he was really too big for the tunnel, he dove through it, hauling himself out the other side. He vaulted onto the balance beam and crossed it in three strides, passing one of the other fathers who was taking the final leg for his team.

Adam's long arms and legs took him quickly over the wall. He jumped down the other side, made the basket in one throw, then sprinted back, neck and neck with the first-place father.

Nicole and Belinda screamed their heads off. Laura, Kyle and the girls added their voices, too. All the kids jumping up and down on the spot.

Haley was too mesmerized to yell. She could

barely breathe as Adam sprinted barefoot across the field, all muscle and sinew and determination.

It looked like he'd pulled into the lead, but it was hard to tell from her angle. He pumped his arms, stretched his legs out, pounding his feet across the grass.

He flashed across the finish line a good yard in front of the other man. His time lit up on the scoreboard.

"We won," Belinda screamed, hugging Nicole. "We won the cake."

"Yes!" Haley punched her fists into the air. She sprinted to Adam, amazed by his performance. As proud as if he really was a member of her family.

"You did it," she cried, spontaneously wrapping her arms around his neck and squeezing tight. "You *did* it," she whispered in his ear.

Deep breaths made his chest rapidly rise and fall.

Nicole and the girls surrounded him, squealing, hugging and congratulating. It was a ridiculous reaction for a chocolate cake, but Haley didn't care.

He gave her a quick, hard squeeze. "It was *so* worth it," he whispered before letting her go to turn his attention to the kids.

10

"ANOTHER PIECE OF CHOCOLATE cake?" asked Ellen, standing up at the dining table, knife at the ready.

"I couldn't possibly," Adam replied. "But it was absolutely delicious." He shifted Nicole, who was cuddling drowsily on his knee.

"Can we all sleep in the motor home again tonight?" Belinda asked her grandmother. "There's no school tomorrow."

School was now out for the entire summer.

Ali nodded in rapid agreement from the other end of the table.

"Sure you can," said Ellen, with a fond smile at her grandchildren. "I'll tell your mom when she gets out of the pottery room," she said to Belinda.

To Adam's disappointment, Haley had disappeared into her pottery workroom before they even had a chance to cut the cake. The hum of her electric potter's wheel through the closed door was the only evidence that she was even in the house.

"Can we stay, Mom?" Ali asked Laura on behalf of herself and her sister.

"It's okay by me. If you're sure, Mom?"

"No problem," said Ellen, ruffling Caitlin's hair.

"Is it okay with you, Daddy?" Nicole sat up straighter in Adam's lap, tipping her chin to look him in the eye.

"Sure, it's okay." He smiled and gave her a kiss on the tip of the nose. "Better run home and get your pajamas."

"Let's go, Nicky," Belinda called, immediately heading for the front door.

"You sure she won't be too much trouble?" he asked Ellen as Nicole slid off his lap.

"She's an angel," said Ellen.

Nicole's smile grew until she positively glowed. She and Caitlin and Ali took off after Belinda.

"Guess I'll go get the girls' things," said Kyle. He glanced at his wife. "You want to head home now or stay a while?"

"I'll stay," said Laura. She winked at Adam, confusing him for a moment.

"Back in a few minutes then," said Kyle.

While Kyle headed out the back door, Laura picked up a few of the cake plates. Brushing past Adam on her way to the kitchen, she paused to whisper, "Just follow my lead."

Her lead? He stared at her as she deposited the plates into the sink.

Ellen was quick to follow suit, scooping up the rest of the cake and taking it over to the counter.

"It's a surprise, so you can't say anything." Laura turned to include both of her parents in her gaze. Her smile was secretive. "But, Adam was thinking about buying Haley an engagement ring."

Ellen let out a delighted gasp.

Warren sat up straight.

Adam's jaw nearly dropped to the floor.

This was what Laura had meant by "follow my lead?"

"Adam," Ellen rushed forward. "We couldn't be more delighted."

He quickly stood up and gave her a quick hug. "Thank you. I'm…" He had absolutely no idea what to say. When he'd talked to Laura about unleashing the formidable weapon this afternoon, he had no idea she'd mean so quickly, or so dramatically.

Haley was going to…

Oh, good grief. He didn't even want to think about what Haley was going to do.

Warren stood up and held out his hand. "Welcome to the family, son."

Adam reached out to shake. "Well, uh… She hasn't exactly said yes yet." She hadn't exactly said yes to a date yet, never mind a wedding. "And I think she's a little reluctant," he finished, deciding he'd better prepare them.

"Oh, pooh." Ellen waved a dismissive hand in the air. "Don't you worry about that."

Well. In fact. He was *very* worried about that. Haley was still hell-bent on finding him a wife. And he knew she wasn't thinking about herself for the position.

"They're having a diamond sale over at Haversham's," said Ellen. "Now, where did I put that catalog?" she said half to herself, heading for the living room.

Warren began picking up the remaining cake plates from the table.

Adam sidled over to Laura. "Are you crazy?" he muttered under his breath.

"Like a fox," said Laura. "You just watch. If you want to convince my stubborn sister to do something, you definitely need my mother's help."

"What if she really doesn't want to marry me?"

"She made love with you, didn't she?" Laura whispered while Warren started a sink full of water for the plates.

"Yes."

"She threw herself into your arms after the race today, didn't she?"

"Yeah." He smiled at the memory. He'd bust

a lung any day of the week if it meant Haley would hug him like that.

"Do you think she loves you?"

Adam looked at Laura, his mind going back to the night they shared lasagna. He smiled. If that wasn't love, he didn't know what was.

If Haley felt only half what he did, she was head over heels.

"Yeah. She must." Then he sobered. "But there's no way in the world she's going to admit it. Not even to herself."

"That's okay. You're the right man for her, so it'll all work out. You do love her, right?"

He closed his eyes for a long second. Love Haley? Oh, yeah. In fact, loving Haley had become his full-time occupation. He loved her when he woke up. He loved her when he fell asleep. He loved every little thing about her. Every smile, every impulse, every silly lie.

"Absolutely." He wanted to grow old with her. He wanted to have babies with her. He wanted to spend every night making love with her, and wake up every morning in her arms.

But, most of all. Most of all, he wanted to hear her say the words. Because he needed to know that she could put her fears aside and build a life with him.

"I knew I'd seen it yesterday." Ellen pushed open the kitchen door. "Come and look, Adam."

She motioned to him with her hand, and he smiled in return.

"You sure this is a good idea?" he whispered to Laura.

"Trust me." She headed after her mother into the living room.

Adam followed, trying to quell the trepidation bubbling up inside him. They were her family, he told himself as he settled on the couch with one woman on either side and a catalog of engagement rings on his lap. They knew Haley better than anyone.

"A solitaire?" asked Ellen, flipping pages. "A cluster?"

"What about a colored stone?" Laura turned another page. "A ruby or an emerald along with the diamonds. That would be different."

"What did she have last time?" asked Adam. He wanted it to be different. He knew that Haley hadn't been in love with Stephen. And he didn't want his proposal to bring back any kind of sad memory.

"A solitaire," said Ellen.

Laura nodded. "Yeah. Nothing big. They were pretty young when they got engaged."

"Maybe I will go for an emerald," said Adam. "She looks great in green." And maybe he'd buy one tomorrow.

He formed a mental picture of Haley happily

accepting his ring. This was going to work. He was going to make it work. They were perfect for each other. He just had to help her see that.

"Coffee anyone?" Warren asked from the kitchen door.

"I'd love some, Dad," Laura answered. "You want some help?"

"I'm just fine in here," said Warren.

"No coffee for me," said Adam. Sexy memories of Haley were bad enough for keeping him awake at night. He didn't need any help from caffeine.

Warren disappeared again behind the swinging door.

"Look at this," said Ellen, flipping to another section of the catalog, pointing to a page of smiling models in elegant bridal gowns.

"That one looks like mine," said Laura, pointing to a full-skirted, lacy white dress.

Adam was partial to the champagne color and a simpler style.

"Remember how cute Haley looked as a bridesmaid at your wedding," said Ellen, turning the page. "And, look, we can put Belinda and Nicole in something like this." She pointed to a little girl all dressed in yellow with wildflowers in her hair.

A picture of Nicole in the wedding ceremony planted itself in Adam's mind. She was smiling up at her new mother, and Haley was radiant. He knew in that moment that he'd found his fantasy.

Nothing was going to stop them.

Warren appeared with a tray of coffee, setting it down on the low table in front of them.

"Doesn't this bring back memories?" Ellen asked him. "I bet your tux still fits."

"I'm sure it does," said Warren, striking a pose.

Adam could suddenly see it all clearly in his mind.

"Mom can bake the cake," said Laura.

"Haley loves spring bouquets," said Ellen.

"Do you think she'll go for a veil or just some flowers in her hair?" asked Laura.

"*What* are you doing?" Haley's stunned voice from the kitchen doorway instantly silenced everyone.

Adam jerked his head up.

"Just browsing, honey," said Ellen cheerfully as she stood up from the couch. "We wouldn't make any final decisions without you."

Haley's eyes got wider and wider. She opened her mouth. Then she closed it again. Then she tried to form a word, but apparently failed.

"Adam," she finally rasped.

"Yes," he sort of squeaked, guiltily shoving the catalog back on the coffee table. This sure wasn't the way he'd planned to broach the subject of marriage with her.

"In the kitchen, please." She turned on her heel and left the room.

Adam shot Laura a helpless look.

"It'll be fine," she assured him, but she didn't look all that convinced.

"You go on." Ellen patted his shoulder consolingly. "Just make sure she knows she'll have all the final decisions. That's important to a bride."

He had a feeling it wasn't the final decisions that had Haley upset. He had a feeling it was the initial decisions. Like the one to actually date him before he started planning the rest of her life.

THE KITCHEN DOOR SWUNG shut behind Haley, and her heart pounded hard against her chest.

How could he? How could he? *How could he?*

She gripped the edge of the counter, her knuckles turning white under the pressure. Had she not tried to *warn* him?

"Haley?"

She heard Adam open then close the kitchen door behind her.

She whirled to face him. "Are you out of your *mind?*"

He grimaced. "Uh…"

"What? Did you wake up this morning and

think 'I know, let's see how *impossible* I can make Haley's life'?''

"It's not—"

"Did I not *warn* you about her?"

He was an intelligent man. Had he simply not believed her?

"We were just—"

Haley stretched her arm out, pointing toward the living room. "There is no 'just' about it where my mother is concerned. She's probably out there right now renting a hall."

"I'm sure she's not—"

"When were you planning to tell her we were playacting? When the invitations went out? When the gifts started to arrive? At the bridal shower?"

"Haley, listen—" He took a few steps toward her.

"Don't *Haley* me. Do you have any idea how hard her wedding train is to stop once it gets rolling? I sure do. I've been there. Ask Kyle. He knows."

Haley lifted her hands in the air in a gesture of utter frustration. She took a couple of paces into the middle of the room. "And what on earth was Laura doing out there? Is she in training to take over when my mother retires? I mean, we do have four daughters to think about here."

"Haley—"

"Don't." She held up a warning finger. She

didn't need to hear arguments from him. She just wanted apologies. Apologies and strategies for undoing the damage. "I'm going in there right now to tell her this is all a lie."

"No." He reached out toward her. "I've been thinking."

"Not rationally," said Haley, stopping in order to avoid him. The last thing she needed right now was his touch. She still remembered touching him this afternoon, in Technicolor.

All she had left at the moment was her shaky resolve.

"I'm thinking perfectly rationally," said Adam. "Maybe it's not such a crazy idea…" He paused and took a breath. "For you and I to think about something real together. Something serious. Maybe something permanent."

"Permanent?" Haley drew back farther, the bottom dropping out of her stomach.

He'd lost his mind. Was he abandoning his list? Had he forgotten everything she'd ever told him about herself?

She stared at the earnest expression and realized she needed to be strong for the both of them.

"Why is it so crazy?" he asked.

She fought the enticing look in his eye, fought her memories. She couldn't afford any weakness right now. And remembering Adam's whispered words while he held her naked in his arms definitely made her weak.

"She got to you," Haley whispered.

"Nobody got to me," he scoffed.

Haley nodded her head vigorously. "Oh, yes she did. She's brainwashed you." That was the only explanation. If Adam would just stop and think about it for a few minutes, he'd realize it was true.

"Haley, I haven't been brainwashed. I just happen to think—"

"You have a list—"

"That's true, but—"

"And it's a good list. A great list. You are being intelligent and rational about finding a mother for Nicole. I know we can still do it."

"That doesn't mean—"

"Yes, it does." She nodded vigorously. "It does mean—"

"I told you before, I could change it. The list is not the be-all end-all—"

"Oh, no, no." She took another step back, bumping into the counter behind her. "That's my mother talking. You remember when I told you she'd make me the only item on your list? Do you?"

He slowly nodded, an uncertain expression crossing his face. Good. He was starting to see the light.

"Don't you find it just a little bit strange that I'm suddenly the person you want?"

His expression hardened, and he shook his head. "Haley, I'm—"

She'd almost had him there. But she'd lost him again. Darn it. Panic was starting to creep in. "Adam. Remember? Back when you were thinking rationally, you made some good decisions about finding a wife."

"I realize now that my list was wrong," he stated baldly.

"No, it wasn't. It was a great list." Why was he doing this? They'd agreed that she would help him find a wife. A wife that *wasn't* her.

"I changed it."

"To what?"

"Two things." He took a step toward her, and she inched toward the door. "Just two."

She had to be ready to escape. She couldn't let him touch her again. If he touched her, he'd start to confuse her. Okay, he'd finish confusing her, since she was already halfway there.

She couldn't do another relationship. No matter how seductive it might feel going in, it was always a disaster coming out again.

"Criteria one," he said, taking another step forward. "I love her."

Her heart stopped beating, and she felt her eyes widen.

"Big check mark beside that one," he continued before she could even form a thought. "Criteria two. She loves me…"

Haley slid sideways along the counter, a trembling hand going to her lips. How had her life gotten so far out of control?

She fought the panic that threatened to engulf her. She couldn't let Adam become another Stephen. She had to stop this.

No matter how she felt about making love with him, no matter how much a tiny, contrary part of her wanted to consider a future together, she knew they were being railroaded.

"Do you have any idea how many times she's done this?" she asked, forcing herself to maintain focus, refusing to get caught up in her mother's wedding fantasy.

"I have no idea," said Adam.

"Kyle and Stephen are just the tip of the iceberg."

Adam crossed his arms and shook his head. He was looking calm, reasonable, deceptively rational. "Will you give me a little credit?" he asked.

"I know her better than you do," Haley insisted.

"Granted. But I know *me* better than you do. And I know exactly how I feel about you."

Oh, no. He was *way* too good at this.

"Adam." She crossed her own arms, forcing

herself to sound reasonable and rational right along with him. "Two weeks ago, you had a plan. I had a plan. We were intelligent, reasonable people. Our thinking wasn't clouded, and we knew where our lives were leading. We were right."

"You were planning to be a lesbian."

"I didn't say my plan was perfect." Just reasonable and rational and unencumbered by those man-chasing Nelson hormones.

Now she was being forced to fight her man-chasing tendencies with ever fiber of her being. But it was hard, because she was weak. Part of her honestly wanted to let Adam talk her into perusing the bridal catalogs, buying a dress, waltzing down the aisle, throwing herself into his open arms...

"Will you at least let me—"

"No." She shook her head, forcing out every one of the compelling visions. "I can't do this." She backed toward the door.

She had to get out while she could. Another few minutes, and she'd be lost. "Tell everyone I went out for a while. Get Mom to watch Belinda." It was the least her mother could do.

"Haley." He stretched out his hand. "The girls are—"

"No, Adam." She shook her head. "We have to stop. We can't do this. We can't be this. We have to end it all right now."

11

ADAM'S SHOULDERS SLUMPED as the door slammed and Haley disappeared into the backyard. He leaned against the kitchen counter with a thump.

He'd blown it. He'd absolutely, completely blown any chance he'd ever had with her.

He never should have listened to Laura. He should have taken his time, slowly showed Haley he loved her, let her get used to the idea of the two of them as a couple, made sure there was never the least little suspicion in her mind that her family had anything to do with his feelings.

What was the all-fired hurry anyway? He sure didn't know.

Kyle peeked into the kitchen. "I heard the door slam."

"Come on in," said Adam with resignation.

Kyle pushed through the door, letting it swing shut behind him. He cocked his head back toward the living room. "They filled me in."

Taking up a spot next to Adam, he leaned

against the countertop. "I take it, it didn't go so well?"

Now there was an understatement.

"Could've been worse, I suppose," said Adam. "If the kitchen caught fire in the middle of the fight."

Kyle shook his head. A dark chuckle broke through. "I can't believe you took relationship advice from my wife and my mother-in-law."

Adam shook his head in agreement. Another moment of twenty-twenty hindsight. "Well, they seemed to know what they were talking about," he defended weakly. "And they sure know Haley better than I do."

Kyle grinned. "Differently. Probably not better." He paused. "So, what are you going to do?"

"What can I do?" Adam was pretty sure this was the end of the line for their relationship. When a woman said no, she meant no. And Haley had said no in the plainest of terms.

"Well—" Kyle straightened "—you want my advice?"

Adam tilted his head sceptically. "I don't know. Is it better than your wife's?"

"Maybe."

"Now that's reassuring."

"If I was you, I'd back off. Haley's worst fear has just come true."

"You mean she's being railroaded into a marriage she doesn't want?'' Adam was beginning to feel like a heel. A stupid, unthinking, unfeeling heel.

Kyle crossed to the fridge and pulled out a couple of beers. "I mean she's fallen in love, and there's nothing she can do to stop it.''

He tossed one to Adam and popped the top on the other.

"Wouldn't *that* be advantageous?'' Adam snapped opened his own beer. He'd thought Haley must love him. But now he wasn't so sure.

He'd been single-handedly holding up the idea of this relationship for a long time now. It seemed well past time for him to accept what she said at face value.

"That's what I thought earlier.'' He shook his head as he held the can up in a mock toast. "But I'm starting to think she's being honest with me.''

"She's in love with you. I know it. Laura knows it. Her mother knows it.''

"Unfortunately the majority doesn't rule in this case.''

"She's scared,'' said Kyle. "Back off. Let her come to you.''

"And, if she doesn't?'' Adam stared at the full can of beer, unable to bring himself to take a drink. His stomach was rolling with nerves.

Kyle tapped his can against Adam's. "I said it

was my best advice. I never claimed it was fool-proof.''

"YOU WANT SOME COMPANY?" Laura caught up to Haley a couple of blocks from the house.

The sun was setting and the neighborhood was growing quiet. It should have been a relaxing walk around the block on a summer's evening, but Haley's mind and stomach were in a turmoil.

She shook her head in response to her sister's question, not trusting herself to speak, still wondering what her sister's role might have been in the debacle.

"You okay?" Laura gave her a quick squeeze around the shoulders and fell into step beside her.

Haley shook her head again. She definitely wasn't okay. She was being sucked into the wedding vortex once again. And this time she'd dragged innocent Adam in along with her.

Everything was a complete mess. She should have been able to find Adam a nice wife, or at least a few good prospects for a wife.

She should have been able to keep her perspective, to keep her unruly feelings for him under control. And *he* sure shouldn't have caved to the pressure from her family. Could they have made any more mistakes? Even if they'd tried?

"He loves you," said Laura.

Haley made an inarticulate exclamation of disbelief deep in her throat. Adam wasn't in any position to decide if he loved her or not. And, even if he did, Stephen had loved her, too. That didn't mean it could work out between them.

"What? You think he's lying when he says he loves you?" Laura asked.

Lying? No. Confused? Yes.

"He's confused," Haley choked out.

"By Mom?"

"Who else?" Her voice and her conviction grew stronger.

"You know, Haley. It was Adam that told Mom he wanted to marry you. Not the other way around."

"Adam actually told Mom he wanted to marry me?" Haley paused. The brainwashing must be worse than she thought.

"Well. Okay, it was me who told Mom he wanted to marry you," said Laura.

Haley shook her head. "Oh, great. Tag-team steamrolling. No wonder he's confused. The poor man never even had a chance."

"Haley, Haley, Haley." Laura put her arm around Haley's shoulders again. "Has it occurred to you that Mom and I might not have anything to do with Adam's feelings?"

"Ha."

"Maybe he decided all by himself that he loved

you. Maybe you decided all by yourself that you loved him.''

Haley stared at her sister from beneath raised eyebrows. ''There is no all by myself. She's *living* in my driveway.''

''Okay, admittedly, she's taken a personal interest in this relationship.''

''She's taken a personal interest in *every* relationship.''

''Do me a favor,'' said Laura.

''Does it involve wearing white and carrying flowers?''

''Ask yourself a question.'' Laura steered her around a corner so they were heading back toward the house.

Okay. That sounded harmless enough. ''What question?''

''If you weren't in love with him, would you have a problem?''

Haley's heart faltered. Maybe harmless had been the wrong word. ''What do you mean?'' she asked.

''Think about it. Easiest thing in the world would be for you to tell Mom and Dad that you and Adam broke up. But you didn't.''

''There was never—''

''It would have taken all of two seconds.''

Haley didn't know how to answer that. The right time had never presented itself.

"He dates Kimberly, and you make love with him the next night."

Haley hated it when Laura used that knowing tone of voice. "It just sort of—"

"Happened?" Laura laughed. "I don't think so. Today I saw you talking to Elsa at the funfair. Adam was sure you were going to try to match make again. But, you didn't. Why not?"

Haley could feel the trap her sister was leading her into. If Haley didn't end the dating charade, and if she didn't match Adam up with every woman in Hillard who had a pulse, then she was, de facto, in love with him herself. No way she was falling for that.

"Elsa wasn't right for him—"

"That's because—"

Haley held up a hand to stop her sister. "It's not because I want him for myself." Well, it *wasn't.* "I've gotten to know him better in the last couple of weeks. I have a better idea of the kind of woman he likes, that's all."

"You're lying." Laura stopped, folding her arms over her chest.

"Am not." Haley turned to face her sister.

"Are, too. You couldn't stand the thought of Adam with Kimberly. And you couldn't stand the thought of him dating Elsa. You are such a fraud."

"She wasn't the right woman. Simple as that." But even Haley was starting to question the simplicity of her motivations. How would she have felt if Adam had dated Elsa? What did she feel when he told her he'd kissed Kimberly?

White-hot jealousy.

"At some point," said Laura, "you have to ask yourself what it means. When it's getting harder to stay away from Adam than it is to be with him."

Laura nodded toward Adam's house. They'd circled the block and were standing in front of it.

"Nicole's in the motor home with our kids," said Laura. "He's all alone in there."

Haley turned to gaze at Adam's front door.

Was Laura right? Was it easier for her to walk up and knock than it was to go back to her own house and bury her head under the covers?

Her chest tightened, making it difficult to breathe.

Oh, boy. Adam wanted her to buy a white dress, take the leap of faith, trust that *this* time it might actually work.

Tears burned the back of her eyes as she realized how very, very much she wanted that, too.

"Ask yourself," Laura continued. "If there was no Mom, no Stephen, no Tony or Raymond, how would you feel about Adam? What would you do?"

Truth was, Haley would run to Adam's front

door, throw herself into his arms, and tell him he was the best thing that had ever happened to her.

"Do it," said Laura. "Whatever it is you're thinking, just do it." She grinned. "Good sex is always better than freedom."

Haley shakily smiled back and took the first step down Adam's front walkway.

"See you tomorrow," Laura called.

Haley absently waved to her sister. Her feet felt like lead. Her palms were sweating and her knees were weak as she took another step, and then another.

Adam had to be mad at her.

He might not even open the door.

If *she'd* confessed her everlasting love to *him* and he'd thrown it back in her face, she'd be pretty upset.

Twenty steps later, she stopped in front of the door. She took a breath deep into her tight chest, knowing this was the point of no return. Slowly letting the air escape from her lungs, she raised her fist and knocked.

Adam opened the door. Okay, step one complete.

He drew back in obvious surprise at the sight of her, blinking in silence for a moment.

"Hi," he finally said.

"Hi," she managed to say in return. She fought

an urge to run, fought another urge to throw herself in his arms.

She did neither.

They stared at each other for a long minute, and it was more than Haley could do to break the silence.

"You want to come in?" he finally asked, opening the door fully and stepping back out of the way.

"Yeah." She nodded, forcing her lead feet to move again.

"I'm—"

"I—" they both started together.

"I'm sorry," he said. "That was unfair of me. I shouldn't have involved your mother, and I shouldn't have tried to—"

Haley put her index finger across his lips to silence him. She shook her head. "I'm the one who's sorry."

"You have nothing to be sorry about," he said.

"I'm sorry for being obstinate, for being scared, for refusing to recognize what you've come to mean to me."

His eyes lit up at her words. "You serious?"

She nodded.

A grin spread over his face, and he reached forward to take her hands in his.

"I love you," said Haley.

"Oh, man." He closed his eyes and sighed, his

grin growing wider. He tightened his grip on her hands, drawing her against him, pulling her into a big, satisfying hug.

"I was going to buy a ring tomorrow," he whispered. "But, I can't wait. Will you marry me?"

Haley nodded, all the tightly held tension from the past days seeping out of her. "It's not like I have a choice. Quite frankly, I don't think there's any way in the world to stop the wedding at this point."

"Would you marry me anyway?" he asked, drawing back to look into her eyes. "Even if we could stop it?"

"I think you misunderstood." She tipped her head and smiled at him. "The reason we can't stop the wedding is that *I'm* completely determined to marry you. And you know what I'm like once I get an idea in my head..."

Adam laughed. "Do I ever."

She pulled her hand from his, and walked her fingers along his chest. Even through the fabric of his T-shirt, she could feel the heat of his body. "As a matter of fact, I'm having another one right now," she whispered.

"Another one of your ideas?"

"Yeah."

"Tell me about it."

She leaned forward and nuzzled her face up to his. "It has to do with kissing you and tearing off your clothes and making love to you for the rest of the night.''

''That's the best idea I've heard all day.''

''Yeah?''

''Well, except for the one where I marry you.''

''SISTERS!'' BELINDA squealed, grabbing Nicole and pulling her into an exuberant hug. Both were still in their nightgowns, having just come in from the motor home for breakfast.

Haley leaned against Adam's solid body. She was tired, but relaxed and unbelievably happy. She and Adam had spent the rest of the night at his house exploring her latest great idea. But they'd roused themselves early to come over and give everyone the news.

''Can we share a bedroom?'' asked Nicole, breaking away from the hug but keeping a grip on Belinda's hand. The two girls skipped around in an impromptu dance.

Haley glanced at Adam for his opinion. They hadn't discussed living arrangements yet. It was enough that they were getting married, enough that they were in love.

''Bunk beds!'' Belinda jumped up and down once again. Then she turned to Nicole, her jumps turning into more controlled bounces. ''You want the top or the bottom?''

''We can take turns,'' said Nicole.

"Bunk beds it is," said Adam with a chuckle, tightening his hold around Haley's shoulders.

"I wouldn't advise bunk beds," said Ellen, bustling in from the kitchen with a coffeepot and a tray of muffins in her hands. "A husband and wife should always have a double."

"We meant us," called Belinda. "Are those blueberry?"

"They're blueberry," said Grandma with a wink to Haley as she set the tray down on the dining-room table.

Warren followed her from the kitchen.

Belinda and Nicole immediately headed for the muffin tray.

"I assume you're going ring shopping today," said Ellen to Adam. It was more a command than a question.

"First thing," said Adam.

"Mom," Haley protested. Just because she and Adam were right for each other didn't make the whole matchmaking tendency acceptable.

"Oh, pooh," said her mother, waving her hand in the air. "You know as well as I do that men need a little prompting for this sort of thing."

"It's nice to see you so happy, sweetheart." Haley's father gave her a quick hug. "I can't wait to escort another bride down the aisle."

"I can't wait, either."

It was true. She returned her father's hug, knowing that she couldn't wait to start her life with Adam.

Then Warren turned his attention to Adam, reaching out to shake hands. "We couldn't be happier for both of you, Adam."

"Here comes Auntie Laura," called Belinda, pointing out the front window.

"Hey, I can call her Auntie Laura now, too," said Nicole.

Belinda gave another little squeal.

"Have you set a date?" asked Haley's mother, glancing from Haley to Adam and back again. "Early July would be nice, before the real heat sets in. Sandra and the family could drive down from Dakota. And you two could honeymoon in New York. Take in the sights, see the shows. We'd be more than happy to take the girls."

The front door opened and Kyle, Laura and their two girls burst in.

Belinda announced the engagement, and the girls immediately started celebrating with their new cousin-to-be.

"Four little flower girls," said Ellen, watching the children with a happy sigh.

She turned her attention to Laura. "Yellow would be nice. Don't you think? And I think we should go with a tea-length dress for Haley."

Haley leaned over to Adam. ''I hope you didn't plan on making any of the wedding decisions.''

''I got everything on my wish list,'' he whispered, kissing her temple. ''That's enough for me.''

* * * * *

Look for Barbara Dunlop's latest
Harlequin Temptation in August 2003!

Mad About Mindy... and Mandy

Toni Blake

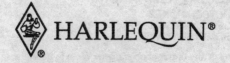

HARLEQUIN®

TORONTO • NEW YORK • LONDON
AMSTERDAM • PARIS • SYDNEY • HAMBURG
STOCKHOLM • ATHENS • TOKYO • MILAN • MADRID
PRAGUE • WARSAW • BUDAPEST • AUCKLAND

Dear Reader,

When a recent skiing accident left me with a bone fracture and some stretched and torn ligaments, I was pretty sure nothing good could come of it. Turns out I was wrong, though, because it was one night as I lay awake, unable to sleep due to the ache in my knee, that I thought, Hmm, maybe I'll try writing a Duets novel. I started with one simple question: What if the heroine was a matchmaker? By morning I knew Mindy and Benton's entire story.

Of course, I encountered a lot of fun twists and turns along the way, discovering that Mindy was even more impulsive than I had realized, and that Benton had an untapped dark side when it came to paying Mindy back for her misdeeds.

Writing *Mad About Mindy...and Mandy* has been a true pleasure, and I hope it will leave you with a smile on your face.

Sincerely,

Toni Blake

P.S. Visit me on the Web at www.toniblake.com.

Books by Toni Blake

HARLEQUIN TEMPTATION
800—HOTBED HONEY
825—SEDUCING SUMMER
870—SOMETHING WILD

This one is for my critique partners
Dave Borcherding and Roger Collins,
the only people I know willing to engage
in lively discussions about proper comma placement,
misplaced modifiers and those pesky dangling participles.

1

"BLOND BOMBSHELL at ten o'clock."

Mindy McCrae subtly shifted her gaze from the Mates By Mindy shopfront across the street to spy the cute guy her assistant, Jane Watkins, had just spotted. He strolled with purpose through Hyde Park Square wearing flip-flops and baggy shorts and looking…young. She cast Jane a sideways glance on the bench where they sat indulging in after-lunch ice-cream cones. "He's about twelve years old, Jane," she exaggerated.

Jane's brown eyes chided her through thick glasses. "He's not a day under nineteen, and who says you can't go for younger men?"

Mindy wrinkled her nose in reply. She wasn't into cradle-robbing, really not into guy-chasing at all, but Jane had made it her mission in life to find Mindy a man. Mindy might run the hottest matchmaking service in Cincinnati, but she'd never had as much luck fixing *herself* up with anyone as she had other people.

Fortunately, however, carving out a love life for Mindy was Jane's ambition, not her own. After all, she had plenty in her life to be happy about already. She had friends and parents who loved her, she owned a modest but quaint home and she operated a highly successful business that was the talk of the city. And since most of Jane's date suggestions were preposterous anyway, Mindy was glad she didn't care very much about finding her own mate.

"Mmm, hot Latin lovah heading from three o'clock toward two."

Mindy glanced up, and the guy, who was indeed hot and Latin, caught her looking. And—yikes—so did the woman clutching his arm. Mindy jerked around to scowl at Jane. "He's with a girl."

Jane shrugged, her dark shoulder-length hair bouncing slightly. "I'm sure you could change that if you wanted to."

Mindy rolled her eyes and reminded Jane, "I bring people together, not split them up."

"You're so darn noble," Jane complained, but Mindy knew she was only kidding. Jane had been happily wed to her husband Larry, for eighteen years and was the mother of three boys, ages fifteen, twelve and ten. Jane claimed she considered her hours at the shop her quiet time, and had ever since coming to work for Mindy three years ago. She openly admitted wanting to live vicariously through Mindy, a single woman whose life should theoretically be blooming with romance. She also admitted to being disappointed when Mindy didn't give her any adventures.

"Ooh la la, be still my heart." Jane's tone had reached a new level of lechery, drawing Mindy's eyes to the impeccably dressed man who'd just pulled his deep green Mercedes convertible into a parking space directly in front of them. "Tall, dark and steamy at high noon."

Mindy couldn't argue with Jane's assessment; in fact, she could only stare. He possessed classic good looks—dark, well-trimmed hair that brushed the edge of a crisp white shirt collar, a strong jawline, well-defined cheekbones and eyes she thought were probably blue and piercing, even though she couldn't tell because of the glare in his windshield. Turned out he was tall and pleasantly broad-shouldered when he exited the car, and his black suit had to be custom-made from the way it fit him.

"Bond," Jane rasped lowly. "James Bond."

"Shh," Mindy insisted. He was far too close to be whispering about him, and they were already gawking as it was.

"It's a bird, it's a plane, it's…"

"A customer!" Mindy gasped as Mr. Tall, Dark and Steamy crossed the street and approached the black awning dotted with fluffy red-and-pink hearts. She'd made the assumption he was headed to the jewelry store to the right of her shop or perhaps the art gallery to the left—because even though good-looking people used matchmaking services all the time, they weren't usually people *this* good-looking. Nonetheless, he reached for the door handle, then spotted the Be Back At sign, its little blue animated clock currently set at one. The hot, dreamy man instantly transformed into a client in Mindy's mind as she snatched up her purse and darted across the street. She reached him just as he turned toward his car, an expression of annoyance gracing his—yes, they *were* blue—eyes.

"Wait, don't go, I'm back."

He blinked upon realizing she was talking to him. "I was looking for—" he motioned slightly over his shoulder to the Mates By Mindy logo emblazoned in red on the door "—Mindy, I suppose."

"At your service." She smiled and peered up at him; he stood a head taller than her. Then she reached to shake his hand, only to realize she'd shoved a mint chocolate chip ice-cream cone at him. "Oops," she said, thrusting it into her left hand, which also clutched her purse, then watched as the entire scoop of ice cream plopped onto the sidewalk directly between his black wing tips.

Mindy cringed, then tentatively lifted her gaze to his. "I'm really not this clumsy."

Unfortunately, the dream man appeared unamused. "Okay," he finally said, although he looked far from convinced.

But this was all right, Mindy told herself as she managed to dig her keys out of her purse, get the door unlocked and let them both inside. Some clients were a little more straitlaced than others, but she could handle it. She was great with people, after all, and some required a slightly different approach than others. It wasn't too late to get this encounter on track.

Mindy showed him to the chair across from her desk, then dropped her beheaded sugar cone in the wastebasket as she sat down on the other side, somewhat relieved to be at eye level with the intimidating man. "How can I help you?" she asked, glad to have her game face on.

"I need a wife."

He'd said it as simply as if he were ordering a burger and fries at the drive through, and Mindy's first impulse was to say, "That'll be four-fifty at the first window." Instead, however, she held her tongue and struggled to keep her expression blank as she took a deep breath, lifted her elbows to the desk and steepled her fingers.

"As you can see by the pictures behind me," she began very calmly, motioning over her shoulder to the numerous snapshots of happy couples arranged on the long, pink wall, "Mates By Mindy has an astonishing success rate—"

"Yes, I know," he interrupted dryly. "Ninety-five percent. I've read your literature. That's why I'm here."

She lowered her gaze, not sure if it was because his eyes were so intense or because he was starting to annoy her. She got the distinct impression he thought she was wasting his time. "Yes, well, as I was starting to say, despite the number of my matches that have gone on to marry, I don't emphasize or promise marriage. I'm interested in helping you find that special someone with whom you can build a meaningful long-term relationship. I believe—"

"I have a meeting in half an hour," he said, checking his watch. "How can we expedite this? Do I need to fill out a questionnaire, speak into a video camera?"

Mindy took a deep breath. He didn't sound rude exactly, but like a man intent on getting things done. Even things, Mindy noted, that shouldn't be rushed, like finding a life mate, for instance. "No." She spoke very slowly, clearly, hoping to calm things to a more gradual pace. "At Mates By Mindy, matches aren't made through the modern selection process, but with a more old-fashioned approach. I make all the matches myself, and I do so by interviewing all my clients extensively in a relaxed setting that allows me to get to know them, their likes and dislikes, their general personalities, their day-to-day lives, their future plans." She reached for her appointment book and flipped through the coming days. "Let's see, I'm busy with another client tomorrow, but I could meet you for a long lunch on Friday. Across the street at Teller's? And we'll need to meet for two to three hours, so if that's not a good day for you, perhaps we can look at next week.''

When she lifted her gaze to the dream man, who was, frankly, seeming a little less dreamy with each passing minute, he was scowling. "I'm far too busy to block out that kind of time during the workday, but it's not necessary, anyway. I've written down everything you need to know.'' With that, he reached into the breast pocket of his jacket and produced a slip of paper folded in half. He placed it on Mindy's desk and slid it toward her as if he were making a bid on something, in this case, she supposed, a wife.

She plucked up the paper and opened it to find, in neat block lettering, a list. "Blond, shapely, classy, petite, intelligent when necessary, knows how to entertain—'' and Mindy's favorite "—knows when to defer to my judgment.''

Struggling to maintain a pleasant expression, or at least not to snarl, Mindy gently lowered the paper to her desk, shoved a lock of short, auburn hair behind one ear and resumed her finger steepling in an effort to stay calm and polite. "Clearly, you have some very, shall we say, *concrete* ideas about what you're looking for in a woman. But I'll still need to interview you.''

"Fine,'' he said shortly. "Let's do it now.'' He checked his watch again. "I have ten minutes.''

"Well, ten minutes isn't much, so…why don't we start like this. Just tell me about yourself, things you think a prospective match might like to know.''

"All right.'' The ex-dream man gave a short nod. "My name is Benton Maxwell the third.''

Oh, so he was a third. *That* figured.

"I'm the CEO of a well-established investment advisory firm with thirty employees and I have an income in the mid six figures.''

Okay, that one caught her a little off guard. *Wow.*

''I live not far from here in a large, refurbished home with an English garden and a swimming pool, and I own two condos—one in the Caymans and another in Colorado for the ski season. I can basically offer my wife-to-be any amenity she may desire, although—'' he raised one finger ''—I don't like cats and I do work long hours. She should *not* plan on working, as I travel extensively and may want her to travel with me, but she may feel free to do volunteer work or involve herself in other community activities that won't interfere with my schedule. She may redecorate the house as she wishes, so long as it looks dignified.''

When he finished, it was Mindy who let out the long breath. Sheesh. ''I was actually interested,'' she began, again slowing the pace of the conversation, ''in finding out more about *you*. More personal things. For instance, what do you do in your spare time? If you're going out to a movie, do you prefer a comedy or a drama? Where did you grow up and what was your family like? That sort of thing.''

Benton Maxwell III grimaced again, looking distraught at the questions, then finally formed a reply. ''I spend most of my time working, if not at the office, then at home. As for my family, they're a lot like me. My father founded our business before I was born and also worked long hours. My brother is a team-building consultant currently residing in Tokyo, and my sister is a tax attorney in New York City. My parents have retired to Boca now, but as you can tell, my father instilled a strong work ethic in all of us. Speaking of which, I *do* have a meeting to attend. Are we done here?''

Mindy pursed her lips and could no longer resist giving her head a caustic tilt. ''Do you think, Mr. Maxwell, that you'll have time to go on a few dates, or did you want to forgo that, too, and have me arrange your first date right at the altar?''

He lowered his eyelids, flashing a derisive look that somehow managed to be disarmingly sexy. ''No need for sarcasm. I'll work the dates into my schedule, Miss...''

''*Ms.* McCrae.'' Mindy met his gaze again, having concluded that she didn't like looking at him because, all sexiness aside, he had irritated her completely. But she had one more pointed question for the man who sat so stiffly across from her. ''Tell me, Mr. Maxwell, why exactly do you wish to get married?''

Benton Maxwell stared at her long and hard, his eyes mellowing to a deeper color than they'd appeared in the sun. They were the kind of eyes you could get lost in, she thought, if they weren't planted in the middle of a face belonging to such an opinionated, chauvinistic jerk. She began to wonder if the question had stumped him or if he was refusing to answer when finally he said, ''I need a wife, Miss McCrae. Can you assist me or should I go elsewhere?''

She held his gaze in order to let him know she was sizing him up, seeing him for what he was—a man making a mockery of love, looking to marry a piece of arm candy. He wanted a trophy wife, the perfect accessory for his champagne and caviar life. She'd never met anyone who managed to be so domineering and such an all-business stick-in-the-mud at the same time, and if he wasn't rich and devastatingly handsome, she decided, he'd have nothing going for him at all.

Frankly, she didn't want to accept his application.

So, in keeping with Benton Maxwell's style, Mindy grabbed a square of paper from the plastic cube next to her phone and scribbled an exorbitant dollar amount, then folded it in half before sliding it across the desk to him. "This is the fee, payable up front, for our deluxe dating package, which includes up to three handpicked candidates, dating suggestions, pre-date counseling and a debriefing session, if desired." She removed her fingers from the paper knowing full well that no one in their right mind would pay the amount she'd proposed. Let Benton Maxwell darken the door of some other unsuspecting matchmaker.

Of course, that was her first mistake—thinking the man was in his right mind. After taking but a brief glance at the number, he whipped out a credit card and thrust it toward her. "I won't need the suggestions," he said pointedly, "or the counseling. Just the women."

Mindy's jaw dropped. *Oh drat, what have I done?*

BENTON MAXWELL sped toward downtown on the expressway, late for his meeting. And Benton was *never* late for meetings. He pressed the buttons on his cell phone as he drove.

"Maxwell Group," said the voice of his elderly receptionist, Claudia, a moment later.

"It's me, Claudia."

"You're late," she lectured.

"Yes, I know. Can you connect me to Miss Binks in the conference room?"

A moment later, his faithful assistant, Candace Binks, picked up the phone.

"Hello, Miss Binks."

"Mr. Maxwell!" As usual, she sounded far too happy to hear from him. Miss Binks had been in love with him for years. Or maybe *love* wasn't the right word—Benton wasn't sure because he didn't know much about the emotion on a personal level—but she certainly had a thing for him. "We were beginning to worry."

He wasn't surprised; his reward in life for being extraordinarily punctual was that on the rare occasions he wasn't, people assumed something was wrong. "I'm on my way. Fifteen minutes max."

After finishing the call, Benton slid the flip phone into his pocket, then edged into the fast lane.

He'd thought about marrying Miss Binks, finally acknowledging the undying affection she'd been showering on him for so long. After all, she was nothing if not loyal, and she'd likely be more than eager to give up working and be everything he needed in a wife. She was attractive in a small, thin way, well-dressed and well-mannered, certainly knew when to defer to his judgment while at the same time keeping his office running like a well-oiled machine, and on top of all that, she moved in the right social circles.

Yet something about Miss Binks had never felt quite *right*. There was no spark, no chemistry. And even if he wasn't going about procuring a wife in the traditional fashion, he knew there had to be *something* between him and the woman he married, something that felt real and good.

The warm May wind whipped through his hair as he turned up the stock report on the radio, but he wasn't really listening; his mind remained in Hyde Park, at the little shop with the silly hearts painted everywhere. In one sense, he couldn't quite believe that he—levelheaded, sensible Benton Maxwell—had gone to a dating service, but on the other hand, he was a busy man and didn't have time to go out hunting for the perfect wife on his own. According to all he'd heard about this Mindy woman, it would be much easier for her to find him a mate. It had seemed an efficient alternative.

Now that it was too late to change his mind, however, he was having second thoughts. And in actuality, they were probably third thoughts, because his second thoughts had come the moment Mindy McCrae's ice cream had nearly splattered all over his Italian leather shoes.

Even so, clumsiness was something he could live with; his real doubts had developed once they'd started discussing the reason he'd gone there. The small redhead had looked nice enough, even if she didn't particularly fit his taste, her short hair more perky than sophisticated and her casual cotton skirt fitting the same short, perky description. Her bright eyes and smooth complexion were striking if not classic. But the thing that had bothered him was her attitude. She'd left him with the idea that she'd found his simple request for a wife preposterous, and when she'd started trying to pry information from him, her emerald gaze had nearly bored a hole straight through his head.

All Benton wanted was a few good women who had the traits he desired; he was capable of doing the getting-to-know-you part himself. And he certainly hadn't popped into the heart-laden building ready to share personal things with a stranger.

Why exactly do you wish to get married? He could still hear Mindy McCrae's dainty voice curling around the question, which, at that point, had sounded more like an accusation.

So why exactly *did* he wish to get married? he pondered as he tooled across the grid of downtown streets. Well, because he was tired of attending business parties alone, for one thing. For another, he'd wearied of hosting his own get-togethers. He was a rich man with no one to share it with and no one to leave it to. His house was beautiful but felt empty.

And because my thirty-fifth birthday is fast approaching and whatever love is—if it even exists—it hasn't found me yet, so it's probably not going to.

It felt to Benton that it was time, that was all.

But he didn't particularly think any of that was Miss McCrae's—or was that *Ms.* McCrae's—business.

Ten minutes later, Benton exited the elevator on the twenty-fifth floor of the Carew Tower and walked into the Maxwell Group lobby. He nodded shortly to silver-haired Claudia, then headed down the hall toward the conference room. After stepping through the open door and firmly shutting it behind him, he took his place at the head of the oval table, where eight associates waited for him. "I apologize for my tardiness. Let's get started, shall we?"

Miss Binks sat to his right, her long, dark blond hair pushed into a loose, stylish bun, her gold-framed glasses balanced precariously on the tip of her pointed nose, looking as pleased to see him as he would have predicted. "You're here," she said with a half smile.

For a bright woman, Miss Binks had a way of stating the obvious. "Yes, I am."

Young Malcolm Wainscott, Benton's Clark Kentlike apprentice, sat farther down the table, casting Miss Binks an adoring gaze, but as usual, she didn't notice.

Meanwhile, Percy Callendar—a longtime employee and one of the only people in the company, including himself, who Benton thought of as having a sense of humor—grinned, his balding head gleaming beneath the room's fluorescent lights. "Good that you called. We were about to send out a search party."

Miss Binks's small smile persisted as they all opened the binders before them, and Benton felt a short stab of guilt considering how she would feel if she knew what had made him late and how much worse she'd feel when he announced his engagement.

"Would you like coffee before we get started, Mr. Maxwell?"

He looked down to find Miss Binks touching his sleeve. This was new. He raised his gaze to hers, wondering if his surprise showed.

"No, thank you, Miss Binks." He pulled his arm away, hoping no one was getting any funny ideas. Then he shifted his gaze to Percy, who headed the budget committee, a silent indication to get the show on the road.

Maybe, he thought as Percy launched into a long-winded presentation, he'd think about doing a little matchmaking of his own in the near future. It had never occurred to him to push Miss Binks toward Malcolm Wainscott, and it wasn't the sort of thing Benton normally involved himself in, but since he'd be dealing with his impending wife hunt in the coming weeks anyway, it seemed an apropos occasion to deal in such uncharacteristic matters. He didn't need Miss Binks getting any more enamored of him than she already was, and he'd always thought she and Malcolm would be well-suited if she'd only get her head out of the sand.

As for who suited Benton, well, he supposed he'd have to wait and see what Matchmaker Mindy came up with. Yet for some unidentifiable reason, as the meeting progressed, Benton struggled with the niggling idea that he'd made a terrible mistake trusting Mindy McCrae.

"Is something wrong, Mr. Maxwell?" It was Miss Binks again.

Upon lifting his gaze to find her pale brown eyes widened on him, he could only suppose he'd started looking ill. "No," he said staunchly. "Nothing. Nothing at all."

Nothing except that I've placed the search for the future Mrs. Maxwell in the clumsy hands of a woman who can't even manage an ice-cream cone. He had the unshakable feeling his dates were going to end up just as messy.

2

THE FOLLOWING afternoon, Mindy slumped over her desk in despair. She'd been scouring her female client database for hours and had yet to find anyone who fit Benton Maxwell's criteria—at least in the personality department. After all, it was the twenty-first century, and none of the women who used Mindy's service aspired to be someone's lapdog. Today's women had careers, ambitions; they were seeking companions to share their lives with, not pining to be some male chauvinist's lesser half. Besides, she *liked* her clients, and sending any of them on a date with him seemed like client abuse.

The tinkle of the heart-shaped bell above her door shook Mindy from her thoughts, and she looked up to find Jane whisking in with two ice-cream cones clutched in her fists. "You just missed a cutie on the sidewalk, Min. Classic guy next door. Even walking a cute little dog, one of those white ones that look like a mop. He was perfect for you."

Mindy considered asking, "The guy or the mop?" but her heart just wasn't in it. She let out a sigh, caring even less than usual about Jane's manhunting expeditions.

"I'm doomed," she said balefully, accepting her second mint chocolate chip ice-cream cone in two days. She only hoped she could keep this one from spattering on the sidewalk or on a client. Although an evil little part of her did begin to fantasize about yesterday and what would have happened if her melty scoop had landed a little more to the left or the right on one of Benton Maxwell's expensive shoes. Or better yet, had slid down one leg of that custom suit. Shoes could be wiped off; suits were a little more complicated. If the man walked through the door right now, she'd be almost tempted to make it happen. Then maybe he'd demand his money back and go elsewhere. As it was, she felt honor bound to fulfill her obligation to him to the best of her ability, since, after all, she *had* accepted his money quickly enough when she'd seen how much he was willing to pay.

"So he's really that bad, huh?" Jane asked, settling behind her desk with a dip of raspberry sherbet in her hand.

"Yes, for the tenth time, he's really that bad." Jane had missed Benton's entire visit, and had seemed hesitant to believe Mindy's account of what had happened. Mindy took a determined lick of ice cream as if to drive the point home.

Jane seemed devastated, frowning at Mindy over her cone. "But he was so tall and so dark."

With her free hand, Mindy plucked up the now-crumpled list of attributes he'd left for her and waved it in the air. "'Knows when to defer to my judgment,'" Mindy reminded Jane sharply.

Jane tilted her head, as if begging Mindy to say it wasn't so. "And so steamy."

"'Intelligent when necessary,'" Mindy said. "When *necessary!*"

"And don't forget rich. I might be able to figure out

when it's necessary to be intelligent if I could bag a man that rich."

"Jane!" Mindy scolded, glaring in disbelief. "He's a pig! And he didn't even care enough about this process to let me interview him." A glance revealed that her ice cream was melting, so she took a quick lick before adding, "Believe it or not, sometimes there's more to life—and even lust—than tall, dark and steamy."

"Why don't you want a man?"

Mindy flinched, taken aback. "Huh?"

Jane's eyes narrowed on her suspiciously. "You heard me. Why don't you want a man? The rest of us want a man. And it doesn't mean we're weak or spineless or dependent. It just means we want a man. We want companionship, love. If nothing else, we want sex. So why not you? How can a woman who has carved out a livelihood by finding men for other people be truly happy without a man for herself?"

Mindy grimaced as the dismay in her chest tightened into a hard little knot, then she shifted her gaze to the pale green ice cream starting to drip onto her hand. Scowling at the cone, she gave up without a fight and chucked it in the garbage. She grabbed a tissue, wiped off her fingers, then swung her attention to her laptop. "Jane, this really isn't the time for another man lecture. I have to find a date for Benton Maxwell."

"Ah." Jane threw her head back in a short, abrupt nod.

Mindy cast a sideways glance. "Ah? What is ah?"

"Ah just means that clearly there's more to the picture than meets the eye. Ah means I've uncovered a chink in your armor, my friend."

"A chink in my armor? What armor? What are you talking about?"

Jane's mouth curled into a small, self-satisfied smile. "You know good and well what I'm talking about. If you really don't want a man, there's a reason. But you don't have to tell me. I won't pry anymore. I'm sure it'll come out someday, whenever you're ready to share."

"Jane, you watch too much TV, read too many books. In real life, not everyone who doesn't follow the social trends has some deep-seated problem. Some people are just different."

Jane gave her head a thoughtful tilt, then widened her eyes. "Are you a lesbian?"

"Jane!"

"There's nothing wrong with it if you are. I just thought maybe—"

"I am *not* a lesbian, okay? I'm just...not hopeful when it comes to guys, that's all."

What she'd told Jane was true; there was no deep secret, no tragic heartbreak in her past. But there was also no great love. Maybe tragic heartbreak would have been better than the emptiness of not knowing what she was missing. That must be what people meant, she thought, when they said it was better to have loved and lost than never to have loved at all. As it was, she'd never found a guy who made her heart go zing!

Over the years, she'd dated men who reminded her of Benton Maxwell in ways, and certainly that hadn't worked out. And she'd also dated men who were Benton Maxwell's polar opposite, men who were sweet and respectful and sensitive and...boring, when all was said and done. She'd dated men who irritated her, men with annoying habits and men who thought themselves far funnier than they were. She'd dated men who dressed well and men who dressed badly. She'd dated men totally devoted to her and others who were totally devoted to themselves. She'd dated a lot of men, but she'd never found one who truly fit with her, who truly made her get the whole man-woman thing.

Because of her job, she believed in love, of course, wholeheartedly. She'd seen too many happy people to dispute it, and she was downright gifted at putting those people together. Even before opening Mates by Mindy, she'd possessed an undeniable gift for fixing people up, for seeing traits and personalities that meshed—that's why she'd started her business. But at twenty-nine, Mindy had washed her hands of that eternal personal search; she was good at searching for others, but searching for herself had proven fruitless. And she really was fine with her manless life. She didn't know why that little knot grew in her chest when she thought about it sometimes, but she was fine.

Focusing on the computer screen she'd been staring at all afternoon, Mindy finally sighed, slapped her palm on her desk and announced, "I've made a decision."

"You want me to track down the cutie with the pooch," Jane said.

"No, I want you to go down the street to the hobby shop and buy a set of darts."

Jane's eyes widened behind her glasses. "Darts?"

Mindy nodded solemnly. "Darts."

While Jane was gone, Mindy printed out the entire list of her female clients who fit Benton Maxwell's physical parameters. Beyond that, there was no narrowing it down, so Mindy figured there was only one sensible way to approach this problem and end her suffering.

When Jane returned, they taped the list of names to the wall. Mindy removed the flowered scarf from her neck and instructed Jane to tie it over her eyes and point her in the right direction.

The first dart ricocheted off the wall, striking Mindy's desk before skidding across the floor. Jane squealed. "Hey, watch it." The second, however, hit home with a nice, solid little *phlunk*. Mindy removed the scarf and stepped forward to see who the unfortunate girl was. As luck would have it, however, the dart had landed directly between two names, so Mindy looked at Jane and said, "All the better. This takes care of two dates for him instead of just one."

Five minutes later, Mindy was on hold with Benton Maxwell's office. Although she didn't relish the idea of talking to him again, she'd decided to get this over with as soon as possible.

When he finally picked up, he sounded just as rushed as usual. "Benton Maxwell." She'd forgotten how deep his voice was, and it threw her a little.

"Mr. Maxwell, it's Mindy McCrae. I've selected your first two dates and I'm calling to give you their evening phone numbers. I'll contact them both this afternoon, so they'll be expecting your call."

"Very good," he said in a way that irritated her, but as she'd discovered yesterday, *everything* he said tended to irritate her.

After she'd relayed the women's names and numbers, Benton asked, "And these women meet my criteria?"

She sighed, annoyed by his doubt even if she

couldn't completely deny it was well-founded. "Yes, they're both lovely, intelligent women."

"What about the third woman? You did say I get three, right?"

"I'm...still working on that one." She tried to sound far more cheerful than she felt. "But hopefully, one of the first two will turn out to be the woman of your dreams and we won't even get to the third."

BENTON BREEZED through a yellow light, anxious to get his second date, Kathy, home and out of his life. That Mindy woman was a nut. She had to be a nut if she thought either of the women she'd chosen was a good match for him.

This evening had been a nightmare from start to finish, even worse than the date with—what was her name? Anita—earlier this week.

"Are you trying to kill me?" Kathy asked, referring, Benton presumed, to his rate of speed. What he'd thought at the beginning of the date was a beautiful lady now looked like a piranha sitting next to him. The small blond predator clicked her long red fingernails together as she sneered at him beneath the dim glare of streetlights. The talons looked as deadly as any weapon he'd ever seen.

"No, just trying to bring this evening to an end and put us both out of our misery."

The first sign of trouble had come when Kathy had informed him that if it were up to her, it would be illegal for anyone to own such an extravagant car when there were children starving in Ethiopia. Benton had explained that a man of his position had a reputation to maintain, a certain image to present, and that he also thought hard work deserved rewards, but she hadn't bought a word of it.

Things had gotten seriously worse, on a life-planning level, when she went on to say she was a professor of communications at the University of Cincinnati. She loved her job, was working steadily toward tenure and intended to be there until retirement.

"You wouldn't be willing to change your plans if something life-altering happened? Say...marriage? To a man who might require your assistance in certain social aspects of his business?"

She had glared at him and clicked her nails a little more furiously. Okay, so he hadn't been subtle, but he'd thought Mindy of the Fluffy Hearts would have filled Kathy in on what he wanted from a woman.

After that, they'd bickered through dinner, and Benton got the idea she sincerely hated him, although he had no idea what he'd done to offend her so. Of course, when she mentioned that her sister's cat had just given birth to an adorable litter of kittens, it had probably been a bad move for him to reply, "I hate cats." But by that point, he'd long since given up on having a pleasant evening.

Coming to a halt in front of Kathy's building, Benton was prepared to at least walk his indignant date to her apartment, but she exited the car, said, "See ya around," then slammed the door in his face before he had a chance to react.

That's it, he thought, driving blessedly away from the piranha lady. He'd paid good money to meet females who wanted a life of luxury and leisure, and he wasn't getting what he'd asked for. Frankly, he'd assumed it would be easy, that women would be champing at the bit to fill the role. How hard could it be to find someone like that? So much for Mindy McCrae's astonishing success rate. Tomorrow he was going to pay her a little visit and give her a piece of his mind.

"AGAIN, KATHY, I'm terribly sorry things worked out so poorly, and I'll make certain it doesn't happen again." Mindy hung up the phone, feeling like a heel for the second time in just a few days.

Earlier in the week, Anita Barker had called to complain that Benton was nothing like any man her profile could possibly suggest she'd be attracted to, and although Mindy didn't admit it, she knew truer words had never been spoken. "I got the idea he was just in a rush to get the date over with," Anita had complained. "We rushed to the restaurant, we rushed through dinner and—oh my God—he even *ordered* for me. Have you ever heard of anything so archaic?"

Not before Benton Maxwell, Mindy had wanted to say, but held her tongue. Frankly, she wasn't the least surprised that Benton Maxwell would think he could choose a woman's meal better than she could. And obviously, Anita was not interested in deferring to Benton's judgment. Not that Mindy could blame her, but a desperate matchmaker could hope against hope, couldn't she?

Kathy had told her Benton had clearly been threatened by her intelligence, another occurrence that couldn't have surprised Mindy less. "And he implied that if I got married, I should give up my professorship!"

The phone calls made Mindy want to hang her head in shame. Deep inside—oh heck, maybe even on the surface—she'd known the dates wouldn't go well. Couldn't go well. The vast majority of her female clients were smart and independent, very today sort of women. And both Kathy's and Anita's profiles had clearly clashed with Benton's. Kathy wanted a down-to-earth guy she could be herself with, while Anita had requested a man with a great sense of humor. And Mindy had possessed the nerve to stick them with *him?*

Yet the problem remained—*no* woman wanted a man like Benton Maxwell, and she'd promised him three.

"Let me guess," Jane said, seeing Mindy's frown. "Mr. Tall, Dark and Steamy's second victim?"

"You got it. And she had every right to be angry. I never should have sacrificed a good client—*two* good clients—to a wolf in tailored clothing."

Jane gave her head a sympathetic tilt. "Don't be too hard on yourself. It could happen to anybody. I'm sure all matchmakers occasionally have off days."

"But that's just why I feel so terrible. It wasn't an off day. I knew *exactly* what I was doing. I was leading those two women to the slaughter, making them my sacrificial lambs in exchange for money."

Jane flashed a skeptical look. "Don't be so dramatic. It was a couple of failed dates, not the end of the world. Nobody died."

"Even so, I feel I have an unspoken vow with my clients to use my matchmaking abilities for good, not evil, to try my best to make matches that will work for each person involved. I'm not sure I can send another poor, unsuspecting woman out with him, Jane. After all, I've probably lost Kathy's and Anita's faith in me and I don't want to risk losing anyone else's."

"Well," Jane said, "I guess you could give Benton

Maxwell back a third of the money he paid and tell him adios.''

At that precise moment, the door to Mates By Mindy burst open and a tall, angry man came marching through.

"Speak of the devil," Jane whispered, and Mindy cast her a quick look of reproach before rising to round her desk and meet Benton Maxwell head-on.

He looked as devastatingly handsome as she remembered, every hair in place, today's suit a charcoal color that enhanced his eyes, even if they were brimming with displeasure at the moment. And unfortunately, he was still much taller than she—something she'd forgotten about—and she became keenly aware of the disadvantage it gave her.

"Ninety-five percent!" he said, towering over her small frame. "Ninety-five percent?"

He leaned so near that their noses were practically touching, and for one shocking, almost horrifying moment, Mindy froze. She caught the unmistakable scent of musky male and—wait a minute! That didn't matter. Who did he think he was, barreling into her shop like this, throwing her success rate at her as if it were a lie!

Catching her breath, she took a step back and quickly focused, narrowing her gaze on him. "Ninety-five percent. Before *you* came along, that is."

"Considering the choices you made for me, I can't believe you have a success rate of *five* percent. I don't know what you were thinking when you selected those two women, but you couldn't have been following the list I gave you."

Mindy had had just about enough of this man. "Take a seat," she said, then planted one hand firmly on his chest and nudged him into the chair across from her desk.

As Benton Maxwell landed, he looked entirely perplexed, as if he didn't know what had hit him, as if no one had ever taken the upper hand with him before. Which was probably his problem, Mindy thought. She liked putting him off balance.

"That's better," she said, and she considered returning to her chair behind the desk but decided she liked being the one who got to tower for a change. She held her ground and crossed her arms. "You, Mr. Maxwell, have a lot to learn about women."

"Is that so?" He looked a bit less cowed, to her disappointment.

Yet Mindy was far from deflated. "Yes. For one thing, you cannot narrow a woman down to a list of attributes and expect to find a suitable life mate. And if you *are* going to present a list of attributes, it helps if they don't sound like they came straight from the 1950s."

Benton Maxwell sighed. "I simply told you what I'm looking for in a wife and asked you to find some suitable candidates."

"Easier said than done in your case, I'm afraid."

"Then you're saying you can't do it? You aren't capable?" He tilted his handsome head, his voice going a bit softer, his eyes taking on a look of bewilderment. "Let me ask you something, Miss McCrae. Is this how you treat all your clients? Lecturing them, berating them for their preferences—" he glanced around helplessly, then motioned vaguely to the chair he sat in "—and *pushing* them, for heaven's sake?"

And that was when it hit Mindy, a revelation as pure and clear as a cloudless summer sky. She gazed into this man's bluer than blue eyes and finally understood. He didn't know.

He didn't know he was overbearing. He didn't know he was unreasonable. He didn't know he was a chauvinist. He didn't know he was seeking a woman who had gone out of style decades ago. He just plain didn't know.

And he clearly thought *she* was crazy; the look in those eyes said so.

She held the gaze and for a few short seconds hoped that he could see she wasn't crazy, that she was really a nice, normal, friendly person.

When his sexy eyes remained baffled and half-angry, though, she gave up and decided she didn't care what he thought of her. After all, what self-respecting woman would care about this guy's opinion? She might have glimpsed him in a whole new, almost innocent light, but that didn't excuse him for not having a clue.

Nonetheless, she realized, she did want to fulfill her obligation to him, and she would. She felt challenged, and more than that, suddenly tempted to do something that *was* just a little bit crazy.

"Listen," she said in a calm, firm tone, "I *will* find you a third date, someone who fits your criteria, someone you can at least tolerate."

"Frankly, I'm not sure you're up to it."

Well, that figured. The last remnants of Mindy's strange empathy fled the scene. "Is that so?"

"Yes, that's so."

Mindy uncrossed her arms, planted her fists on her hips, and attempted to raise subtly on her tiptoes in order to tower over him even more. "Well, Mr. Maxwell, we'll just see about that, won't we?"

"WELL, you've got yourself in a pickle now," Jane said as the door shut behind Benton Maxwell a few minutes later.

Mindy turned to her assistant with a thoughtful expression. "No, as a matter of fact, I don't." Because Mindy had made a decision concerning Benton Maxwell's third and final Mates By Mindy date in the time it had taken to usher him from the office. It was an outlandish decision, but the notion had come to her when she'd realized he honestly didn't know how unreasonable his expectations were. In fact, the more she thought about it, the more all the pros of her crazy ideas outweighed the cons, of which there was only one, the fact that it was outlandish.

"I'm waiting," Jane said, sounding completely impatient.

"*I'll* go," Mindy said.

"You'll go where?"

"On a date with him. I'll be his last date."

"*What?*"

"Of course, I can't be me, I can't be Mindy. So I'll pose as…Mandy, my imaginary evil twin."

Mindy smiled in triumph, but Jane looked as if Mindy had suggested she eat worms.

"Quit looking so horrified," Mindy demanded. "Your face might stick like that."

"But I *am* horrified."

Mindy shook her head; she wasn't explaining this right. "Listen to me. This will work perfectly—I can fit the criteria. I'm petite, I have a nice enough shape and I'm certainly intelligent, but I don't have to let it show. Unless it becomes necessary, of course, which I presume means if he needs help solving a problem or wants to impress someone. And I'll wear that blond wig I bought for your Halloween party last year—you remember, the time I came as Dolly Parton?''

Jane looked completely bereft. "How could I forget? My poor boys drooled over your fake boobs for weeks.''

"So I'll wear the wig and claim I'm my sister." Mindy went on. "And I'll let him order my dinner and I'll defer to his judgment and I'll pretend my greatest goal in life is to throw tasteful garden parties for the ladies at the club. I'll seem like a completely appropriate candidate, one he can't complain about. See? It's perfect.''

"Uh, just one problem, Min. What if he *likes* you?"

Mindy let a wicked grin take shape on her face. This was the best part. "Easy. He won't. Because while on the surface Mandy will appear to be the perfect woman for him, once the night progresses, I plan to shake up his world a little.''

Jane looked skeptical but undeniably intrigued. "Shake up his world?"

Mindy nodded. "By evening's end, I—I mean Mandy—will be the antithesis of everything he wants in a woman, and in the process, I'll kill lots of birds with one little stone."

"These birds being?"

"Well, I'll succeed in showing him that I—the real I, Mindy—can indeed find a woman who at least *appears* to be what he wants. But I'll also succeed in showing him that women, even seemingly docile, dependent types, are more complex than a list of silly attributes. Most importantly," she concluded, "when the evening draws to a close, my obligation to Benton Maxwell will be over, and I'll never have to see him again.''

3

"ANOTHER DATE tonight, huh?" Phil Harper asked Benton over lunch at Pigall's, a downtown eatery near both their offices.

The third member of their party, Mike Kelly, slid into his chair in time to hear Benton's answer, which he kept short and simple. "Yes."

They were his best friends—buddies from college—but Benton hadn't chosen to tell them his means of procuring his recent dates lest they think he was desperate instead of busy.

Mike grinned hopefully, a slightly crooked tie hanging from his white shirt collar. "Well, maybe this one will work out better than the last two. Carrie's always saying it's time you settle down and find yourself a good woman."

Benton nodded. His happily married friends had been offering such comments for the past couple of years, but he hadn't told them he'd recently decided they were right. It didn't come naturally to admit anything in his life was less than perfect.

"And hey, the big three-five is coming up soon, isn't it?" Phil asked. "Seems just about the right time for a wedding."

If they only knew how closely his thoughts mirrored theirs.

Mike laughed and added, "Yeah, before you're too old to enjoy the nighttime perks."

Again Benton ignored the joke and kept it simple. "We'll see."

Because the sad truth was that he didn't hold out much hope for his last Mates by Mindy date and was almost sorry he'd mentioned it to his friends.

Unfortunately, this one felt much different than the other two already. The other two he'd looked forward to. The other two had made him feel optimistic and hopeful. The other two, he'd mistakenly believed, had held a chance of working out. But Benton no longer remained so naive.

And hours later, as he stepped from the shower and slapped on aftershave, he felt the same way. He knew, either by instinct or habit, that it would be another disaster. As he dropped the towel circling his waist, then got dressed, he considered calling this Mandy woman and canceling the whole thing. She'd seemed nice enough on the phone when they'd spoken last night, but he couldn't be fooled that easily anymore. After all, the same person had planned all three dates. An image of a little redhead with flaming green eyes filled his mind. A spitfire, he thought.

More than once while he was growing up, his father had laughed and said, "You wouldn't know it now, but your mother was a spitfire when we were young."

"Ben," his mother would scold from the opposite end of the dining room table. But then his parents would share a private wink or a special look, and in those moments Benton had realized they had a pre-children history he knew nothing about, and he understood there must be more to their relationship than met the eye.

He'd never really known exactly what his dad had meant by the term *spitfire,* but now he thought he did. Mindy McCrae had unwittingly enlightened him.

It wasn't the first time in the last two days a vision of her had assaulted him. When they'd stood in her office yelling at each other, she'd looked cuter than he'd recalled. She'd worn a casual yet shapely lime-green dress, which, although rather loud, had somehow suited her. Well, not that it mattered what suited a crazy lady, but…he'd noticed her in a way he hadn't on their first meeting. It probably had something to do with the way she'd pushed him into that chair—another image that kept entering his head unbidden. He wasn't used to women getting rough with him. In fact, he was fairly certain it was a first. As he straightened the knot in his silk tie, he realized he remained as baffled about the incident now as he'd been the moment it happened.

Besides filling him with the sense that he'd entered some alternate universe where things didn't work quite the way he was accustomed to, the encounter had left him shaken in another indefinable yet intense way. It made sense that his heart had been beating wildly in his chest when he'd left, that his palms had grown sweaty, his breath short; he'd been angry. But it made less sense that he still felt the same way each time he relived the moment in his thoughts.

Because Benton Maxwell was nothing if not in control—of himself, his life, his relationships. Take Miss Binks, for example. She was crazy about him, and her feelings didn't affect him, emotionally or otherwise. And he possessed that same control in business situations—nothing ever got to him. He was cool under pressure. Yet one little redhead knocks him into a chair and he's sweating. He gave his head a slight shake as he grabbed his suit jacket and exited the bedroom.

Do not think about Mindy now, he commanded himself. This was no time to sweat. Yet as he reached up to slide one finger between his neck and crisp white shirt collar, Benton already wished he could loosen his tie.

AS THE MERCEDES pulled to the curb outside Mindy's house, her heart leaped. Oh sure, this had seemed like a barrel of fun when she'd come up with the idea, but now she had to go through with it, pretending to be someone she wasn't. *What have I done?*

With no time to worry over bad decisions, she let the sheer curtain drop into place over the window, then pivoted toward the full-length mirror on the back of her bedroom door. Not one red hair peeked from beneath the platinum-blond wig that hung neatly past her shoulders. With the ends slightly curved, the style was a bit tame compared to the way she'd worn it on her Dolly outing. Pale shades of pink lipstick and blush complemented her new hair color, as did her cool pink suit with decorative cutouts at the lapel. The stylishly fitted suit stopped several inches above her knees, yet it said *classy,* allowing Mindy to check another attribute off his list.

"What do you think, Venus?" she asked the slender tabby cat who watched from a windowsill across the room.

Mindy took the feline's silence, as well as the fact that she didn't seem too freaked out over Mindy's appearance, as a good sign. Mindy stepped into the hall, closing the door behind her as the doorbell rang.

Okay, she thought, looking around and checking

things off her own personal list. Cat hidden in bedroom. House much more tidy than normal, which was something she'd figured would matter to Benton. Yes, everything was in place.

When the doorbell buzzed again, she turned a derisive glare toward it. "Impatient as ever," she murmured, then started across the room. Taking a deep breath, gathering her courage and putting on her practiced Mandy smile, she whisked open the door.

"Hello, you must be Benton!" she said cheerfully, and oh my, was he ever Benton. She kept forgetting how good-looking the man was, how utterly drop-dead handsome from head to toe. As usual, every dark hair was in place, every stitch of clothing lay straight and smooth and creaseless against his broad physique, and as far as Mindy could tell, every inch of him was beyond perfect.

She was so caught up in drooling over him, in fact, that she almost missed the look of shock in his stunning blue eyes. He tilted his head, as if trying to make sense of what he saw. "Uh, Mindy?"

Showtime. She widened her smile. "No, but it's an understandable mistake." She spoke in a softer-than-usual voice and splayed frosty pink fingernails across her chest. "I'm Mandy, Mindy's sister."

Predictably, his mouth dropped open, and Mindy couldn't deny the twinge of pleasure that bit into her. She definitely enjoyed catching this man off guard. "Mindy has a sister? A *twin?*" He said it in the same tone one might say, "A monster?" and appeared horrified when she nodded.

"We're not much alike, though," she rushed to add, lest he turn and flee the scene. "We have very little in common."

"You definitely look alike."

"Not really," she claimed. "Especially not since…Mindy cut her hair and dyed it red."

Benton blinked. "She's really a blonde?"

She nodded again. "Just like me." For fun, she almost instructed him to look for Mindy's roots the next time he saw her, but caught herself. No, that would sound tacky. Tonight, at least for a while, she had to be the woman of Benton Maxwell's sophisticated dreams. "Would you like to come in for a moment?"

She wasn't sure why she asked, only that she'd felt the conversation ball was still in her court and she didn't have a good return ready. Benton stepped uncertainly across her threshold, and she hoped the simple, down-to-earth qualities of her small home wouldn't turn him off.

"Can I get you something to drink?"

He checked his watch. "Well, our reservations are in half an hour at the Greenwood Room downtown."

Typical, she thought. Rushing the date. But no matter. She was his dream woman, and dream women never balked; they smiled, so that's what Mindy did. "All right then. Let me turn off the lights, and I'll be ready."

As Mindy crossed the room, flipping off first one lamp, then another, she couldn't deny hoping Benton was taking in her form from behind. After all, he'd asked for petite and shapely, and she'd worked hard to keep her figure the last few years and didn't mind having it noticed.

"So, Mandy, what do you do?"

She turned toward him with another angelic expression, pleased to have this part all worked out. "I'm a receptionist." Receptionists had to be smart, of course, but men who had them, which probably included Benton Maxwell, didn't always realize just how smart they were. Besides, it wasn't a career that required years of schooling, so it would be perfectly believable if she claimed readiness to give it up. It seemed the perfect profession for Mandy.

"Very good," he said in that annoying you-have-my-approval way that made her want to smack him, but she kept on smiling. "Where do you work?"

Mindy stopped dead in her tracks. It was a simple question. Preposterously simple. Yet she hadn't bothered to think ahead to that part, assuming he wouldn't care enough to ask. But with her smile still pasted in place, Mindy calmly scanned her surroundings until a glance through the wide doorway to her kitchen drew her attention to the bottle of dishwashing liquid on the sink.

"Procter & Gamble," she said, naming the biggest, most historic business in the city. Not just anyone could snag a job there, and being a receptionist at P&G said smart when necessary as well as anything possibly could. Benton's impressed nod seemed to agree. "But not downtown," she added. "I work in the complex in Blue Ash." She knew he worked downtown, and couldn't risk discovering his offices were right next door or something.

Mindy hadn't realized she was such a good liar. But she supposed she was glad to find out, since she had a whole evening of it ahead of her.

WHEN BENTON held open his car door a few minutes later, he watched Mandy's long, slender legs stretch from beneath her little skirt as she climbed inside. And as the Mercedes headed down I-71 toward the city,

Benton kept stealing glances at his date. Mandy. Mindy's twin. He couldn't believe it. Other than the hair, the resemblance was amazing. He still suspected the night would be a washout—he couldn't imagine any sister of Mindy's being wife material for him— yet he couldn't quit looking at her.

She was really quite hot in an elegant way, a trait Benton found highly appealing. Her suit was sophisticated yet profoundly feminine, the fabric hugging her curves in a way that drew his attention without shoving them down his throat. And her shimmery pink lips were downright tantalizing. Pink wasn't usually a color Benton would choose for a woman—he thought it was too froufrou—but Mandy pulled it off perfectly. Everything about her was refined but demure and sexy.

"How long have you been at P & G?" he asked, hoping to build on their earlier conversation.

"Since college." She flashed another glistening pink smile. "Eight years now."

Benton figured that made her about thirty. Perfect. Mature enough to have a firm sense of herself and what she wanted in life, yet young enough to remain attractive and vibrant, and also still young enough to have children, something Benton definitely wanted.

"So you're happy there," he said.

She gave her head a thoughtful tilt. "I've enjoyed my job immensely over the years, but I don't want to do it forever."

Curiosity pinched at him. "No? What else are you interested in pursuing?"

She gave a hesitant half smile, which for some reason made his groin tighten a little. "Well, this may sound rather old-fashioned, but I suppose if I ever find the right guy and settle down, I'd like to try a simpler, less hectic life. Perhaps be a full-time wife and mother.''

She was blushing, looking to him for approval. Little did she know pure happiness was flooding Benton's entire body. No wonder his groin had tightened; already he had a feeling about this woman, a big feeling. He was sexually attracted to her, but also sincerely enjoyed her company. He might be jumping the gun—he was a sensible enough man to know that—but he didn't think any woman he'd ever met had set off such a perfect combination of emotions inside him, let alone done it ten minutes after meeting her. Even if she *was* Mindy's sister.

''I hope you don't think that sounds…unambitious,'' she offered.

He shook his head quickly, gazing at her. ''Not at all. I think it's great.''

''Benton, the road!''

Benton yanked his eyes to the windshield to find himself bearing down on a semi moving at a crawl in the fast lane. He pressed on the brakes, slowing the car, then felt a peculiar warmth climb his cheeks. Oh God, he was blushing. He couldn't recall the last time *anything* had made him blush. He didn't look at Mandy, just said, ''Sorry about that,'' as he veered into the Third Street exit lane of the Lytle Tunnel.

He didn't risk glancing at her again until they left the tunnel's dimness, emerging into the city. When he found her smiling, he sheepishly returned it and felt as out of sorts as a sixteen-year-old kid on his first date.

He pulled up to the Greenwood Room, accepted a ticket from a valet who greeted him by name, then met Mandy on the sidewalk. She took his arm as they proceeded toward the red-carpeted entrance, and Benton felt like a king—not only was he walking into his favorite restaurant with a pretty woman, but he really, truly liked her. He kept reminding himself that it would be wise to keep his doubts in place, not to trust in something so contrary to the rest of his Mates By Mindy experiences, but Benton had to admit maybe he'd misjudged the matchmaker. After all, how bad could she be if she had a sister this pleasant? And Mindy *had* fixed him up with her. Benton decided to officially forgive Mindy for the bad encounters they'd shared getting to this point. If this worked out, it would all easily be worth it.

After they were seated at an intimate table for two in the candlelit room, a black-and-white clad waiter approached. "Good evening, Mr. Maxwell."

"Good evening, Henry."

As Benton ordered a 1994 Pinot Gris, he felt Mandy's admiring gaze and thought, finally, someone who appreciated a man with his particular set of skills! When the waiter departed and Benton drew his gaze to hers, she didn't look away, didn't even blink. The instant chemistry he'd felt with her was beginning to override the other more logical reasons he was attracted to her, and the sexy spell between them was broken only when another waiter arrived with two menus.

"The baked lobster here is excellent," he began to say when the waiter walked away, but he recalled thinking the other two women he'd taken out hadn't been pleased about his ordering for them, and he didn't want to screw this up. "If you like lobster, that is. I'm sure everything here is quite good."

She flashed a smile overtop the leather-bound menu.

"I'd love to try the baked lobster. And I so respect a man who knows his way around a fine restaurant. I adore extravagant evenings out like this, but being with a man like you does take the pressure off."

They both laughed, and Benton wondered what good deed he'd done to make fate smile upon him this way at last. "I'm discovering it's rare to find a woman who really values fine dining these days. I'm glad you're enjoying it."

"Well, I've happily indulged in my fair share of pizzas and hamburgers, but I can also embrace the better things, too. I'm always eager to expand my horizons."

Benton decided he was probably smiling way too much for someone always so serious, but at the moment he didn't feel nearly as in control as usual. With each passing second, he became more taken with her, and on impulse, he reached across the table to touch her hand, smooth and delicate beneath his. "May I tell you something?"

"Sure." She peered at him over the candle burning between them, her eyes like two fine-cut emeralds.

"You have the most brilliant eyes." Even as the words left him, Benton couldn't believe he'd uttered them. He'd dated dozens of women, but he'd never felt compelled to say such a thing. Yet just watching her was making him feel ridiculously romantic.

"Why…thank you."

Loving the crimson blush that stained her cheeks, he let out a small laugh partly at himself and at the unlikely situation he found himself in. They were both clearly a little nervous with how fast things were moving, with the instant magnetism tugging at them, and yet it was so obviously mutual that the embarrassment almost didn't matter. "That wasn't actually what I wanted to tell you," he admitted. "It just came out."

Her gaze stayed locked on him. "What else did you want to tell me?"

Benton sighed. This was the sort of thing you should probably say at the end of a date, when you asked a woman to see you again, but he wanted to say it now. "The truth is, when I first came to your door and discovered you were Mindy's sister, I didn't hold out much hope for the evening. You see, your sister and I haven't really hit it off."

She nodded knowingly. "She mentioned."

"But you're right. You're nothing like her. And I'm having a wonderful time. I hope you are, too."

Her smile lit him up inside. "Yes, Benton, I am." Then she squeezed his fingers, which had curved around hers, and the sensation shot straight between his thighs.

Mindy couldn't stop gazing into Benton's blue eyes, nearly the color of midnight in the dimly illuminated room. His large hand on hers was making her skittery inside.

What was she thinking?

Well, she was thinking about being his dream woman, of course, answering every question just as he'd want her to, casting worshipful smiles across the table. And it was all an act. Wasn't it?

Yes, yes, of course it was an act…but when he'd said her eyes were brilliant, she'd believed it. Way down deep. She'd even blushed, for heaven's sake.

To her surprise, she'd found Benton much less abrasive than before, and if she didn't have good reason to think differently, she'd suspect he was sincerely interested in getting to know her, learning about her, listening to her. In fact, now that she thought about it, he didn't even seem rushed anymore. Everything about the evening was dreamily pleasant and made Mindy feel sort of heady. She couldn't help beginning to wonder if maybe, just maybe, she might have judged him too harshly.

But even if she had, she still had to squelch the giddy, romantic sensations swimming through her veins. She still had to go through with her plan, the big switch that would take place at some point, the point where she changed gears and did something to turn him off. She had no choice, not just because it was part of the plan but because she was masquerading as someone she wasn't. Someone who didn't exist. Liking him was not an option.

Of course, hearing how happy he was to discover she was nothing like Mindy did help inspire her, harkening back to her previous impressions of Benton. Just keep thinking about that, she instructed herself as he ordered their dinner. She had to remember that he didn't like the *real* Mindy, she told herself as the waiter poured their wine.

"To special evenings," Benton said a moment later, lifting his glass. She followed suit. "And to you, Mandy, for making this one of them."

Mindy bit her lip, swallowed a sip of the fruity wine and almost forgot that quickly whatever crazy things she'd just been telling herself. He was too...perfect. And he continued to be no less than charming as the meal progressed.

He asked her more about Mandy's job, which forced Mindy to spin numerous additional lies yet served to remind her that nothing taking place here was real. And when he asked about her family, she mentioned her parents' divorce a few years ago, explaining that she kept in close contact with both of them, even though her father, an ex-army lieutenant, lived in Arizona now. She'd thought perhaps a divorce in the family would be the thing to turn up Benton's nose, but he'd looked much more sympathetic than judgmental. Of course, she was suddenly no longer an only child, but a twin, and she tried to keep conversation on *that* topic to a minimum.

He talked about his job, his company, and he told Mandy far more about his family than he'd consented to tell Mindy during their initial meeting. What he'd broadly painted to Mindy as a cold, success-driven family suddenly sounded warm and inviting. He talked about how much he looked forward to the holidays since it meant seeing his brother, sister and parents, along with his four nieces and nephews. "We usually try to plan a beach trip in the summer at my parents' place in Boca, too, but that's always trickier, trying to arrange all of our schedules."

"Now that your parents live in Florida, where do you go for Christmas?"

"Here, where we all grew up," he told her. "At my house. I enjoy it because it's the only time all the extra bedrooms and bathrooms get used. The rest of the year, the place stays empty. Except for me, that is."

Mindy's heart contracted a little, thinking he sounded sad about that. No wonder he wanted a wife. Despite his list, maybe his desire to marry *wasn't* so cold and calculated. "Why," she began tentatively, "do you have such a large house? Were you planning for the family gatherings or…"

"When I bought it five years ago, it mainly seemed like a good investment. But now that I've lived there alone all this time, I guess I'm hoping to...eventually fill it. With a family.''

Mindy didn't answer, just dropped her gaze to her lobster. This was bad, really bad. He liked her, a lot. She could tell he thought she was the one, the wife, the prize, the trophy. Which, of course, was exactly what she'd *wanted* him to think; she just hadn't expected to feel so utterly lousy about it. Because she hadn't expected him to turn so darn nice!

When they left the restaurant an hour later, Benton said, ''I thought we might take a stroll since the weather's so pleasant.''

He was right—a light breeze had cooled the May night. Darkness had fallen, and street lamps turned the city dusky and romantic. And the wine, she supposed, had left her just a little tipsy, making her follow her wants more than her plans. She'd find a way to ruin the evening eventually, just not yet.

''Or maybe you'd enjoy a carriage ride instead?'' he asked.

A horse-drawn carriage ride. The ones that left from Fountain Square and clopped their way leisurely through the city. For years, every time Mindy had seen some couple curled up in one of those carriages, she'd dreamed of being with the sort of man who would want to share something so romantic. And, of course, she had eventually decided that no such man existed, not for her. She clutched Benton's arm a little tighter, bit her lip with the small sexual thrill that came from pressing the side of her breast against him in the process, and smiled into his eyes.

She had to stop this. Now, this very minute, before things progressed any further. It was time for a major about-face, time to totally change his mind about her, time to become…the anti-Mandy.

Just then, a heavy disco beat echoed onto the street from somewhere nearby and supplied Mindy with a solution. As they continued walking, nearing the music, she glanced through a window to see countless bodies gyrating behind the glass to an old Blondie song.

"Or…we could hit the dance floor!" Mindy said.

"Huh?"

She avoided looking into Benton's eyes. Instead, she grabbed his wrist and dragged him toward the open door from which the music spilled.

"Mandy, what are you doing?"

She pulled him along behind her until they were immersed in the sweaty, smoky, crowded room, the beat pounding so loudly Mindy could barely hear herself think. She stopped at the bar and yelled, "Screwdriver!" to the bartender.

"Mandy!" Benton bellowed, trying to be heard above the din. "Why are we here?"

"Just had the urge," she screamed back.

"The urge to what?"

As Mindy's drink appeared, Benton hurriedly fumbled for a credit card, but Mindy pulled a ten from her pocket and slapped it on the bar. "I got this one," she told him, then picked up the small glass and drained it. She needed a little more courage to go through with this next part of her plan, which originally had been a loose, wait-and-see-how-you-can-incorporate-this-into-the-evening thing, but now Mindy knew exactly what she must do to show Benton the dark side of Mandy, the side he'd never want to marry.

"Let's dance!" she said. She flicked open the three

pink buttons on her jacket and ripped it off, revealing a daring black-beaded bustier underneath. She'd bought it the year she'd gone to Jane's Halloween party as Madonna and knew it gave her serious cleavage.

She looked up in time to catch Benton's wide eyes and nervous swallow. "Mandy," he chided her.

Mindy tossed her jacket on the bar, then strode confidently onto the dance floor, yelling over her shoulder, "Come on, Benton, loosen up, have some fun. Let's party!"

"Party?" he yelled, tentatively following.

Benton felt as if he'd just been hit by a truck. One minute things had been going great, the next, he'd been yanked off the street and thrust into the center of several hundred undulating bodies. But what blew him away even more was seeing Mandy's bare shoulders and what appeared to be truly incredible breasts! The tight thing she wore shoved them together and up and...well, if Benton had been mildly aroused during dinner, nothing compared to the instant response in his pants now.

Without warning, Mandy turned to face him, having apparently decided they'd reached the right spot on the floor, then threw her arms around his neck, pressing her body flush against his. She swayed and gyrated against him, which forced him—however stiffly—to sway and gyrate, too, although he never made the conscious choice to do so. He hadn't danced to music like this since college. And he'd never particularly missed it or hoped to do it again, but Mandy felt far too good against him to put up much of a fight.

As the Blondie tune faded, the song changed, and Mandy suddenly backed away from him to—oh

God—start doing very enticing things with her lithe little body. She watched only him as she danced, although numerous male eyes followed *her*. Her every move screamed sex, her breasts shimmying and straining against the black fabric, her hips rolling in a liquid rhythm. Then, as if she hadn't excited him enough, her hands descended slowly over her breasts before inching down the front of her thighs until they played at the hem of her skirt. She eased it upward, gradually, teasingly, until Benton glimpsed the tops of lace stockings and the pink garter belt that held them in place.

Part of Benton didn't want to be here, watching this. It felt more foreign to him than being in another country, another universe. He'd never been attracted to this kind of a woman, the wild, uninhibited, anything-goes type, and he had no idea what had happened to the sweet yet sophisticated lady he'd had dinner with. He should demand she stop dancing and take her home.

On the other hand, she was driving him mad with wanting. He was only flesh and blood, after all. Blood, which at the moment was gathering in all the right places.

Suddenly something unfamiliar and almost dangerous grabbed Benton and drove him forward. He reached out and hauled Mandy against him until they were moving together to the rhythm, hot and sexy.

At this point, Benton had to wonder if he even *knew* what he was looking for in a woman. He was almost past caring about his ideas of the perfect wife, past caring about anything but the heavy heat of sensuality vibrating through him. He'd never thought he wanted *this,* but maybe he did!

Mindy was equally lost—to the music, the man and the excitement pumping through her veins. Hungry for more, she instinctively pressed her thigh between his to discover that he'd become a column of solid rock there. *Hello!*

As difficult as it was, she disengaged herself from him and took a big step back. But she didn't quit dancing and couldn't quit giving him what she feared was a look brimming with blatant sexual invitation.

Her whole plan had gone awry! Her wild public display was supposed to be freaking Benton out, turning him off, totally ruining his image of her. He was supposed to be outraged and embarrassed, dragging her out of the nightclub to his car, then dropping her at her doorstep thinking, Good riddance! He was supposed to be learning a lesson, that a woman couldn't be categorized by a list of traits.

But instead, he was aroused, and his eyes glimmered with wild abandon, and he was dancing—*dancing,* for heaven's sake! And the little bit of perspiration that edged his slightly unkempt hair somehow made him all the more sexy, all the more human to Mindy.

And perhaps even *more* startling than Benton's reaction to her teasing was her own. She'd never dreamed she could dance like this in public—or even in private—without totally humiliating herself. In what she supposed, technically, qualified as underwear, too! It had been a desperate move to turn the evening's tide, but she'd thought she was far too mature to act like this and enjoy it!

Nonetheless, she found she was thrilled to be dancing with this gorgeous and surprisingly unpredictable man. And she was just as thrilled, although in a different way, to know she'd aroused him. It made her feel sexy and desirable in a way she never had before. The Mandy she'd unveiled at dinner—the Mandy who'd let him order for her, who'd hung on his every word—that had been mostly an act. But the frightening truth was, maybe *this* side of Mandy *wasn't* an act; maybe it was a part of herself she'd never encountered before.

So as the music played on, one classic seventies hit dissolving into another, they danced. Sometimes she ended up pressed close against him, other times she found the will to pull back. Even then, their gazes kept them connected, and Mindy became absorbed in the pure, sexy fun of it all. She didn't think she'd ever felt so free.

When a slow, sensuous song pumped through the already heated air, Benton drew her against him. They swayed together, and she looked into his eyes and heard herself singing slightly suggestive lyrics. As his hands slid from her hips to cup her bottom, she bit her lip.

"Mmm." He breathed hotly in her ear, then she felt his kiss, whispery soft on her neck. The tiny titillation sent shivers through her, and she turned her face to his. The kiss he brushed across her lips was just as gentle, just as fleeting, just as tantalizing.

"Kiss me more," she heard herself whisper, unplanned.

His mouth sank onto hers with slow greed, and Mindy kissed him with all the passion that had likely been hibernating inside her for years. Without forethought, she pushed her tongue into his mouth and felt the heat spiral through them both.

This was wrong; she knew that. Her behavior had been intended to appall him, not entice him. But right and wrong seemed distant ideas at the moment, and only Benton's mouth, only his hands and his body, seemed relevant.

As he broke the kiss, his breath came warm on her neck. "Let's get out of here. Let's go to my place."

Abort! Abort! Every alarm inside her head went off, screaming at her, urging her to do something to keep this situation from getting any more out of control. Turn and run! Leave him behind and forget this night ever happened! Leave Mindy to pick up the pieces and make the excuses! Nothing was more important than getting away from him immediately!

Mindy braced her hands on his broad shoulders, pushing away from him, but he gently curled one hand around the back of her neck, halting her retreat.

"Benton, I…" She looked into his hungry eyes, sparkling beneath the glittering lights of the disco ball overhead, and couldn't think how to turn him down, how to explain after all they'd just shared.

When she hesitated, though, he tenderly grazed his fingertips downward, over her collarbone, until they paused, lingering on the exposed ridge of her left breast. "Yeah, honey?"

She swallowed, determined to try again. "I…" Then she dropped her gaze to his fingers, aching for more of his touch. "I…want to go to bed with you."

4

AS THEY MADE the tense drive to Benton's house, Mindy occasionally caught him studying her in the car's darkness. His eyes were filled with anticipation, and maybe even a little apprehension that this was happening so fast. But she also witnessed a sureness there, a certainty that thrilled her.

Of course, more than once, she felt a niggling little miniature version of herself perched on her shoulder, screaming, "Stop this! Are you crazy?" Each time, though, she mentally reached up and brushed it away. She couldn't think about anything right now besides Benton and how much she wanted him.

His hand enclosed hers as they practically ran up the stone steps to the double doors of his stately home. Mindy's heart pounded a hard, insistent rhythm in her chest. Upon entering a foyer large enough to create an echo, Benton looked at her, his eyes blazing with the same passion that coursed through her veins. "Do you, uh, want a tour of the house?"

She widened her gaze. "Only your bedroom."

Sheesh, Mandy had no shame! But being so utterly forward tripled Mindy's already increased pulse, especially when Benton gave her a sexy looks-like-we're-on-the-same-page smile. "This way."

He led her up a palatial curving staircase and down a dark, plush hallway, then let go of her hand to thrust open the double doors at the corridor's end. The enormous oak bed suited the house's size and looked good for rolling around in. Mindy had never been much of an acrobat in the sack, but she had the funny feeling Mandy might be.

Benton turned toward her to lift one palm to her face. Tipping her head back, she got lost in his gaze. Oh drat, maybe a part of her had thought the time spent traveling from the nightclub would cool the heat between them, bring Mindy to her senses, but that wasn't happening.

"You're beautiful." His deep, throaty voice spiraled through her, twisting her desire into an even tighter knot waiting to unwind and explode.

"Benton—" her speech was breathy and anxious "—I want you to know I don't usually sleep with someone on the first date."

He gave his head a light shake. "Doesn't matter."

"Really?" She'd assumed a rigid, old-fashioned man like Benton would believe in the double standard, and this only proved further that he was far more evolved than she'd thought possible.

He slanted her a playful grin. "Don't get me wrong. I'm *glad* you don't." The smile faded to an earnest expression. "It makes me feel special."

Mindy's voice quivered as she pressed her hands against his chest. "You *are* special." Then, just as it had at the club, her desire broke through the thin dam of her defenses to flow rough and hot and uncontrollable, and she couldn't wait another grueling second. "Oh Benton!" Flinging her arms around his neck, Mindy forcibly drew him into a kiss, the heat of his mouth swirling through her like liquid lightning.

Things moved quickly. His firm kisses intensified as

his hands molded to her curves. She moaned when his thumb passed over her breast, then she fought to loosen his tie, grapple at the buttons on his white shirt. He deftly pushed her pink jacket from her shoulders.

Resting his hands at her waist, he looked at the bustier clamped around her torso. "How do I get you out of this?"

"From the back." She spun to offer up the small black hooks and suddenly found herself looking into a dresser mirror, Benton behind her.

Their eyes connected briefly before he dropped a slow, sensuous kiss to her bare shoulder, then moved his hands to the fasteners. Within seconds, the confining piece of lingerie loosened around her, freeing her, until it fell away completely, leaving her bared before their eyes.

An expectant flush rose to Benton's cheeks as he studied her breasts, and when his hands came up to cup them, any lingering shreds of anxiety inside her faded to nothing. She met Benton's gaze in the mirror. "Don't go slow."

Without hesitation, he scooped her into his arms and carried her to the bed. And it turned out Mindy's first thought about the piece of furniture was accurate—they rolled wildly on the soft mattress as they struggled to remove each other's clothing. He stripped away her skirt and panties, leaving only her stockings and garter belt. She stripped away his attire and left *nothing.*

Benton's hands moved across her skin with unparalleled skill, and she gazed into his eyes the whole time, thrilled when he looked back. The suit and bustier lying on the carpet belonged to Mandy, and so did the blond hair Mindy prayed would stay snugly in place even if she did choose to get a little acrobatic. But when he peered into her eyes…well, those belonged to Mindy alone, and it somehow made the moment seem a little more real, as if it belonged to her.

When he lifted one hand to her hair, she flinched.

"What's wrong? Did I pull—"

"No, just…a little nervous." Which was not a complete lie. She had *plenty* of things to be nervous about at the moment, even if sex with Benton wasn't among them. About that she was nothing but eager.

His expression filled with adoration. "No need for that. Just let me make you feel good."

And then he was inside her, and her world transformed into something far sweeter, hotter, more fulfilling than it had ever been before. It was like finding a piece of herself that had always been missing, the connection profound.

She was in way too deep here, she knew that. But right now, there was only Benton, his body, his mouth, his sexy whispers. There was only Benton, making love to her, Mindy, not Mandy.

HOURS LATER, Mindy awakened. She turned on her pillow to study the gentle expression on the face of the man sleeping next to her.

She shot upright in bed. *What have I done?*

Okay, she'd had marvelous, stupendous sex with Benton. Three times, in fact. But what had she been thinking? She must have been out of her mind! And then it hit her—she *had* been out of her mind, she'd been in someone else's mind, someone imaginary, no less. Talk about your evil twin. All that stuff about Benton looking into Mindy's eyes, not Mandy's, making love to Mindy, not Mandy, was hooey. Every bit of it was romantic hogwash she'd invented to try to make what she was doing seem a little less heinous.

She glanced at him, biting her lip. Oh no. She'd slept with this sweet, wonderful, passionate man, and she'd let him think she was someone she wasn't, someone he could love. She *was* evil. Scum of the earth. Scum of the entire solar system. There was no point in denying it; she knew it better than she knew her own name, whatever *that* was. It had been challenging to remember the last few hours.

Well, there was only one thing to do. Sneak out.

Hardly honorable, but that ship had sailed long ago.

Mindy eased from the bed, gathered her hastily removed clothing and purse, then slipped into the bathroom and gently closed the door. She'd programmed the number of a local cab company into her cell phone, thinking maybe she'd need a ride home after she repulsed Benton with her anti-Mandy act, but never in her wildest nightmares had she imagined placing the call from Benton's bathroom while she was naked. She was only glad she'd had the foresight to key in the number or she'd have been stuck stealing Benton's Mercedes. She would have done it, too, if she'd had to—desperation made people do crazy things.

After making the call, she hurried into her clothes, then dug a pen and notepad from her purse. *Thank you for a beautiful evening,* she wrote before skulking into the bedroom and swiftly placing the slip of paper on his bedside table. Then she crept toward the door.

Upon pausing to look at Benton's sleeping form, she wished she could return to his side, gently kiss his cheek, tell him goodbye in some better way than her silly note. But she couldn't wake him, couldn't risk it, so she forced back her emotions and quietly shut the door behind her.

SUN BLASTED through the split in the draperies and onto Benton's face. Letting out a frustrated growl, he rolled over, reaching to curl one arm around the sexy woman at his side.

Just one problem. His arm landed on a limp pile of disheveled sheets. He opened his eyes to discover that, sure enough, he was alone in the bed, just as he was any other morning.

He hadn't dreamed last night, had he? No. No way. His subconscious wasn't capable of such feats.

"Mandy? Where are you?"

Probably in the bathroom. Women *loved* bathrooms, Benton had observed. Only she never answered, so he yelled again, louder this time, deciding maybe she'd ventured down to the kitchen, seeking breakfast. Sharing morning coffee with her sounded appealing, but he didn't smell any brewing. And still no answer came, leaving him surrounded by the echoing silence of his large, empty home.

Rising up on one elbow, Benton was about to go looking for her when he spied a note on the table beside him and reached for it. It took a long moment to believe—to accept—that she was gone, but slowly, surely, a sinking feeling grew in his stomach. He was alone. As always.

What he didn't understand was why.

Glancing at the pillow where he'd expected to find her, Benton recalled their fabulous night together. It had felt like a dream. But it *hadn't* been, he remained sure, despite the vacant spot in bed.

Much about Mandy had turned out to be different

than what he'd been seeking in a woman, yet she'd been undeniably perfect. As he'd run his hands over her body, listened to her soft sighs, he'd been reminded of the docile yet refined female who'd shared dinner with him. And when she'd pushed him to his back and straddled him in the bed, he couldn't help recalling Mandy's unexpected wilder side. To his vast shock, he'd found he liked each side equally well. Maybe even *loved* each side equally well.

Too quick, a voice echoed inside him. Far too quick to even be *thinking* about that word.

But no, it wasn't. Any fear of the word he harbored could be chalked up to immature emotions left over from his youth. The truth was that he wanted to be in love. And Mindy had indeed found the ideal woman for him just when he'd begun to think she might not exist.

Only now she was gone. She'd left him. It was the last thing he'd expected when he'd fallen asleep in her arms.

Trying to push the disappointment from his mind, Benton glanced to his bedside clock to see it was after nine; he'd never set the alarm last night. His office was likely in chaos by now, fearing he'd been hit by a bus or some such catastrophe. Shoving one hand through his hair, he reached for the phone and dialed.

"Maxwell Group."

"It's me, Claudia."

The older woman sighed with relief. "Glad to hear you're all right. You *are* all right, aren't you?"

"Yes, I'm fine."

"You're making a nasty habit of this."

Her tone was the slightly playful scold of a grandmother, but Benton had no intention of discussing his tardiness in any detail with his receptionist, no matter how sweet she was. "Evidently so. Can I have Miss Binks?" He cringed as soon as the words left him. "I mean, put me through to her, will you?"

As Claudia made the connection, he imagined her likely amusement over his faux pas. No one had ever said so, but he suspected some of the staff might have noticed Miss Binks's attraction to him; it would be hard not to.

"Benton Maxwell's office."

"Miss Binks."

"Mr. Maxwell! What a relief to hear your voice! I was worried!"

The emotion pouring through the phone added to his various frustrations. After last night with Mandy, after seeing how good things could be with a woman, he couldn't believe he'd ever even *thought* about trying to form a relationship with his assistant. He kept his voice stern and businesslike. "No need for concern. All's well. I'm just running late."

"When will you be in?"

Benton thought ahead to his plans for the morning. "I'll be another hour or two, at least."

"Oh." She sounded let down. "I wanted to go over the portfolio status report with you."

"Tell you what," he said, taking a new tack. "Why don't you work on it with Malcolm?" Benton was hardly in the mood for matchmaking, but the suggestion would at least help to keep him and Miss Binks apart.

Her hesitation was slight but evident. "Malcolm?"

"He's as in tune with those reports as I am, and you keep telling me I need to delegate, so I'm officially delegating this. From now on, you and Malcolm deal with the portfolio reports and send me a memo outlining your discussion. All right?''

"But I..."

Benton didn't say anything as her voice trailed off, knowing Miss Binks was nothing if not professional—most of the time, anyway—and she'd likely get herself on track if he didn't interfere.

He was right. "Of course, Mr. Maxwell," she finally said, even if she didn't succeed in covering the severe note of defeat in her voice.

"Very good."

After Benton hung up, he glanced again toward the empty spot in the bed beside him. He'd been feeling uncharacteristically hurt and betrayed a few minutes ago, probably because his ego had recently been bruised by the outcome of his first two Mates By Mindy dates before waking to find his third date had vanished sometime before dawn. But his conversation with Miss Binks had restored his confidence.

He knew good and well Mandy had experienced the same magic last evening he had, and he wasn't about to let her get away without an explanation. He didn't know why she'd gone dashing out of his bed in the middle of the night, but he intended to find out.

"YOU *WHAT?*" Jane's eyes grew as big as the doughnut she'd been preparing to bite into.

Mindy hadn't exactly planned on telling Jane what she'd done, but trying to hide it seemed fruitless. So she'd spilled as soon as her friend had settled behind her desk, bakery bag in tow.

"You heard me. I slept with him."

Jane cast a dry look. "Well, that'll really teach him to go around stereotyping women."

Mindy cringed. "I didn't *mean* to sleep with him. It just...happened."

"How? When were you someplace private enough for that? In the car? Did he start kissing you in his car and you couldn't stop?"

Mindy pursed her lips, knowing her explanation was weak, considering the many opportunities she'd had to say no. "Actually, it was more like we were dancing and he invited me back to his place for sex and I said okay."

As if needing it for sustenance, Jane bit into her doughnut, then spoke with her mouth full. "And you couldn't get hold of yourself at some point and realize you were letting him have sex with someone who doesn't exist?"

"Apparently not." Mindy slumped in her chair.

Jane sat a little straighter, mouth empty. "All right. Two questions. How was it, and what are you going to do about it now?"

"The earth moved, and I don't know."

"I knew this was a bad idea." Jane scowled. "And sneaking out hardly solved anything. He knows where you live. He knows your phone number." She used her doughnut to gesticulate.

Mindy smirked at her, wishing she had a doughnut to wave so dramatically. "Yes, I realize that, but at the time, sneaking out seemed like a perfectly valid thing to do."

"And he's not going to let this drop if he's as crazy about you as you say."

"*Mandy,*" Mindy said. "He's crazy about *Mandy.* Not me."

Jane gave her head a caustic tilt. "Is there a difference?"

Mindy spread her arms wide. "There's a *huge* difference. Mandy is some bizarre cross between June Cleaver and Madonna during her Erotica phase. And I'm just me. Normal Mindy."

"Well—" Jane glanced toward the front of the shop "—don't look now, normal Mindy, but Mr. Tall, Dark and Steamy has come to see you."

Mindy's eyes darted toward the plate glass window and, sure enough, between the pink-and-red hearts painted there, she spied Benton crossing the street, heading straight toward her door.

"Me," she said softly, more to herself than Jane. "He's coming to see me, not Mandy." She'd never dreamed she'd have such a hard time keeping track of her identities. Her heart rose to her throat as he reached for the door handle.

She focused desperately on her computer, wishing she could erase the grim expression she knew she wore, but when the bell above the door jingled, she looked up. "Benton," she breathed at the sight of him. "Maxwell. The third," she added awkwardly. Mindy had never called Benton by his first name before, and now seemed like a highly suspicious time to start. She coughed into her hand to cover her blunder. "What can I do for you?"

"It's about your sister."

He sounded so solemn that a ray of hope swept through her. Maybe he was angry over Mandy leaving. Maybe the light of day had reminded him he didn't want a wild woman who wore underwear as outerwear. Maybe he was here to complain or demand his money back or something she'd come to expect of Benton before their date last night. Encouraged by the thought, Mindy put on her game face. It was much easier to argue with the man than feel mushy about him. "Let me guess. You don't like *her,* either."

He gave his head a slight shake. "No, that's not it. I'm crazy about her."

Mindy's heart swelled—with joy or disappointment, she couldn't discern which—but she tried to act cool. "Oh."

He took on a painfully earnest look. "In fact, she's the best thing that's ever happened to me."

Whoa. Mindy's imaginary twin was the best thing that had ever happened to him? She barely knew whether to kiss him or throw up. She felt dizzy as visions of their night together raced through her mind. "Really? I mean, that fast?"

He nodded. "Sounds quick, I know. But the truth is, I owe you an apology. I had you pegged all wrong. You *do* know what you're doing. After all, you brought Mandy into my life."

Nearly breathless, Mindy spoke quickly, suddenly anxious to get him out of her office so she could cry or bang her head against a wall or something. "So all's well that ends well. That's great. Congratulations and good luck."

"But there's a problem."

She blinked. Twice. Thrice. Oh no, it was becoming a tic. "A problem?"

He glanced at Jane, who had lowered her doughnut to her desk and pretended to dig madly through a nearby file cabinet, despite having glaze-covered fingers. Then he drew a little closer to Mindy and lowered his voice. "Mandy sneaked out of my house in the middle of the night."

Mindy met his gaze. Blinked again.

He leaned slightly forward, appearing confused. "Are you okay?"

"Just—" she pointed to her eye "—a speck of dust or something. I'll be fine."

"Well, about your sister. She and I went back to my place and—"

"Yes, actually, she called me this morning," Mindy blurted. There was no way she was going to let Benton relay all the sordid details about what he'd done with Mandy, with her...whatever.

He perked up. "Really? What did she say?"

She said she changed her mind about you. She felt it was a mistake. She doesn't want to see you again. Mindy thought all those statements fell firmly into the category of "obvious things to say right now," and she truly tried, but for some reason, she couldn't spit them out. Benton's eyes shone so sweet and hopeful. And her heart beat so hard. She couldn't do it this way, couldn't crush him. It had to be *his* decision—he had to see for himself that Mandy wasn't the girl for him. He had to want Mandy out of his life.

"She said she got scared," Mindy finally replied. "She was embarrassed."

"Embarrassed?"

A thin veil of heat climbed Mindy's cheeks as she peeked at him from beneath bashfully lowered eyelashes. "She doesn't usually—*you know*—that quick."

Benton's handsome face colored slightly, as well. "She shouldn't be embarrassed. Everything was...extremely mutual, if you know what I mean."

Oh boy, do I.

Before she could summon a reply—after all, what could she say—he tilted his head and gave her a sincere smile. "Thanks, Mindy." Then he turned to go, rather abruptly, she thought.

"Thanks? For what?"

He stopped, looking back. "For filling me in on Mandy's feelings. It explains everything."

"So…what are you going to do?"

"I'm going to call her tonight and work this out. We'll be back on track in no time."

Mindy blinked again. Twice. "Then you plan on seeing her again."

His grin widened. "Oh yes. I want to see a *lot* more of Mandy."

Well, there's not a lot more for you to see now, is there? Mindy thought, but instead she blinked a few more times and attempted a smile. "Great. Swell."

Benton reached for the door, then turned one last time. "I hope your eye feels better."

"Okay. Thanks. See ya."

Mindy sat very still as the door shut behind the man she'd made love to less than twelve hours ago. The only good news was that she'd quit blinking.

As Jane rotated her chair away from the file cabinet, Mindy felt her glare. Jane spoke very calmly. "Have you lost your mind?"

"Yes?" Mindy answered uncertainly. She released a huge sigh and let her head droop over her desk. "Jane, I just couldn't hurt him that way. Did you see the look in those gorgeous eyes?"

"Oh yeah, I saw it. He's got it bad for Mandy, all right. You are in so much trouble."

"I know," Mindy lamented.

Pausing to pick up her doughnut, Jane wheeled her chair a little closer to Mindy's desk. "Of course, you could always tell him the truth."

Mindy bolted upright. "The truth!" It was unthinkable. "Have *you* lost *your* mind?"

"Maybe he'd understand. Then you could live happily ever after and all that."

She shook her head vehemently. "No way. First of all, as I explained to you before, he wants Mandy, the doormat with a dark side, not me. Second, I've committed the worst of all matchmaker crimes imaginable. In fact, scratch that, because what I've done is *un*imaginable. If I tell him the truth, I—I could be disbarred!"

Jane flashed her driest look. "Matchmakers don't take the bar exam."

"Well, if the world knew how evil we could be, how we can ruin people's lives—" Mindy gave her chin a defiant tilt "—they'd realize there should be some standards, tests to take, qualifications to prove." Then her fervor wilted. "Oh Jane, I never meant to be such a sham."

"Then tell the truth."

Mindy narrowed her brow. Since when was Jane so forthright and honest? She was as irritating as that little Mindy angel on her shoulder last night. And since when was *Mindy* not forthright and honest?

Still, as horrible as she felt, she was sure she could get out of this unscathed. Well, sort of. There'd always be the memories of his bed. And the knowledge that she could have been the woman of his dreams—if she weren't such a crazy, masquerading liar. But all that was secondary to her need for self-preservation, which meant she needed to solve this dilemma without admitting to Benton that she'd done something horribly wrong. And she really didn't want to hurt him. She wanted *him* to decide to toss Mandy back.

So Mindy held up her hands as if to say stop. "Wait, listen. I've got a plan."

Jane rolled her eyes. "This should be good."

"I've just got to be the anti-anti-Mandy."

Jane thought Mindy's words through slowly as she nibbled her breakfast. "Anti-anti? Theoretically, wouldn't that be…the regular you? You know, the way a double negative goes back to being a positive?"

Mindy shook her head, annoyed. "What I mean is, I have to be even *worse* than the wild dancing woman he met last night, worse than the seductress who told him she wanted to go to bed with him."

Jane's eyebrows shot up. "You said that? You actually asked him to—"

"Don't change the subject, I'm on a roll. I have to do things that are even *more* embarrassing, maybe even *dangerous* somehow. I have to leave him totally mortified. That way he'll want nothing more to do with me—I mean Mandy—and life will get back to normal."

"So, any idea what these embarrassing, dangerous things are?"

Mindy's mind whirled with possibilities. "Well, I don't have them all pinned down just yet, but trust me, they'll be perfect."

5
_____

BENTON GLANCED from the financial report in his hands to the small engraved gold clock, a too-expensive gift from Miss Binks last Christmas, that sat on the corner of his desk. Ten after six, well past time for the gift-giver herself to have headed home. Benton knew she was still here, however, because she always said good-night, without fail, and always checked to make sure he didn't need her for anything before leaving.

She had become more aggressive since he'd shown up late after his initial visit to Mates By Mindy, the day she'd first touched his sleeve. She'd made the same move several times since, and the adoring look in her eyes had grown more intent. So the fact that she remained in the office with him long after everyone else had left made him feel a little like…prey.

Or maybe, he reasoned, he was imagining it. Maybe he was noticing her attentions more than usual because lately he'd become more attuned to the feelings of *all* the women in his life. After all, it would have been impossible not to see how Anita and Kathy, his first two Mates By Mindy dates, had regarded him. With total detestation. Conversely, Mandy had been as wildly enamored of him as he'd been of her, and his conversation with Mindy this morning had shored that up. The matchmaker herself, on the other hand, fell somewhere in between. Sometimes he thought she hated him, other times he thought she liked him. Then there were times, like today, when she acted nervous around him, which seemed completely contrary to his earlier impressions of her. Odd. Not that she was really on his mind. She wasn't. There would be no reason for his thoughts to dwell on the little redhead with the sometimes fiery attitude and serious blinking problem.

No, his thoughts ran firmly toward her delectable sister. And, well, to Miss Binks, too—although that was due to forced proximity, not choice. And to the fact that it was possible nothing with Miss Binks was really changing at all; maybe he'd simply become more aware of her affection.

As soon as Miss Binks vacated the office, he intended to call Mandy. He knew he could close his door if he wanted privacy—maybe that would tell Miss Binks he no longer needed her today—but he wanted his full concentration on the conversation. He had to make Mandy understand she had nothing to fear, reassure her that nothing she'd done last night had disturbed him in any way whatsoever. Which was surprising, but true. It upset him to think she'd rushed out of his house at three or four in the morning, worried over her actions. He needed to clear up the confusion and get them back to that perfect place they'd been last night.

"Mr. Maxwell."

Benton glanced up to find Miss Binks posed in his doorway. He couldn't have called it a seductive pose exactly, but she leaned against the door frame, one hand resting on her hip, so she appeared more relaxed than usual. He had the distinct worry that she'd been standing there longer than he realized, watching him.

And he also had the feeling he'd been right in the first place; things were definitely escalating.

"Miss Binks. You're working awfully late tonight."

She lowered her gaze, hesitating. "There's something I've been wanting to discuss with you."

It wasn't so much the words that alarmed Benton, but the look in her eyes when she raised them again. Still not quite seductive, but perhaps her best shot at it. It set off warning sirens inside him. He couldn't let her do it, couldn't let her ruin their working relationship by expressing her true feelings for him. So he shifted his gaze to his computer screen. "Unfortunately, I'm very busy right now and expecting an important call from the west coast any minute. Catch me another time."

A bit cold, perhaps, but warranted. And Miss Binks, more than anyone, was accustomed to his shifting moods when he was immersed in business.

Normally such a response would have her saying something like, "Certainly," then she'd walk away, but now, without looking, Benton knew she remained at the door, mooning at him. "If you're planning to work late, would you like me to pick up some dinner for you?"

This was really getting out of hand. "Thank you, Miss Binks, but no." He *was* planning to work late, but the deli across the street delivered. "Why don't you head home? And have a nice evening." He avoided looking at her and began keying gibberish into his computer to make himself appear busier.

"All right, Mr. Maxwell," she said on a sad sigh he felt all the way to his bones. After another slight hesitation, she finally departed, disappearing down the hall.

When he heard the ding of the elevator, he couldn't help thinking, *Alone at last!* He wanted to feel badly for Miss Binks, but he was too anxious to patch things up with Mandy to spend any more concern on his assistant. Benton snatched the phone and dialed.

"Hello?" The familiar, airy voice gave him goose bumps.

"Mandy." He spoke deeply, letting determination rule his tone. "This is Benton."

"Oh, Benton. I'm…so sorry about last night."

"I'm sorry you left. But I'm not sorry about anything else that happened, and I hope you aren't, either."

He detected her uneasy swallow on the other end of the line. "It's just that I was so…embarrassed by my behavior. And not only about the sex, but also about the way I acted at the club. I'm not usually like that."

"No?"

"It must have been the wine. And the screwdriver afterward. I've always heard you're not supposed to mix alcohols, and now I know why. It must have made me a little loopy, as if I were…someone else." She coughed, then sounded as if she were choking a little.

"Are you all right?"

"Yes, yes, I'm fine."

"Listen, nothing you did last night changed the way I feel about you."

Her voice was a little more high-pitched than usual. "Which is?"

"I told you then," he said warmly, a soft smile claiming him. "Repeatedly. Don't you remember?"

"Well, I *was* filled with wine and screwdrivers."

Benton found her frankness incredibly sweet. "I'm

crazy about you, Mandy. Mad about you. And I can't wait to see you again.''

"I see."

"You sound nervous."

"No. It's just that I'm...I'm..." Her voice trailed off into exasperation, and just when Benton had nearly given up on her finishing, she sighed and said, "Benton, the truth is, I'm completely head over heels about you, too!"

MINDY LAMENTED her most recent phone call with Benton as she stood before the mirror in her bedroom adjusting her wig. She'd never meant to tell the man she was head over heels for him. Just as she'd never meant to fall into bed with him the other night, either. Obviously, she had a serious lack of control where he was concerned.

"But no more," she vowed, half to her reflection and half to Venus. The cat lay curled on the bed, still looking less frightened of the blond Mindy than Mindy herself felt these days. "Tonight I'll make Benton rue the day he ever trusted me with his love life. And I'll definitely stick to the plan."

Stick to the plan, stick to the plan. She repeated the mantra in her head, as Jane had counseled her earlier.

"Do you know what happened the last three times I didn't stick to *my* plan?" Jane had scolded during her lecture.

Already feeling contrite, Mindy had shaken her head.

"I ended up with three kids, that's what. I love them, of course, but th y changed my and Larry's life considerably, before we were ready. Do you want to end up like that?"

"Benton used a condom," Mindy told her quickly.

Jane rolled her eyes. "I meant figuratively, not literally."

"All three times," Mindy added before she could stop herself. Then she cringed. Drat, another bit of information haphazardly spilled.

Jane looked at her in shock. "Three times? Does he also wear a cape and leap tall buildings in a single bound?"

Mindy shrugged. "I couldn't say. We haven't spent that much time together. But don't worry, there won't be three times tonight. There won't even be *one* time."

And there absolutely wouldn't, she promised herself, even if she was wearing the slinkiest thing she owned.

"But there's a reason for that!" she announced, turning to point a finger at Venus as if the cat had started spouting accusations. Sheesh, she was really losing it.

The dress was a stretchy, sparkly, skintight, flesh-colored number she'd picked up at a vintage clothing store the year she'd gone to Jane's Halloween bash as Marilyn Monroe. It seemed becoming Mandy required frequent dips into her Halloween boxes, since Mindy didn't have anything flamboyant enough among her regular clothes to suit her alter ego.

She'd worn the Marilyn costume the same year Jane's husband, Larry, had donned his Bill Clinton mask, and Jane had insisted Mindy sing "Happy Birthday, Mr. President" on the karaoke machine she'd rented. Of course, that had taken a lot of drinks beforehand, and it reminded Mindy of her plan for tonight. Step one—have some drinks. Step two—do horribly embarrassing things she would surely regret under any other circumstances.

And she would start by wearing this totally inappropriate dress to dinner. It was shorter and much less see-through than Marilyn's real birthday suit, and of course, Mindy lacked Marilyn's boobs, but she still filled the dress out nicely with her own. She had gone without a bra to ensure an over-the-top look and knew she resembled someone who was more likely heading off to a wild New Year's Eve party than someone on her way to a staid, sophisticated restaurant on the arm of a flawlessly groomed man. For good measure, she added glittery eyeshadow in a bronze shade she'd picked up from the drugstore on the way home, and rubbed a little glitter body gel in her décolletage, as well.

She'd told Benton on the phone that her earlier behavior was out of the ordinary—another flub—but she hoped it would return him to his comfort zone, make the things she did tonight seem doubly shocking. She'd caved under the pressure of hearing his deep, reassuring voice and she'd started letting the real her seep into Mandy with hardly a thought. Which was bad, very bad. She had to learn to keep the two personalities apart, once and for all.

When the doorbell rang, Mindy nearly leaped out of her skin *and* her formfitting dress. Venus jumped, too, and dove from the bed, then raced from the room. Drat. Just what she needed, a runaway cat while her cat-hating date waited outside.

And then it hit her. She had a cat. And a cat-hating man she was attempting to drive away. She couldn't believe it had taken her so long to put two and two together.

Chasing Venus down in her heels was no easy task, especially as Benton's impatient second ring vibrated through the house, but when she flung the door open a minute later, she held the tabby in one arm.

Benton's eyes dropped from hers to Venus, then came back. "You have a cat." He obviously struggled to keep his expression blank.

She tilted her head and shrugged. "Guess the cat's…out of the bag, so to speak." She giggled lightly. "Mindy told me how you felt about kitties, so I kept Venus hidden the first time you were here."

"Venus?"

"Goddess of love," she explained, stepping back to let Benton inside. "I thought it was the perfect name for a cat who belongs to a—uh—" she blinked nervously "—a person whose sister is a matchmaker." Dear God, she'd nearly let everything out there.

Benton blinked, too, and she wondered if it was contagious.

She rushed ahead. "Mindy bought her for me, you see, so that makes sense. Doesn't it?" In a twisted, backward, goofy sort of way.

To her surprise, Benton grinned. "Well, I guess there isn't a goddess of receptionists, so…sure, makes perfect sense."

She automatically smiled in reply. What was going on here? He no longer hated cats? And what about her tacky dress? Why wasn't he noticing how improper she looked?

"So, do you think you can stand dating someone who owns a cat? Because if you can't, I understand. A person has to have boundaries." Not that she did, clearly. But if Mindy had ever met anyone with boundaries, it was definitely Benton.

Nonetheless, he shrugged. "Sure, why not?" Then he reached up to scratch Venus behind one ear. "Seems like a harmless enough little guy."

"Girl," she corrected. "Goddess, you know."

"Right." He still grinned, darn it.

So the cat thing was that easy? It made no sense. But since Venus had proven to be a completely useless deterrent, Mindy lowered her to the floor, the better to show off her dress and get back to the plan.

He noticed right away. "You look fabulous."

Mindy blinked some more. "I do?"

He gave her an appreciative once-over, then a suggestive nod that aroused her a little.

"You see, I was feeling impulsive tonight, just wanted to wear something kind of wild, I guess. But I feared it might be too, um, showy for wherever we're going." He hadn't mentioned where he was taking her for dinner, but she instinctively knew the dress would be too much for any establishment Benton would patronize.

When he merely shrugged again, she wondered if that was getting contagious, too. "I think you look gorgeous. Any man would."

Flash! A humongous imaginary lightbulb finally lit up over Mindy's head, and she felt quite thick, especially after her slow uptake on the cat situation. She'd made an enormous error; she'd forgotten she was dealing with a *man!* Any sane woman would know she looked ridiculous. But most men, apparently even tasteful Benton, could only see her breasts and her hips and the take-me-now air she knew practically dripped from her. Which meant she had to go out looking this way for absolutely no good reason at all!

Calm down, she told herself. Stick to the plan. Yes, that was the key.

And what was the first step of the plan? she quizzed herself.

Drink something. And the sooner the better, at this point.

"Let's go," she said, blinking. "I'm anxious to get the evening underway."

"To ROMANCE," Benton said, lifting his glass.

Mindy gaped at him as she raised hers, too. He was beautiful, and his blue eyes sparkled in the low lighting, and she wanted him. "To romance." *Which I can't have.* At least not with him. She had to stop gaping at his perfectly chiseled cheekbones and his devastating smile. No more drinking in the sheer masculinity that hung about him.

Of course, all of that would be easier if anything at all were going her way. First the cat had failed her, then the dress. In fact, the dress continued to fail her— every man in the place had noticed her, and it had obviously made Benton as proud as a peacock. Mindy swallowed half a glass of wine in one long, indelicate sip. It was time to really get things rolling here, and acting unladylike could only add to the lack of appeal Benton would surely start seeing in her any minute now.

"How's the wine?" He smiled at her across the table.

"Dee-lish." She took another long drink to prove it. "Whew," she added as warmth spread through her glitter-covered chest. "Good stuff."

Just then, the maître d', who had greeted them at the door, appeared at their table. He peered uncertainly at Mindy as he drew a black cardigan sweater from behind his back. "Pardon me, madam. Maybe you would like to borrow a sweater while you dine. Perhaps you feel chilled."

Disdain rested in the little man's beady eyes. Chilled, schmilled. More likely, at first glance across the room he'd thought she appeared naked. Finally, a man who realized she was terribly out of place here! She'd never known they kept sweaters on hand for women at nice restaurants in the same way they kept jackets for men. This presented an opportunity that couldn't be passed up.

"Maybe *you'd* like a pop in the nose," she replied.

The maître d' took a quick step backward, and Benton flinched, cringing inwardly. Had Mandy really threatened to hit the man? Obviously, she'd had too much wine. But that didn't mean he could let the maître d' embarrass her. Benton worked to keep his surprise from flashing across his face before raising his eyes to the small man and speaking in a quiet yet firm voice. "The lady looks lovely this evening. She doesn't need a sweater."

He appeared appropriately cowed by Benton's tone. "Of course not, sir. My apologies."

Benton nodded shortly as the maître d' turned and walked away, defeated. He almost felt cruel; after all, he understood the guy was only trying to do his job, and he respected establishments with certain standards. There was a reason he didn't frequent fast food joints and bars—he liked refined surroundings, and he supposed that applied to apparel, too.

Yet a primal urge to protect Mandy had risen inside him unbidden. Even if she was a little out there at moments, he couldn't resist thinking she was fun and exciting, not to mention incredible to look at in that clingy dress.

He swung his gaze to her, and the mere sight stirred him, removing any momentary awkwardness. Covering that dress would be criminal.

He leaned slightly toward her over the table. "I hope that didn't embarrass you."

What just happened here? Mindy thought. She'd threatened to punch a man in the nose, and Benton wasn't angry? Instead he was gallant? Dear God, it wasn't bad enough that she couldn't do anything to turn him off, now she wanted to kiss him senseless for being so incredibly sweet and indulgent. She'd never dreamed Benton Maxwell III would be so difficult to get rid of!

"No," she said, caught precariously between Mindy and Mandy. "But thank you for defending me."

He raised his eyebrows slightly. "Looked like you were pretty capable of that on your own."

And this amused him? She still couldn't believe he didn't mind having a scantily clad date who picked fights with maître d's in fine restaurants. "I need more wine."

Three glasses later—or maybe it was four, but who was counting—Mindy continued vacillating dangerously between her two personas. When Benton started telling her more about his family and how much he missed them, she couldn't help letting her true self shine through as they talked.

"It sounds like you're close to your brother and sister," she said. She hadn't gotten that idea upon first meeting him, but he'd turned out to be so different than she'd expected.

He shrugged, a slight smile turning up the corners

of his mouth. "Not as close as when we were young obviously, but I miss seeing them and wish they lived nearer. I miss not knowing their kids as well as I'd like."

Of course, that made Mindy want to share more than minor details about her family, too. She explained that they'd moved around a lot when she was growing up, with her dad in the service, and that somewhere along the path, a wedge had slowly been driven between her parents. She admitted she still missed her mom and dad being together; the family had settled in Cincinnati after his retirement only to have him head west a few years later.

Together, they commiserated how, even as adults, it wasn't easy to have parents who lived far away, and Benton told her he really wanted some kids of his own, wanted to get a family back in his life again.

She knew he meant he wanted those things with *her*—he wasn't the least bit subtle. So it would have been a fine time for Mandy to tell Benton she'd fibbed on their first date about wanting to be a mother, a fine moment to say she didn't want to be tied down with that kind of responsibility, but she couldn't bring herself to do it. Truthfully, nothing in the world sounded better to Mindy than sharing Benton's big bed while they lived in his big house with two or three wonderful kids.

"Of course, maybe you're not in as big a hurry for that as I am, since you still have family nearby," he finally said.

She was grateful for the turn in subject. "Yeah, my mom lives just across town."

"And there's Mindy," he reminded her.

"Oh yeah." How could she forget her be-loved twin?

"Are you two close?"

Mindy reached for her wineglass and took another large swallow. "Extremely."

"You seem so different."

"Not always so different. But then again..." She grimaced, uncertain, recalling she'd once claimed she and Mindy had nothing in common. Darn it. When she'd devised this drinking plan, she hadn't considered having to think clearly.

Luckily, though, Benton only laughed, then bailed her out. "Don't worry, I know how it is with siblings. You sometimes have a love-hate relationship."

"That's it exactly! Sometimes Mindy and I are so much alike that it's almost as if we're the same person. But other times, well, she probably feels like she doesn't know me at all."

Benton nodded, appearing profoundly interested. Mindy realized she was babbling and should shut up before she edged any further into the truth. "Are we done?" she asked, looking at their empty plates and drained glasses. "Because if we are, I'm ready to go." Anything to advance the evening by a few more moments without disaster.

"So am I." He put his linen napkin aside, got to his feet, then came to help with her chair.

Mindy was horrified when she realized her legs were wobbly. She had the overwhelming urge to cling to him, because she felt sad about what could never be between them and for physical support. Could be she'd taken this wine-drinking thing too far.

She wanted to tell the truth as Jane had advised, but she still couldn't. It was too humiliating, and she didn't want to hurt a man who really cared about her. Well, the imaginary her, anyway.

He held her hand as they left the dining room and entered the darkly paneled foyer, teeming with patrons coming and going. Mindy concentrated on each step, careful to stay balanced on her heels. It was when Benton rubbed his thumb sensually over the back of her hand and turned to say, "I was thinking maybe we could go back to my place," that Mindy tripped and went sprawling across an oriental rug with a loud *thump*.

She heard several gasps and one "My heavens" from what sounded like a rich old woman, but even as embarrassment and pain racked her body, she was immediately glad this had happened. She'd come out tonight to shock Benton, hadn't she? Surely this sort of drunken display would accomplish that goal.

"Mandy! Are you okay?"

She raised her gaze from the baseboard to find Benton kneeling beside her, his eyes frantic with concern as she lay spread-eagle across the floor. Oh for the love of God, the insufferable man was understanding!

If things weren't bad enough, some frantic restaurant employee entered the fray. "Are you all right, miss? Are you badly hurt? Should I call an ambulance, sir?"

"Dear God, no," she interjected, lifting her head from the plush rug. "I'm drunk, not injured."

"You took a pretty hard fall." Benton gently stroked her shoulder. "Are you sure you're okay?"

"Peachy," she said, although she felt quite sore all over and knew standing would be a challenge. She pushed herself to her hands and knees, figuring she probably looked pornographic from the back, but who cared at this point? Benton was clearly far too concerned for her health to realize how ridiculous she felt. She peered at him from her all-fours position and spoke lowly. "You'll never be able to show your face in here again."

He helped her rise to her knees, then steadied her as she made the final move to her heels. When they stood face-to-face, he winked. "Sure I will. I have a lot of money."

Mindy had probably never been so glad to reach a sidewalk in her life as she was when they finally stepped outside and said adios to Mr. Beady Eyes and his entire staff. The fresh evening air revived her and helped wash away at least a little of her mortification. *Mortification you wanted,* she reminded herself. She'd hoped her suffering would produce some positive—or was that technically negative—results, which she certainly hadn't gotten so far.

She clutched Benton's arm as they stood in line for the valet.

"So what do you say?" he asked.

She looked into terribly sexy eyes, having no idea what he was talking about. "Say?"

"Back to my place?"

Oh yeah, that, the invitation that had sent her sprawling. She bit her lip and sighed. Going to his place sounded *so* good right now, for more reasons than she could easily identify. She could rest her weary body a while and then—

"I could give you a nice back rub," he whispered enticingly, seeming to read her mind. "Maybe we could even take a relaxing bubble bath together, then I could carry you to the bed and—"

"No!" she yelled.

The couple in front of them turned to stare.

"Sorry," she said.

The two looked away, and Mindy shifted her gaze to Benton, who appeared surprised and a little hurt. "No?"

His expression broke her heart. "Well, I didn't mean no, exactly, I meant not yet. I meant I could really go for a walk around the city, like we started to take last time."

His features brightened, warming Mindy from head to toe. "Maybe it would be good for you to walk some, help keep your muscles from getting stiff after that fall."

"Yeah, I was thinking the same thing," she lied as they departed from the valet stand and ventured into a crosswalk, the sign blinking white for them.

"Maybe we could stroll down to Fountain Square, take that carriage ride we talked about."

As before, the suggestion filled Mindy with such affection and anticipation she could barely measure it. But a cluster of pink neon grabbed her attention, and she remembered what she had to do. "Or we could go in here," she said, bringing them to a rough halt before downtown Cincinnati's only bona fide sex shop. A well-endowed mannequin in the brightly lit window wore nothing but scraps of black leather, including a mask, and wielded a rather scary-looking whip.

Ha, this would get him! She was sure of it! No woman Benton Maxwell could ever want to marry would be caught dead in such an establishment, nor would a man like Benton. He was a prominent local business figure, he had a reputation to maintain, and being spotted in a sex shop would be the equivalent of professional suicide.

As Mindy drew her gaze cautiously from the storefront of XXXtra Naughty to her date, he eyed her skeptically. "You want to go in *here?*"

It was working! Her plan was finally working! Now to seal it. "Yes, Benton, I do. I really, really do."

Benton glanced up and down the street, then briefly toward the faceless leather chick before finally returning his gaze to Mindy. A small, adventurous grin quirked up one corner of his mouth. "What the hell. Come on."

Grabbing Mindy's hand, he pulled her in the door of the brilliantly illumined den of iniquity before she knew what was happening.

"Oh my!" Countless cylindrical objects dangled overhead in a dazzling array of colors and sizes. Mindy had the urge to duck and cover, lest they start falling on her like tiny torpedoes. Although some of them were frighteningly far from tiny.

Anxious to stop gaping at them in front of Benton, she swung her gaze to the right, where she found breasts, dozens of them, adorning videos and magazines. A turn to the left revealed something a little more palatable—lingerie. Only…most of it seemed to be missing key bits of material.

Mindy's face burned, and her whole body tingled with embarrassment. This wasn't going at all as she'd hoped. *He* was supposed to be the embarrassed one, and *she* was supposed to be the wild, worldly, free spirit. But then, she'd never thought Benton would agree to go inside. She'd been avoiding his eyes since they'd crossed the threshold, but when she looked at him, he cast a sympathetic grin, clearly seeing her discomfort.

"I…I…I …" she began ever so eloquently.

"Would look excellent in *that*," Benton said, concluding her sentence in a way she'd never intended as he pointed over her shoulder. She risked following his eyes to a mannequin wearing a very skimpy black vinyl teddy, complete with spiked dog collar and tall boots with pointy heels.

Her jaw dropped slightly as she shifted a questioning gaze to the man at her side. "Really?"

He gave a playful shrug. "When in Rome…"

Mindy felt her face go from crimson to beet as she visualized herself in such a getup.

"Although I'll admit," he added, sliding a comforting arm around her waist, "I'm usually more drawn to black lace."

Well, that was a relief. In fact, it was slightly arousing, because Mindy could relate to black lace; she even owned a little of it. Dog collars were another matter.

"Benton?"

"Yeah, honey?"

"Could we, uh, get out of here?"

He grinned. "Sure. It'll save me from having to cover your eyes when you spot what's in the back corner."

She instinctively swung around to look, but he laughingly blocked her vision with his body. "Trust me. You don't want to know."

If Mindy had thought reaching the sidewalk outside the restaurant had been a respite, it was nothing compared to their departure from the sex shop. She felt like an idiot. She wasn't sure what had happened to the man who'd come into Mates By Mindy seeking a twenty-first century Suzy Homemaker, but this wasn't him. Then again, in all fairness, she wasn't sure what had happened to the sensible, honest, well-meaning matchmaker *she* used to be, either.

Total desperation besieged her. Things were going far too well, and it seemed no matter what radical move she made, they *kept* going well. The really scary part was that she feared she could be prodded into his bed with ease if the tide didn't turn soon.

She had to do something, something big, something unimaginable. Something so completely outrageous it would put every other one of tonight's events to shame. And she had to do it very soon because the way he held her hand, the way he smiled, was making her want him so much she could barely breathe. She found herself wondering how he felt about *flesh-colored* lace, like the panties she wore under her Marilyn dress right this moment.

"So, what's next?" Understandably, amusement tinged his grin.

But Mindy was determined to wipe that smile right off his gorgeous face. And that's when she spotted the very expensive-looking cherry-red sports car sitting unattended at a valet stand across the street. Aha! she thought triumphantly, feeling a little crazed. *This is it! This will finally show him what a nut Mandy truly is!*

"Let's go joyriding!" she said, pointing at the convertible. "In *that* car! Let's just throw caution to the wind and do it!" She punctuated the suggestion with her most manic look.

"You want to take that Lamborghini for a joyride, huh?" Benton asked, sounding a little calmer than she'd hoped.

She maintained her wild, anxious expression. "Yes! Yes, that's exactly what I want to do!"

To Mindy's unqualified disbelief, Benton said,

"Wait here," and coolly crossed the street. He disappeared beneath the awning of the restaurant where the car sat and reemerged a moment later, in the red convertible. He pulled up to the curb beside her, engine purring, then leaned over and winked. "Let's go for a ride."

6

BENTON HAD seldom enjoyed shocking someone so much. He and Mandy raced onto Columbia Parkway in the classic sports car, the wind whipping about them. She screamed at him. "You stole a car? You stole *this* car? Are you crazy? We're going to jail!"

He turned to her with a chuckle. "Isn't that what you wanted?"

"To go to jail? No!" She shook her head vehemently, both hands clamped firmly to the top of her head to protect her hair from getting mussed.

"I was talking about the Lamborghini. I thought you wanted to go joyriding!" He accelerated, relishing her panicked expression. She tried to act so hedonistic, yet glimpses of the prim woman he'd first met continued to surface, and he couldn't resist following her lead to see how far she'd go.

"But I…but I—"

"Look excellent in this car." He winked, then turned his eyes to his driving as they careened along the darkened riverside thoroughfare, a full moon shining above the perfectly spaced streetlights. "Isn't this great?"

"No! No, it isn't great at all!" She shook her head some more and kept holding her hair.

Benton leaned his head back and let out a laugh of pure joy.

"We won't even *make* it to jail because you're going to get us killed first! Why on earth did I get in this car?"

He slanted her a look. "Well, it would have been rude not to. After you asked me to steal it, I mean."

"I didn't ask you to steal it! I said joyride. Which is kind of like borrowing."

"Borrow, steal, does it really make a difference? Either way, it's too late at this point, so you may as well sit back and enjoy the ride. Now—" he swung his full attention to the road and reached for the gearshift "—let's see what this baby can do!"

Benton shifted the Lamborghini into high gear and pressed down the gas pedal to send the car soaring like a rocket through the late spring night. He couldn't remember a time when he'd cut loose like this, forgotten all the pressures and responsibilities of running a business. He couldn't remember a time when he'd had this much fun. Benton would never have considered joyriding a pleasurable activity, but teasing Mandy was too entertaining to resist.

Although the night had turned out differently than he'd foreseen, he grew fonder of the woman with each passing moment. He could barely explain it—he only knew that being around her lightened his heart, made him feel younger than his thirty-five years and plunged him into a carefree happiness he'd forgotten existed.

Of course, at the moment she sat next to him with a look of sheer horror frozen on her pretty face, and since he wanted her to have a good time, too, he supposed it was time to let her off the hook.

"I know the guy!" he yelled above the hum of the car as they took a particularly gratifying curve.

She glared at him. "Guy? What guy? What are you talking about?"

"The guy who owns this car. I know him. We manage some trust accounts together. I caught him heading into the restaurant and asked if I could take it for a spin."

He cast a grin, waiting for her to smile back, but instead her mouth fell open in a silent gasp, and her eyes remained filled with horror—or was that anger?

Without warning, she began pummeling his arm with small, determined fists. The car swerved. "Hey, you're going to make me crash!"

She stopped hitting him—he was relieved to see she was at least *that* sensible—but started yelling. "You big jerk! You let me think you stole this thing! You let me think we were going to get arrested! I was envisioning myself in horizontal stripes, which is not a good look for me, by the way!"

He slowed the car somewhat and shot her a satisfied expression. "I got you, didn't I?"

"What?"

He kept his accusing grin trained on her. "I scared you. You like to act so wild, but you're not really *that* wild, are you, Mandy?"

Mindy had never been so confused in her life. She'd thought she'd understood Benton Maxwell perfectly, but as this night wore on, she was beginning to realize she hadn't a clue about him. She couldn't tell if he wanted a wild woman or a staid, obedient one. *This,* she wanted to tell him, *is exactly why I do thorough interviews with all my clients!* But rather than blow her cover after all she'd done to keep her true identity a secret, she bit her lip and weighed her response carefully. "How wild do you want me to be?"

His eyes twinkled in the moonlight as the breeze mussed his thick hair. "As wild as you want. Or as tame as you want. Either way, I'm crazy about you."

Oh no. This meant no matter what she did, she wasn't getting rid of him. Whether issuing her silly tittering laugh in a chaste pink suit or guzzling wine in skintight sparkles, none of it mattered. How had this happened? "But *why* are you crazy about me?" she asked, exasperated.

Benton drove in silence for a moment, finally veering left into the wooded hills along the riverside. He parked the convertible on a quiet tree-lined street, then turned to gaze deeply into Mindy's eyes, the moon cutting through the foliage just enough to illumine his handsome face.

"Why am I crazy about you?" Warmth filled his expression. "Let's just say you've reminded me what I've been missing, that all work and no play makes Benton a dull boy. You make me feel more alive than I have in years."

She held in her gasp. "Really?"

He gave a firm nod, his voice coming deep. "Really."

Mindy bit her lip and tried to hold back her emotions. She could easily cry because this was more serious than she thought. She was changing him, changing the way he lived, the things he thought about, the ways he acted and reacted. And…well, she was afraid it could get pretty serious for her, too.

Maybe it had gotten that way already. After all, she never went to bed with men she didn't know, yet *something* had made her sleep with Benton on their first date. She'd thought it was the atmosphere, the role she was playing, Mandy's fake seductiveness. But as she gazed into Benton's captivating eyes, she began to recognize that maybe she *liked* the wilder, more adventurous woman she became with him—even if she hadn't lasted long in the sex shop. It was exciting to see how it felt to wear more daring clothing, not to care what anyone thought of her, to experience these little snippets of life she never would have otherwise. And most of all, it was exciting to share every bit of it with Benton.

She pushed back the urge to weep, because she could also just as easily kiss him, and that sounded more fun. "Kiss me," she whispered.

"Gladly." His voice came breathy and hot as he lifted both hands to her face and brought his mouth down on hers. Mindy closed her eyes and got lost in the lush emotions, the night air, the moonlight, the man. One soft warm kiss dissolved into another until they grew deeper, tongues twining, hands roaming. Mindy never planned to climb into his lap, and she certainly never planned to get her dress hung up on the gearshift.

"Ow!"

A swift move from Benton disentangled the fabric, and she looped her arms around his neck, sinking into the heaven of his embrace. When his hand slid over her breast, the sensation washed fiercely through her. She kissed him harder, panting with pleasure as he stroked his thumb over her nipple.

As she shifted to straddle him, which was no easy feat in that dress, his hands slid up her thighs past the tops of her stockings. He gazed heatedly into her eyes, and when his palms reached her hips, he cast a wicked grin. "You're wearing lace."

"It's not black," she warned.

"Who cares?"

When he began kissing her breasts through her dress, Mindy groaned, and when he began to rub between her legs, she moved against his oh-so-welcome caress. But it was when he deftly pulled the lace panties aside and she knew he would touch her, flesh to flesh, and then there would be no stopping, that four hideous words pounded through her brain. Worse, they were spoken in Jane's voice. *Stick. To. The. Plan.*

"Stop!" she screeched.

Benton flinched, releasing her breast from his mouth and her panties from his fingers in one fast move. "Huh?"

Cringing at the loss of pleasure, she peered down at him. "We can't do this!"

He looked bewildered. "We can't?"

She shook her head. "We absolutely can't."

"Why not?"

Good question. She had no sensible answer. "Because…because…this is your friend's car, that's why."

He gave a sigh of concession. "True."

"And he said you could take it for a ride, but he didn't say I could take *you* for a ride in it, so…"

He nodded. "You're right."

Whew, she was glad to see he hadn't lost all his conservative qualities. "So we should take the car back."

"And then we should get in *my* car and do it." He flashed an enormously tempting grin. Who'd ever have guessed Benton could be this utterly hedonistic?

It was a major turn-on, and Mindy started to say "Okay!" with the same enthusiasm, yet she stopped.

The plan, the plan. It was not to have sex with him tonight under any circumstances. "No," she replied.

He blinked. Apparently, the habit truly *was* catching. "What?" She couldn't imagine explaining why she was turning him down, so she quickly evaluated her options.

She could stick with no and tell him the relationship was moving too fast, that sleeping together on the first date was a mistake, that it would be smart to take a step back, get to know each other better, then ask him to take her home, concluding the evening with a chaste good-night kiss.

Or she could forget all that and share one last, final, blinding night of passion with him.

"The thing is, Benton..."

"Yes?"

"We can't have sex in *this* car, or in *your* car, or in any other car tonight."

His warm embrace stiffened before he pulled away. It tore Mindy apart, not only because his sexy midnight-colored eyes brimmed with disappointment, but because she thought she must be crazy to be fighting this kind of desire. After all, she'd fallen hard for Benton. Despite everything, being with him felt so right.

"We should go to your house instead," she continued quickly, "so we can do it all night long without interruption."

BENTON LAY in bed naked, covers pulled to his waist, hungry anticipation humming through his veins. When Mandy spotted him upon exiting the bathroom in her sparkly dress, she gasped.

He leaned against the headboard, hands behind his head. "Figured I'd save you the trouble."

Her face colored slightly. He liked it. "Thanks. All those buttons were pretty pesky last time."

She started toward the bed until he said, "Stop."

She stilled. "Why?"

Reaching to his bedside table, he pushed a button on the small CD player he'd placed there while she was freshening up. The funky notes of the song she'd danced to for him on their first date echoed through the speaker, and her eyes went wide.

"You—"

"Bought it after the other night," he said, still grinning. "Couldn't get the song out of my head, and I can't get the way you moved to it out of my head, either."

She looked embarrassed at the memory, and he liked that, too. He couldn't get a firm grasp on who exactly she was, the prim woman Mindy had paired him with or the much freer girl he kept catching sizable glimpses of, but the one undeniable thing about Mandy was that she wore her heart on her sleeve. Benton never found it difficult to discern her emotions, and after years in a stiff business environment where image was everything, it turned him inside out to be with someone so utterly genuine, whichever side of her was currently on display.

"Turn down the lights a little—" he pointed to the dimmer switch behind her "—and come to bed with me."

The sexy tune played as Mandy twisted the indicated knob, shrouding the room in shadows.

Then, with her back still to him, her hips began to sway gently to the beat.

Benton felt a slow smile unfurl across his face.

Spinning suddenly, she looked him straight in the

eye and broke into song with wild gusto. She took sexy steps toward him, then backed up, teasing. She fell off her shoes once, interrupting the lyrics with an "Oh!" but got quickly back into her dance. Coming closer, she held on to the bedpost with one hand, arching her back as she moved down then up slowly, her long, blond waves swinging behind her. Of course, the second time she did it, she nearly lost her balance, but Benton smiled when she regained it.

Letting go of the post, she raised her arms over her head, falling into the same enticing moves he recalled from the last time they'd heard this song together. And when she reached behind her back, he heard the slide of a zipper. His mouth went dry as she crossed her arms over her chest, then slowly, seductively began peeling her bodice down over her breasts. "Stuck," she muttered at one point, struggling to free herself from it, but she soon stood bare to the waist, still swaying to the beat, and he stifled a moan. Then finally— oh yes, the moment he'd been waiting for—she reached down and began to playfully lift the hem of that sinful dress.

He watched impatiently as she painstakingly revealed inch after slow inch of thigh and just when he was about to lose his mind…she inched the dress back down.

That was when Benton decided he'd had enough dancing for the evening, no matter how sexy she was. "Oh no you don't," he said, then he tossed back the covers. She gasped, which he took as a compliment considering where her eyes focused. He pulled her down on the sheets with him, quickly rolling her onto her back.

"Oh Benton," she breathed as his hands molded to her thighs.

Having been repeatedly tormented by that sparkly fabric, he slid his palms upward, taking the thin material with him until the entire dress rested at her hips, revealing a tiny swath of lace just a shade darker than her skin. Gliding his touch around to her bottom, he realized just how small her panties were.

A laugh escaped his throat. "So, tell me, do you always wear things like this?"

"No, but with this dress, any other kind of underwear would just be panty lines waiting to happen."

"Then I think you should wear this dress a *lot*."

Benton ran his fingers lovingly over the lace, listening to her soft, sensual sigh, then slid his thumbs beneath the elastic and drew the underwear past her stockings, over her shoes. "Lift up," he said, and pulled the dress off over her head, although—as expected from his experiences with the dress—it was no easy task.

"Now—" he cast his most devilish smile "—lie back and enjoy."

He'd never seen a more beautiful sight than Mandy lounging naked, nestled in his pillows, her lips lush and full, her eyes shut in sweet abandon. After the last time they'd made love, when things had seemed so hot and frantic, he wanted to take things slow, wanted to make things last.

Running his hands the length of her body, he followed with his mouth, kissing his way down her neck, across her breasts. "Oh," she moaned.

He lifted one hand, pushing her hair aside to whisper in her ear. "Relax, honey. We've got a long way go yet."

Resuming his kisses down her body, he stopped at her navel, then caressed her inner thighs, glancing down to find an adorable little birthmark, shaped something like a heart, just inside her left knee. He gently stroked his thumb over it before easing his hands downward, following with his mouth. Blood thundered through him by the time she climaxed.

After that, he couldn't wait anymore. He entered easily, and as he moved inside her, he knew he'd never felt such a strong connection with another person. Benton had made love to plenty of women, and had often been with the same woman for months at a time, the whole while waiting, hoping he would begin to feel something as powerful as he felt with Mandy. He held back for as long as he could, but soon groaned as the pleasure rumbled through him, heightened by the deep attachment he felt for her.

I love you. He started to say it, but stopped because it was too soon to tell her. And besides, he'd glimpsed something odd, and focusing on it stole all other thoughts.

Was he imagining things or was there suddenly a clump of short red hair jutting through the blond around Mandy's face?

7

USUALLY Mindy was behind her desk by eight a.m. even though Mates By Mindy didn't open until nine. So when she left her house around ten the next morning, feeling like a semi had mowed her down, it was a bit of an aberration in her routine. Then again, being Mandy was a bit of an aberration, too. And having lots of fabulous sex with a man who could qualify for Greek god status was also rather out of the ordinary.

What a night—and she wasn't even thinking about all the stuff that had happened *before* she'd gotten to Benton's house.

They'd made love over and over again. She was beginning to believe maybe he really *was* a superhero. And unlike the last time she'd been in his bed, she didn't even think about sneaking out before morning. For one thing, having to explain such behavior twice would only complicate things, if that was possible. And for another, she *liked* being in Benton's bed. In between sex, they'd talked and laughed, and Mindy had felt so incredibly close to him that it had made her skin tingle to look at him.

So her reason for staying the night was the same reason she kept sleeping with him in the first place—she couldn't seem to help herself. So much for sticking to the plan.

Of course, she'd still woken up with one primary thought in her mind. *What have I done?*

After all, it was very risky business to keep getting naked with him.

For one thing, he'd kept playing with her hair. The wild ride in Benton's friend's car had been stressful enough on her wig, and having him pull her dress off over her head had nearly given her a heart attack until she'd realized he hadn't taken her hair off, too. Having him repeatedly run his hands through the strands or twirl them around his fingers had kept her on edge through the entire passionate encounter.

And clearly, the big issue still loomed, getting bigger with each passing day, each passing lie. She'd set Benton up with an imaginary woman.

She dragged herself into the shop around ten-fifteen. Jane sat behind her desk, elbow propped next to an open bag of M&M's, chin resting in her fist. She gave Mindy a long once-over. "Do you have the flu or just a long story to tell?"

Mindy settled behind her desk, stowed her purse in a bottom drawer and flipped on her computer. She quickly checked her calendar to see she had a lunch date with a new client, and after that a debriefing with a woman who'd gone on her first Mates By Mindy date just last night. Then she turned her chair toward Jane, giving her a look that warned her to tread lightly. "It would seem I have a hangover."

Jane's gaze dropped from Mindy's, suddenly drawn to something lower. She gasped, pointing to Mindy's knees, visible below the hem of her short, rust-colored skirt. "What happened?"

Mindy knew dark brown bruises crowned both kneecaps, but she'd forgotten about them because too many other parts of her body hurt just as badly. "I took a pretty nasty tumble." Similar bruises colored the back of each elbow, and a smaller greenish one hid beneath her chin, but she'd concealed that one with makeup.

Jane hesitated, popped a red M&M into her mouth, then spoke with advisable caution. "Dare I ask where?"

"Expensive restaurant," Mindy said, keeping her voice void of emotion. "And I suppose I'm lucky there was a rug or the injury could have been a lot worse."

Jane tilted her head slightly, as if trying to piece the puzzle together. "And this is one of the things you did to drive Benton away from you?"

Mindy sighed. "Sadly, no."

"Well, *did* you drive Benton away from you?"

Mindy let out an even heavier sigh, then turned to her desk. "Sadly…no."

"I'm guessing," Jane said pointedly, "this means you didn't stick to the plan."

Mindy turned on her, exasperated. "But how could I? He's too sweet, too wonderful!"

Understandably confused, Jane knit her brow, pursed her lips and shoved a lock of shoulder-length hair behind one ear. "Is this the same man who came in here making ridiculous, exacting demands and doubting your ability to do your job?"

"Purportedly. I mean, he doesn't *seem* the same, but…"

Jane raised her eyebrows in sarcasm. "Hey, maybe he's masquerading as someone else! Or maybe he has a secret twin!"

"Very funny." Then Mindy reminded Jane of

something. "You wanted me to have adventures with men, you know. You wanted to live vicariously through me."

"Well, stop the ride, I want to get off."

Mindy glared at Jane. "Easier said than done, it would appear."

"I guess now would be a good time for me to mention he came in looking for you this morning."

Mindy gasped. "He was here? This morning? Already?" He must have come straight to see her after dropping Mandy off at home. "What did he want? Did he say? Was it about last night?"

"He just said he'd stop by later."

"Dear God, what could he want from me? The real me?" She lowered her voice, murmuring to herself. "After last night, I'm pretty sure I know what he wants from Mandy."

"So you slept with him again."

Mindy grimaced, guilty as charged. "But I really tried not to. It was just impossible."

"Oh?"

Mindy nodded emphatically. "Every move I made, he thwarted. I started by wearing my tacky Marilyn Monroe dress, but he loved it. Then the maître d' at the restaurant subtly insulted me, but Benton leaped to my defense. Then, when I tripped and fell on my face, he was there by my side, much more worried about my health than how much I'd just embarrassed him. And after that, I dragged him into the sex shop downtown, which by the way is a—a virtual phallic fest." She spread her arms as if trying to encompass it all.

"Now *that* I'm sorry I missed."

"But he was *still* sweet and understanding. Although everything in the store totally shocked me, he never even asked why I took him there.'' She spoke more slowly, trying to drive her point home. ''Jane, when I asked the man to steal a Lamborghini for a joyride, he did it.''

Jane's mouth fell open. ''He did it?''

''Okay, so it turned out to belong to a friend of his, but still, he never flinched when I suggested it. And when we got back to his place, I discovered he'd bought a CD with a song I danced to for him on our first date and so I danced for him again.''

When Mindy least expected it, Jane quirked her lips into a smile. ''When you say dance, do you mean dance, or do you mean *dance?*''

Mindy rolled her eyes. Drat it all, foiled again by her own babbling. ''All right, so I stripped for him. So shoot me.''

''You stripped for him?'' Instead of reprimanding her, Jane broke into peals of laughter. ''You actually stripped. You, Mindy, the happy, sensible, I-don't-need-a-man-I-just-like-finding-them-for-others match-maker. This is rich. I mean, it's perfect.'' Tears began rolling down Jane's cheeks as she all but threw herself on her desk in reckless, cackling abandon.

Mindy sat calmly watching Jane crack up staight-faced, since she had no idea what was so wildly amusing. Finally, when Jane's crowing faded to a light giggling, Mindy said, ''And what exactly is so funny about that?''

''What's funny is that I've finally figured you out. Your secrets are secrets no more. Your armor has more than a chink in it, my friend—it's fallen off completely.''

''What are you talking about?''

Jane cast a cocky, knowing smile. "You *like* being Mandy. In fact, I think you *are* Mandy."

Mindy raised her eyebrows in utter shock. "What?"

"Think about it. Every Halloween, I invite you to a party, and do you ever do anything simple like rent a gorilla costume, wear an old prom dress and come as Cinderella, stick on some white ears and a fluffy tail and call yourself a bunny? No, you go to great trouble and expense, all to masquerade as some flamboyant woman like Marilyn, Dolly, Madonna."

Mindy swallowed nervously. She wasn't quite getting the point—or maybe she was choosing not to—but she admitted, "I *am* planning a Cher costume for this year, but only a seventies version. I'm not wearing that butt-revealing outfit from the 'If I Could Turn Back Time' video. No way."

Jane held up one finger. "It's my theory, young grasshopper, that you have a secret loud, flashy, devil-may-care side and that every time you dress up as someone else, you're trying to let that part of you out. The same thing happens when you become Mandy. You can go back to being Mindy the next day, so it seems *safe* to act wild and crazy, as if there will be no repercussions."

Ironically Mindy had thought the same thing last night, but she wasn't ready to admit, to Jane or to herself, that maybe she didn't know herself as well as she claimed. "Only one huge hole in that conjecture, Dr. Jane. Everything I do as Mandy *does* have repercussions."

Jane let out a derisive snort. "Not ones that you actually deal with."

"Oh well, repercussions that I *deal* with." Mindy

rolled her eyes. ''That's another matter entirely. From now on you should really be more specific.''

The front door opened with a jingle, and Mindy looked up to see her mother, looking stylishly casual in a green pantsuit that complemented her auburn hair, a trait that ran in the family.

''Hi there, Judy,'' Jane said. Mindy's mom was a frequent visitor to the shop.

''Hi, Mom.''

''Good morning, Min—'' Her mother stopped and flinched. ''You don't look well. Are you all right?''

Mindy sighed, feeling, as usual lately, as if she'd been caught doing something forbidden like lying, shopping in X-rated stores or stealing cars. ''So Jane has informed me. But I'm fine, really.''

''Mindy just had a late night, that's all,'' Jane volunteered. ''She had a date.''

Mindy scowled at her assistant, who might as well have said, ''Mindy was out all night having sex.''

Her mom appeared appropriately worried as she leaned forward slightly, still studying her. ''I see. Well, I hope he's…nice.''

Mindy swallowed, feeling defensive. ''He really is. You'd like him a lot.''

Her mother broke into a smile. ''Then does this mean I'll be meeting him?''

''Uh…'' *Not likely, but if you do, be sure to pretend I was twins.* ''We'll see.''

Hearing the uncertainty in Mindy's voice, her mother knit her brow and shifted her weight from one foot to the other. ''You know, I've often worried that perhaps my divorce has soured you on the idea of commitment and marriage.''

''No such thing, Mom,'' she promised hurriedly.

And before her mom could start asking if this current guy could be *the one,* Mindy said, "So what brings you in today?"

"I'm on my way to a hair appointment, but I stopped by because my bridge partner, Lois, has a son, Todd, who's coming to town next week, and she thought you two might make a cute pair. She's hosting a—"

Mindy decided to nip this in the bud. "No thanks."

"But you don't even know—"

"I know everything I need to, which is that one matchmaker in this family is way more than enough."

After all, she currently had her hands far too full with her *own* matchmaking mistakes.

BENTON SAT at a small round table next to the window of the French pastry shop across the square from Mates By Mindy, nursing a latte. He needed to get to work. But he also needed to see Mindy. And he found it awfully suspicious that she hadn't shown up until some time after he'd dropped Mandy off at home. He'd gone straight to the matchmaking shop after leaving Mandy, hoping he'd imagined the whole red hair incident, hoping to find fiery little Mindy sitting behind her desk, just waiting for new mates to match. The empty desk, however, along with her assistant's bewilderment over where she could be, did not bode well.

He hadn't said anything to Mandy about the red hair he thought he'd seen because he wasn't sure what to say. No sooner had he spotted it than she'd shifted beneath him, and the glimpse of auburn had disappeared. And he couldn't exactly go looking for more—although he *had* played with her hair a lot in hopes of revealing anything that needed to be revealed, and no red strands had appeared. After a while, he'd decided he was being silly, and he'd let himself forget about the sighting and devote himself fully to spending time with her and, of course, making love to her. Which he'd done repeatedly with commendable vigor, he thought, leaning back in his chair with pride. Ah, it was good to be king.

Well, it was good to be king as long as you were having sex with the same woman you thought you were having sex with. That was why he was here, lurking across the street from Mindy's shop. He'd awakened with doubts, still questioning what he'd seen in the dim lighting.

He recalled Mandy saying Mindy dyed her hair red, and the thought had occurred to him that maybe she'd lied, maybe *Mandy* had been a redhead like her sister once upon a time and hadn't wanted to admit it. After all, he'd been pretty specific when he'd given Mindy his requirements for a mate. He'd demanded she be a blonde, so maybe Mandy had been afraid an *unnatural* blonde wouldn't fit the bill. He cringed upon recalling his rigid standards, but he had more important things to think about.

He wasn't sure why Mindy had suddenly popped to mind upon the glimpse of a few auburn wisps, the idea that Mandy could actually be Mindy. Anyone would think he was insane to leap to such a conclusion. Except that, well, the resemblance *was* incredible. And they both had that strange blinking tendency. Now that he thought about it, when Mandy was nervous, her voice sounded more like Mindy's to him.

None of that meant anything, of course. They were twins. From what he'd heard, twins often shared a lot more than looks; they could have similar habits, gestures, facial expressions, even feelings. And he'd certainly seen plenty of twins he couldn't tell apart, so that aspect fit, too.

Still, as crazy as it sounded, a lingering notion swam in his head. If she was nervous about being found out, it would explain her sneaky departure after the first time they'd made love. And wasn't it true, if he chose to be honest, that something indefinable had sparked between him and Mindy before she'd fixed him up with her sister? He couldn't pin down the reason, couldn't call it plain attraction, but she'd stayed on his mind. He'd not fully allowed himself to acknowledge that truth until this very minute because two people had never been more wrong for each other, and the idea of him dating *her* would've sounded preposterous.

Which could explain, he reasoned, feeling a bit like Sherlock Holmes, why Mindy might choose to disguise herself. What if she'd been wildly drawn to him, desperate to go out with him, but had been too embarrassed to say so after their rocky start?

And he *was* her client, after all. Maybe she had a rule about never dating clients since, if it didn't work out, they probably wouldn't trust her to find future dates for them, and if nothing else, it would be awkward. Plus, Mindy was such a purist about the whole matchmaking business, she might think dating a client would sully the process. He could picture her sitting behind her desk, hands clasped atop it, spouting some such nonsense in the calm, soothing voice she used when she thought he couldn't comprehend what she was saying.

So maybe her attraction to him had been too powerful to push down. Maybe it had driven her to do something totally out of character. Maybe this was all an outrageous charade designed to let her spend time with him, in bed and out.

Yes, the more he considered it, the more it made sense. He was mad about Mandy, but this would certainly explain her shifting personality. And come to think of it, it would also explain why she'd been holding on to her hair for dear life last night in the convertible.

The longer Benton turned it over in his mind, the more intent he became on getting to the bottom of things without delay. He drained his cup, rose from his seat, left the café and strode boldly across Hyde Park Square toward the heart-laden shop with the spicy little redhead inside.

AFTER PASSING a small auburn-haired lady on the sidewalk just outside Mates by Mindy, Benton stepped inside, a smile pasted on his face. He focused on the woman in question, wondering if indeed she was the same one he'd parted ways with less than an hour ago. She looked predictably cute, even if a little worse for wear. "Good morning, Mindy."

Her eyes opened wide. "Benton—I mean, Mr. Maxwell." After the slightly off-kilter greeting, she relaxed a little, obviously trying to mask her surprise at his arrival. "Jane told me you stopped by. I'm sorry I missed you. What can I do for you?"

"It's about your sister," he said, coming closer. He bypassed the chair in front of her desk, not stopping until he stood beside the desk.

She peered up at him, blinked.

"More dust?"

"Yes."

"Sorry to hear it." He shifted his weight from one foot to the other, strategically positioning himself to stand directly next to her chair so she had to crane her neck to look at him.

"You said you wanted to see me about Mandy?" She blinked twice after the question, then shut her eyes tight, as if trying to will the tic away.

Benton reached inside his jacket, extracting the greeting card he'd picked up at the gift shop next to the pastry place. "I'm still simply entranced with her, and to show my appreciation, I brought you a—" He dropped his gaze to the card tucked inside an envelope flap, then chuckled at his feigned forgetfulness. "Well, look at that—I bought you a card but forgot to sign it."

"Oh. Well, here's a—"

She held up a standard office pen, but Benton dug quickly into his jacket to pluck out the gold one Miss Binks had given him on his last birthday. "Got one already, thanks."

He gave another fake smile as he stooped over her desk to scrawl his name in the thank you card. At the same time, he lowered his gaze, thinking she might back away, considering his proximity, and show her legs, but damn it, they remained tucked under her desk where he couldn't see them.

This called for drastic measures, but he was desperate to know if Mindy was Mandy, or if Mandy was Mandy, and just who exactly he was so mad about.

So as he straightened and started to return the pen to his inner jacket pocket, he dropped it to the floor— voilà!—beneath Mindy's desk. Knowing time was precious, he knelt and dove for it, mumbling, "Excuse

me," as he wedged his head under the desk, grappling
for the pen between her feet.

She finally pushed her chair backward, rolling away
from him. "Mr. Maxwell, what on earth are you doing?"

Snatching the pen, he rose to his knees and smiled
at her. "Got it." Then he sheepishly explained, "It's
a special pen. It has my name engraved on it. See?"

He held it up, and she looked, and he used the opportunity to steal a peek at where he would find a
birthmark, if indeed Mindy and Mandy were the same
person. Unfortunately, her knees were locked together
below the cute little skirt she wore, inhibiting his view.
But something just as telling caught his eye.

He raised his gaze to hers, trying to sound innocent.
"What happened to your knees?"

Mindy darted an alarmed glance to them, then
looked at his face as she clamped both hands over the
bruises. "I fell."

"Nothing too serious, I hope." He slipped the pen
in his pocket without taking his eyes off her.

She briskly shook her head and spoke with consid-
erable speed. "Nope, this is the worst of it. Otherwise,
I'm right as rain."

"This is really quite a coincidence. Mandy took a
fall, too, just last night." He stayed on his knees as he
studied hers, despite how peculiar it surely seemed.
But he wasn't quite done investigating yet.

After only a hint of hesitation, Mindy let out a been-
there-done-that sigh, then gave her head a short shake.
"Not again. You wouldn't believe how often this happens to us." She rolled her eyes. "It's the twin thing.
You've probably heard about twins feeling each
other's pain, feelings? Well, Mandy and I sometimes

actually copy each other's actions. Case in point, she falls, I fall. It's really quite eerie.''

''Downright spooky,'' he agreed.

Time for drastic move number two. He wasn't buying a word she said, of course, but he had to be one-hundred percent certain his suspicions were correct. So, reaching to move one of her hands away, he gently grasped one kneecap with his fingertips, wiggling it from side to side, as if he were her attending physician.

He knew even before he spotted the birthmark on the side of her knee that she was Mandy, not only because the bruise story didn't wash, but because under any other circumstances, the Mindy he'd originally met would have already slapped him silly for touching her so forwardly. As it was, she was saying, ''Benton, uh, Mr. Maxwell, what are you…?'' She spoke in a shivery little voice that told him she was a bit confused.

He raised his gaze to her face, which looked panicky. ''Just making sure your knees seem okay. After all, Mandy fell quite hard, so I'm sure you did, too.''

She didn't answer, but Benton's work was done. He pushed to his feet.

So he'd been right. Mindy *was* posing as Mandy, lying to him, making a fool of him, letting him fall for her under false pretenses. A slow anger began to assail him, seep through him. He didn't like being duped. No matter how he looked at it, he should be spitting nails, spouting accusations, threatening legal action of some sort.

But a softer part of him, the part he'd started to uncover since meeting her, stopped to think about her motives as he had at the café. And the longer he examined it, the more he realized he was *flattered*. She'd gone to all this trouble, all this risk, just to be with him. She'd wanted him that much.

He remained angry about the lies, of course, and he wondered how long she intended to let this go on before being honest. Yet like it or not, despite the thin tendrils of irritation curling through him, he was still mad about the woman.

Maybe he was happy to find out he had them *both*— the spitfire Mindy, who didn't let anyone push her around, and the passionate, adventurous Mandy, who grabbed life by the horns and held on for the ride, whatever it may bring. And this did simplify one thing—at least now he didn't have to worry about falling for one sister while he carried a secret torch for the other.

Not that Benton was going to let her off the hook with a wink and a smile, though. No way. You didn't tell a lie this big for this long without deserving to be taught a lesson. So he decided he was going to keep playing along with her. After all, it appeared that Mindy liked games, so he'd play one of his own and make *her* suffer for a while until she finally told him the truth.

And he had a feeling he was going to enjoy it immensely.

"Can you keep a secret?" he asked, peering pointedly at his split-personality lover.

Mindy gaped at him, clearly still puzzled over the whole knee-grabbing event. "Um, yes. Sure."

"And you, Jane?" He turned to Mindy's faithful assistant, who always sat quietly, watching their exchanges without a word. He suspected the two women were close and that Jane knew everything.

"Me?" She flinched in surprise at suddenly being

drawn into the conversation. "Oh yes, ask anyone. I'm an ace secret keeper."

"I'll bet." He shifted his smile between them, then spilled the beans. "Don't tell Mandy, but the next time I see her, I'm going to ask her to marry me."

Mindy gasped and flung her chair backward. Jane let a bag of M&M's fall from her hand, sending the candy clattering across the floor. Mindy attempted to speak, but it took her a while to get anything out. "D-d-don't you think this is a little fast?"

Benton smiled. This was even more fun than the drive in the Lamborghini. "Not at all. That was my goal, after all. Finding a wife. Remember?"

"Well...well, you don't really know her yet!"

Benton countered by raising his eyebrows. "Oh, you might be surprised. Just last night I discovered she's into kinky things." Both women gasped. He went on. "But hey, who am I to complain if she wants to spice things up in the bedroom?" He finished with a suggestive wink.

"I think," Mindy began slowly, her face turning a delightful, familiar shade of red, "that she was probably just *curious* about those things but not really *into* them. In fact, I think you should ask her about it and give her a chance to explain."

"Nope, doesn't matter. Besides, the next time we're together, I'll be too busy asking her to be my wife to discuss anything else."

"But, Benton, you don't know the real Mandy!" Mindy claimed, her green eyes looking as if they'd pop from her head. "She's impossible to live with! She leaves the cap off the toothpaste! She never puts her clothes in the hamper! And she—she lets dishes pile up in the sink until there are bugs! It's disgusting, I tell you!"

Benton raked a dismissive hand through the air without bothering to hide his smile. "I'll get her a maid. Or better yet—" he lifted one finger triumphantly "—I'll get her a maid *outfit*. You know, one of those sexy ones with the short skirt and the fishnet stockings? Now that I know she's into experimenting, this'll be perfect. Thanks for helping me think of it, Mindy. But I really have to run now—money to invest, empires to topple, that sort of thing. Take care, and, hey, be careful with those knees."

With that, Benton swept out the door, glad when it shut behind him so he could finally burst into the laughter he'd been struggling to contain.

It really *was* good to be king.

MINDY SAT on her couch in a pair of cut-off sweatpants and a T-shirt bearing a picture of Eeyore. She *felt* like Eeyore. *Woe is me. Everything's depressing.*

She'd dressed intending to go for a run before her date with Benton, but about two strides into it, she'd realized her knees hurt too much. She didn't run often, had just thought it might clear her head. Did she really think *anything* was going to clean up the mess currently cluttering her brain?

Glancing at the clock, she realized she should be donning some Mandyish apparel right about now, lowering her blond locks onto her head, standing in front of the mirror honing her Mandy smile and her Mandy voice. The fact that she wasn't preparing for her date could only mean one thing—she wasn't going and she wasn't letting Benton propose to her tonight.

She shook her head, reliving the horror of his most recent visit to Mates By Mindy. She still couldn't believe the man intended to ask for her hand in marriage! *And* buy her a French maid outfit! It wasn't even Halloween! Then again, she didn't exactly think he intended to take her to a party in it. Well, perhaps a *private* party, which, although Mindy had never thought about such a thing, might not be so bad.

What am I thinking? Everything had gone so awry, gotten so terribly out of control, that she clearly couldn't process it anymore.

Since she wasn't busy practicing her Mandy voice, it seemed much more apropos to get started on her Cher impression. She shifted her gaze toward the phone, thinking of Benton's impending arrival, and belted out the first couple of lines of "If I Could Turn Back Time."

Well, she thought, she couldn't turn back time, but she *could* freeze it for a while, at least as it pertained to the progression of her relationship with Benton. Without another second's delay, she picked up the phone and dialed the direct line to his office. When he'd called to make the date, he'd mentioned he'd probably work late and head straight to her house afterward.

He answered on the first ring. "Benton Maxwell."

Mindy held her nose closed with her free hand in an attempt to sound congested. "Benton, it's Mandy."

"Mandy? Are you okay? You sound—"

"Sick. I'm sick."

"Oh no, honey, that's awful." The concern in his voice shifted to disappointment. "Does this mean you're calling to postpone our date tonight?"

"Yeah. Sorry."

He sighed. "Me, too, but if you're ill, it's better not to go out."

She still pinched her nose. "I was really looking forward to seeing you, but—" she coughed for good measure "—you're right. I should stay in."

"Well, I hope you're taking care of yourself."

"Oh, don't worry, I am." *I'm taking care of myself by canceling this date.* That was one way to keep from sleeping with the guy.

"By the way, how are your knees?"

She let go of her nose just long enough to make some snuffling noises. "Sore. They're very sore."

"Well, take care of those, too."

When Benton asked to reschedule, she told him she'd rather wait a few days, see how long it took her illness to blow over. By the time she hung up the phone, she felt like a heel. A *relieved* heel, but a heel just the same. *He'd hate me if he knew what I'd done,* she thought. *He'd despise me.* One more reason to keep up the charade until she could figure out how to drive Benton away without the truth coming into play. She didn't think she could bear having him hate her.

Venus bounded gently onto the couch next to her, and Mindy reached out to give her a soft scratch under the chin. "Hey, V, looks like it's just you and me tonight." Despite herself, she was disappointed, too. A part of her really *had* looked forward to seeing Benton this evening. She was crazy about him, after all. But she was also tired of pretending to be someone she wasn't, tired of knowing nothing real would ever come of their relationship, as wonderful as it was.

Lifting the cat so they were face-to-face, Mindy decided to cheer herself up. "You know what, let's not sit here and mope all night. Let's work on my Cher costume." Although she knew May was awfully early to start planning for an October event, it sometimes took her a while to perfect her Halloween look, so she figured it was never too early to start. And it would take her mind off her troubles. "This will be my first time as a brunette!" she said, cheered by the change.

"Let's head up into the attic and see what we can find."

Two hours later, Mindy stood before her long mirror, admiring the floor-length red-sequin dress she wore. Her mother had bought the gown for some formal event in the eighties, and Mindy had cut out the neck so it scooped low between her breasts, and she'd pinned the waist tight. It would take some sewing, of course, but add a slit up one side and it would be perfect for her seventies Cher. As Venus stood at her feet, giving a gentle meow, it finally dawned on Mindy why Venus was never alarmed by her Mandy costume. She'd seen Mindy in disguise so many times before!

That was when the doorbell rang.

She glanced toward it, annoyed. "Who could that be?" Probably her neighbor, Mrs. Weatherby, who was always borrowing an egg or a cup of sugar as if it were 1950 and there wasn't a convenience store two blocks away. She had also recently commented on having seen Mindy coming and going in a blond wig with a handsome fellow and wanted to know what that was all about. Put on the spot, Mindy had told Mrs. W. that she had seen her twin sister, Mandy, and had confused the two of them. "Happens all the time," she'd said. Oh, what a tangled web.

Scurrying to the window, she pulled back the curtain, squinting when the setting sun flashed bright and blinding in her eyes. Yet it didn't take long to discern that the silhouetted figure on her front stoop wasn't Mrs. Weatherby; it was none other than Benton Maxwell III. As her heart beat faster and fresh panic set in, Mindy figured any minute now that web was bound to strangle her.

8

"WHAT NOW?" Mindy murmured. Think, think. Fast! Dropping the curtain into place, Mindy yanked and pulled and scrambled to get the long sequin dress over her head, then flung it against the wall. She scanned the messy room, littered with open boxes from the attic. Where on earth were her shorts and T-shirt?

Aha! She snatched the shirt from under the edge of her bedspread and tossed it on. The doorbell rang again, his familiar impatient ring. Shorts, shorts, where were the shorts? MIA. This wasn't good. She'd have to go without them.

Yanking open her closet door, she grabbed her big pink terry-cloth robe and threw it on, cinching it at the waist. Then she dashed from the bedroom, turning back after getting halfway down the hall to close the bedroom door, concealing the array of fabrics and hairpieces and exotic garments that didn't say "sick in bed."

Skidding to a halt before the front door as Benton rang the bell once more, Mindy caught sight of herself in the little decorative mirror hanging in her entryway. Oh no! No wig! "Just a minute!"

She scurried back to the bedroom and threw the door open. "Wig, wig," she whispered. She'd made such a mess she didn't see the darn thing anywhere!

"Come on, where are you?" she muttered through clenched teeth.

Just as pure dread spiraled through her, she caught sight of one blond curl protruding from under a bolt of brightly flowered fabric. She dove for it, thrilled to discover it was the Dolly wig and not the Marilyn wig, since she was in no state of mind to explain a major haircut. Tugging the fake hair onto her head as she sprinted toward the front door, she paused before the mirror again just long enough to tuck in a few renegade strands of auburn.

"This is another fine mess you've gotten me into," she murmured to her alter ego's reflection with a scowl.

Just before she greeted Benton, she remembered she was supposed to be sick. She forced herself to slow down and take a deep breath, then she feebly twisted the knob. "Benton," she uttered weakly, tacking a little cough on the end of his name.

Worry colored his expression. "What took you so long? Are you all right?"

"Had to, had to—" she glanced down "—find a robe. Because I'm not wearing any shorts, see?" Using both hands, she parted the pink terry-cloth beneath the tie, flashing cotton undies.

He lifted his eyes to hers. "You sound a lot better than you did on the phone." Stepping over the threshold, he didn't give her much choice but to back up and let him in.

"My, uh, nose cleared. Wonder drugs."

Benton glanced around her small living room, looking perplexed. "Really? Where? When *I'm* sick, I usually gather everything I could possibly need and keep it with me at all times."

He was smiling as he spoke, yet clearly he'd expected to see tissue boxes, cold pill packages and half-eaten bowls of soup strewn about, which would have been the case had she really been ill. But to her annoyance, the place was neat as a pin. Since originally tidying the house for Benton before their first date, she'd kept it that way. And after Mindy had claimed Mandy was such a slob, too. As usual, nothing was going right.

"They're in the…bathroom medicine cabinet. I just straightened up a little, right before you came."

"When you should be resting," he scolded. "Which is why I'm here. I've come to take care of you."

Mindy wasn't sure if it was guilt or happiness that trickled through her as she gazed at him, but she chose to believe it was the latter, and she wanted desperately to throw herself into his arms, yet refrained from doing so. "You are the sweetest man."

He shrugged, one corner of his mouth quirking up. "You're easy to be sweet to. What's this?" His focus shifted to her neck as he reached gentle fingertips to pluck a lone red sequin from her skin.

"Um, looks like a sequin."

He appeared a little dumbfounded. "Have you been *wearing* sequins lately?"

She swallowed, then summoned an answer. "Actually, I was just cleaning out the attic when I started feeling bad. Old Halloween costumes and that sort of thing. It must have come from something in the boxes I was going through."

Benton nodded, and Mindy realized it was among her most sensible lies. She almost hated to think she was getting better at this. She wasn't really a liar—

usually—and she didn't want to be a person skilled at the art.

Too late, Mandy murmured viciously inside her.

She changed the subject, peering at the shopping bag at his side. "What's in the bag?"

Benton smiled and, moving into the room, lifted it to the coffee table to reach inside. "I rented some movies." He set a handful of tapes on the table. "I got you some ice cream." He extracted a large tub of mint chocolate chip. "And I picked up some catnip for Venus at the pet store since I didn't want her to feel left out."

Mindy stood before him, nonplussed. *Sweet man* didn't even begin to describe him. "You got a special treat for my cat when you don't even like cats?"

He tilted his head, gave a quiet laugh. "Guess I wanted to show Venus my intentions are honorable."

That makes one of us, unfortunately. "And you got my favorite ice cream. How did you know?"

He smiled. "Lucky guess. Actually, the first time I met your sister, she was eating—well, dropping—a cone of mint chocolate chip, so, thinking you might share common taste buds, I took a shot."

"Uh…good one," she said, swallowing the guilty lump in her throat as she recalled how cold Benton had seemed to her on that first meeting. She'd judged him so wrong. "What movies did you get?" She lowered her eyes to the videos to keep from looking at him.

"A little bit of everything." He picked them up and flipped through the stack. "*When Harry Met Sally* for laughs, *E.T.* for comfort, *Titanic* for romance, and *Casablanca*…well, because it's *Casablanca*." He concluded with a smile. "I figured I'd get lucky and you'd like at least one of these."

Watching Mindy pretending to be Mandy, staring at him as if he were the greatest thing since sliced bread, was almost enough to make Benton forget his *own* end of the pretense.

"I love them all," she said.

But he was pretty certain Mindy wasn't sick, that she'd been trying to outrun his marriage proposal, so he still had to teach her a lesson, even if, at the moment, he wanted to forget it and just kiss her.

He settled on the couch, prepared to tease her mercilessly as she lowered herself beside him. "If I'd had more time, I'd have run downtown to that shop where we stopped the other night and picked up a *different* kind of video." He raised his eyebrows at her for good measure.

It took her a minute to figure out what he was saying, but mortification slowly crept into her gaze. "You're not serious."

He wanted to laugh—from the look on her face you'd think he'd asked her to star in one of those movies. Feeding on her shock, he slanted an extralascivious grin in her direction. "I thought maybe you were...into that sort of thing. I figured that's why you dragged me into that place."

Mindy blinked at him. "See, the thing is, I was just...curious about what kind of stuff they had in those stores. But that certainly doesn't mean I want to *buy* anything like that."

"Okay, whatever you say." He gave her a humoring wink, then got to his feet, leaving her no time to dispute him as he headed to the kitchen. "I'd better stick this ice cream in the freezer before it melts. Now,'' he called, ''I have something to ask you.''

Mindy went as quiet as a mouse in the other room, and Benton smiled. Despite what he'd told her and Jane in the matchmaking shop, he really wasn't ready to marry Mindy. God knew they had some things to work out, like what her name was, for instance. But under the circumstances, he thought it only fair to pretend he was, and he knew it would be entertaining to watch her sweat. A little more torture was the least she deserved for her ongoing lies. Teasing her about the sex shop had only been an appetizer for what was to come.

When she hadn't responded by the time he returned to the couch, he dropped down next to her, threw an arm around her shoulder and pulled her close. She turned toward him, bringing them practically nose to nose.

She looked worried. ''I'm probably contagious, you know.''

He grinned. ''I have an excellent immune system.''

''Aren't I lucky?''

''Now, on to my question.''

The muscles in her throat contracted. ''Y-yes?''

He hesitated long enough to drive up her blood pressure a bit, then said, ''Which movie would you like to watch first?''

As her eyes opened even wider, he held in a chuckle. ''Which movie?'' Breaking free from his hold, she scrambled through the videos on the table, then struggled to speak in a slightly calmer voice. ''*When Harry Met Sally,* of course. Because I could really use a laugh right now.''

THEY WATCHED *When Harry Met Sally* and *Casablanca,* deciding to save Benton's other choices for another evening, since it was well after midnight by the time Bogie told Ingrid they'd always have Paris. Benton had reclined on the couch at some point long ago, propping his head on throw pillows, and Mindy nestled against his chest, still wrapped in her big pink robe. Benton had never enjoyed watching movies more than he had tonight.

Of course, there were moments when he wanted to pluck that blond wig off her pretty head and tell her he knew everything and that it was all right and that he loved her. Because he did. He'd fallen in love with Mindy McCrae, a woman who was the absolute opposite of everything he'd ever thought he wanted. There was no denying it, and no fighting it, either. As they lay silently waiting for the movie to rewind, he understood why he'd never found a woman he could love before; he'd been looking in all the wrong places, at all the wrong females. No wonder he couldn't care romantically for Miss Binks. It had taken Mindy and all her conniving to show him he hadn't a clue what attributes he desired in a companion. He only knew he'd found them in *her.*

So of course he wanted to do away with the pretending, work out their differences, admit how he felt about her in spite of it all. He wanted to get on with things, take this relationship forward, build on it in a real and lasting way.

But as he peered at the little blond head tucked beneath his chin, seeing that wig of hers galled him just enough to keep him from coming clean. No, *she'd* have to confess first, and he'd continue threatening her with his impending fake marriage proposal until she did. Admitting the truth was the least he could ask of her. Only after that could they move ahead.

Just then, Mindy looked at him. "This has been really nice. Thanks for coming over."

He held in the compassionate smile that wanted to leak free, vowing again that she wouldn't get the best of him by being adorable. "You seem to be feeling a lot better."

"I'm sure it's because you're here." She lowered her eyes, let out a sigh, then lifted them again. "Can I tell you something?"

"Anything," he said, thinking, wondering, hoping. Maybe this was it. Maybe she was going to tell him who she really was.

"Sometimes I…don't feel like I'm living up to the list of attributes you gave Mindy. I feel as if…well, as if I was a bit of a fake with you at first. I must seem so different now than when we first met, when we had dinner."

Benton shifted the woman in his arms so she lay beside him, still wrapped in his embrace. One bare leg sneaked free from the terry-cloth robe to loop affectionately over his. "Maybe," he whispered, leaning to drop a small kiss to her forehead, "you've helped me see that my list of attributes didn't really matter all that much."

He watched her intently. *Tell me,* he willed her. *Tell me you're Mindy. Tell me the truth.*

Instead, she pulled him down into a long, warm kiss, which he figured was the next best thing. Her tongue wove around his, made him forget the truth mattered and gave rise to his wanting her, *both* of her, *all* of her.

He hadn't come here with any intention of making

love to her tonight—she'd supposedly been sick, after all—but his hands roamed beneath her robe, moving up to mold to her breasts over her T-shirt. He looked down as the terry cloth parted beneath his touch. "Eeyore," he said with a small smile.

She grinned at him. "Are you a fan?"

He glanced at the shirt, her breasts, his hands covering them. "I am now."

Twenty minutes later, they lay on the couch after a tender—if brief—intimate encounter. Mindy's robe lay on the carpet, and he'd seen her flowered panties disappear between two couch cushions, but her T-shirt remained on. She lay snuggled against his bare chest. She'd undressed him, too. And considering that he'd just made love to a woman who thought she was keeping a huge secret from him, he'd never felt more whole, more relaxed or happier in the afterglow of sex.

As she twirled one finger through the hair on his chest, he reached up to grab her hand. Their eyes met, and he spoke in a low, gentle tone. "I have something to ask you."

Her mouth fell halfway open, and her eyes filled with distress. She looked nearly as sick as she'd claimed to be earlier. "Wh-what's that?"

Will you marry me, Mandy? The words sat on the tip of his tongue, but he didn't say them. Instead, he shifted his gaze to a framed picture he'd noticed on a table at the foot of the sofa. The photo was of Mindy with three other young women, smiling as they gathered around a birthday cake. "Who's in the picture?"

Relief softened her expression as she looked. "Oh, that's me—me—me sister and some friends on her twenty-fifth birthday."

A small smile found its way to his mouth. "Me sister?"

Mindy reached up to cover one eye with her palm. "Yes, me sister. Argh, I'm a pirate." Then she giggled playfully, and Benton was too amused and content to persecute her for the screwup at the moment. He still planned to ask Mandy to marry him and make Mindy deal with it.

But he wouldn't make her deal with it tonight.

MISS BINKS stuck her head through Benton's door, looking nervous. Unfortunately, she'd been wearing that expression a great deal lately, every time he'd suspected she was about to admit her romantic feelings for him. He'd always managed to stop her by changing the subject or pretending he had an urgent phone call to make. Once he'd rushed from the room, claiming he had to go to the rest room, *now*. Why wouldn't she get the message?

He didn't want to hurt Miss Binks, he just thought it would be better for both of them if the issue of romance was never raised. He could only assume the poor woman's love for him had blinded her to the obvious—that he didn't wish to hear the something she had to tell him. Although it almost made him sympathize with the look Mindy had gotten in her eye each time she'd thought he was going to propose to her. Waiting to have something sprung on you was excruciating. Still, Mindy wasn't nearly as innocent as Benton was in this situation with Miss Binks, so he didn't sympathize *too* much.

"Mr. Maxwell, I'm sorry to interrupt you, but I know your schedule is free this afternoon, and I really *must* have a few minutes of your time."

He'd have felt like a horrible boss for repeatedly putting her off if he didn't know exactly what she wanted to say, if it hadn't been so evident from the adoring look in her eyes. But he had devised a new way to handle this, something that should bring the problem to an end once and for all. "Come in, Miss Binks. Sit down." He motioned to one of the leather chairs across from his desk.

She settled there, smoothing her skirt and pursing her lips. It made him uncomfortable. "Mr. Maxwell, I have—"

"Miss Binks—" he spoke loudly, drowning her out, "—there's something I want to share with you." Benton had decided he had to tell Miss Binks the truth, and he intended to do it before giving her any opportunity to express her affection for him. His announcement would surely hurt her, but it was something she needed to know, and he delivered the news as gently as possible. "I've recently met someone. A woman."

Her gasp was so slight it was almost inaudible, so he pretended he hadn't noticed and went on.

"The relationship is getting serious rather quickly, and I felt it might be wise to tell you." He met her gaze to find she'd gone as pale as a ghost in a designer suit.

"Why is that, Mr. Maxwell?" The question sounded innocent, although sad.

He made up a lie. "Because it may affect my work schedule, which means I'll be spending a little less time at the office and delegating more responsibility your way."

She nodded slightly and rose hurriedly to her feet, apparently ready to end the conversation. "Thank you. For telling me." She made her way to the door, then stopped, as if something had just dawned on her. "I suppose this might explain your uncharacteristic tardiness lately."

Speaking of uncharacteristic, her words had sounded almost scolding. But he decided to let it go. "Yes," he said simply.

"I see." She swallowed visibly, then offered a thin smile. "I wish you well with your new relationship." She disappeared before he could reply.

He sighed, watching the space in the doorway where she'd been. He *had* hurt her, and he felt badly about it. She'd always been so loyal to him in every way, so faithful. But better to hurt her like this than to let her admit she was in love with him and then hurt her. At least he'd saved her the humiliation and saved them both a great deal of awkwardness. Now, this matter could be laid to rest.

Which carried his mind to another, more pleasant subject. He dialed Mandy's cell phone—which was, of course, *Mindy's* cell phone—and listened to her cheerful "Hello."

"Hi, there." He used his most seductive voice.

Affection spilled from hers instantly. "Hi, Benton."

"Did you decide what you want to do tomorrow?" It was Friday and he'd told her to pick an activity, anything she wanted, for the weekend. After all, Benton generally equated a date with dining at a nice restaurant, but Mindy had begun showing him there were other ways to have fun. He'd decided to be a little less rigid about his idea of a good time, and this seemed a fine way to start. He also thought it might make her truly understand that his wish list no longer mattered. Once that clicked, once she really believed it, there'd be no reason to keep pretending.

"I thought we might go see the Reds play."

Hmm, a baseball game. Benton's dad had taken him to a few Reds games when he was a kid, but it wasn't usual Maxwell fare. Even when he came by free tickets from a client, he gave them to one of his employees.

Apparently, his lack of a fast response worried Mindy. "I know it's out of the ordinary for us, but…my sister suggested it. She likes that sort of thing and said it would be fun."

Her continued pretense made him smile. "Mindy suggested it, did she? Well then, sure, we'll go."

No, baseball wasn't his usual taste, but Benton quickly decided that under the circumstances, it could be fun. He reached up to stroke his chin with devilish intent, a private—and very wicked—grin on his face.

IT HAD BEEN Jane's idea. Together, she and Mindy had decided Benton's next date with Mandy must happen someplace public, someplace loud, someplace where he couldn't conceivably propose marriage. As she and Benton found their seats, Mindy was pleased to see a sizable crowd for the matchup between the Reds and the Dodgers.

She'd been a wreck the other night, waiting for him to pop the dreaded question. But she knew Benton well enough to know he wouldn't propose marriage in a crowded stadium. Despite her initial impressions of him, he was a romantic at heart—he'd proven it over and over again—and doing it someplace unromantic just wasn't his style. In fact, that was probably what had kept him from asking her during her pseudo-illness; he'd likely envisioned wine and roses for such an event, not terry cloth and germs. She hoped peanut shells and beer vendors wouldn't meet his standards, either. She was convinced he was waiting for the right time, so her first dating priority at the moment was not to give him one.

She'd bought the tickets and had selected seats behind the Reds' dugout, where she and Benton would have to stay on the alert. One more thing to distract him from his goal. "Keep an eye out for foul balls," she warned as a Dodger stepped up to the plate.

"Why? Are they collectibles or something?"

Mindy tilted her blond head. Poor, dear Benton. He hadn't been lying earlier when he'd said he wasn't into baseball. "No, honey," she explained gently. "Because they'll hit you in the head and kill you. So if you see one coming, duck!"

Benton nodded. "Duck. Got it." He was clearly out of his element, yet being a trouper. He'd bought them hot dogs and beer and had insisted on purchasing a big red foam We're #1 finger when Mindy had seen one and laughed. The acquisition had made something scathingly clear. There was *nothing* she could do to drive him away at this point.

Normally, she'd have worn a pair of cutoff denim shorts on such an outing, but in keeping with Mandy's usual wardrobe, she'd instead chosen a dressier short white wraparound skirt and a fitted red tank top. Benton sat next to her in khaki shorts and a burgundy polo shirt, looking as handsome as ever.

As they watched the first few innings, she found herself explaining some of the game's finer points, but she tried not to sound too well-versed, often throwing in "I think" and Mandylike giggles, claiming she knew all this because Mindy sometimes made her watch baseball on TV. Not that it would be a crime for Mandy to like baseball; Mindy just didn't feel it fit her twin's persona.

A part of Mindy wished she could just rip off her wig and be herself. She'd dropped her Mandy voice for the most part, but she did try to add an occasional bit of Mandy's personality to her remarks, actions, expressions. The truth was, as awkward and silly as the lies had become, and as much as she wanted to be her true self with him, a part of her really *did* enjoy being Mandy, just as Jane had accused. Mindy had just had a hard time completely admitting it to herself before now.

Mandy was more feminine, the kind of woman guys usually went for. Heck, no wonder Benton was nuts about her. And Mandy really was more fun-loving, more carefree. In fact, without intending to, Mindy found herself on her feet, waving her big foam finger boldly overhead when a rock song played between innings. Mindy, conversely, often cheered when a game got exciting, but she blended in with the crowd and would *never* leap up and start dancing in a stadium. And being the girl who danced, instead of the girl who just sat there was a lot more fun.

"Thanks for giving me the finger," she said to Benton when she sat down, then laughed along with him at her unintentional double entendre. "Hey, could you split another hot dog with me?"

"Still hungry, huh? Sure." He chuckled. "Never let it be said I don't take my girlfriend to the finest establishments and order only the best food."

In the next inning, the Reds earned two runs, tying the score, and Mindy sank into a baseball state of mind, thoroughly enjoying the game on the sunny, eighty-degree day. She held the hot dog in one hand, waved her big foam finger with the other and watched as Ken Griffey, Jr. stepped up to bat.

That was when the faint, distant buzz of a small airplane caught her attention, and she glanced to the sky. She expected to see a banner ad for one of the downtown bars or restaurants being dragged behind the aircraft, trying to lure customers after the game, but it was a skywriting plane, beginning to paint snowy trails of smoke across the sky.

After watching the letters *M* and *A* take shape high above her, Mindy's heart began to beat a little faster. *That plane isn't spelling Mandy, is it? Oh God. Please, no.* But when the next letter to curl across the blue backdrop slowly became an *R* instead of an *N,* she relaxed and smiled lazily at Benton as the crack of a bat drew her attention to the game.

Griffey had knocked a grounder to left field and made it easily to second. Mindy waved her foam finger and yelled with the crowd as the announcer heralded the play, and the words *Great Hit!* flashed on the JumboTron. The Reds were poised to take the lead, so Mindy shifted her gaze to home base, where the next batter took a few practice swings.

Then Benton gave her a gentle nudge. She found him pointing up, so she followed his eyes skyward to see MARRY ME, MANDY plastered across the cloudless expanse of blue.

Mindy went numb. She couldn't breathe.

Unless there was really some woman named Mandy here with her boyfriend today, this meant Benton had just proposed to her!

In front of thirty thousand people!

Yep, wine and roses, all right. Yep, she really knew Benton like the back of her hand.

Don't panic. There *were* thirty thousand people here, after all—maybe a real Mandy actually existed.

She hadn't gathered the courage to look at Benton and was formulating her next move when the older woman on her other side tapped her arm and motioned to the JumboTron. "Isn't that you, dear?"

Flicking a dumbfounded glance to the huge screen mounted over the stadium, Mindy saw herself close-up, big foam finger and all. The words MARRY ME, MANDY appeared there, too, flashing—*flashing,* for God's sake!—in bright red-and-yellow neon.

She felt like a cornered rat. No, she *was* a cornered rat. One look at her face should tell anyone that, but a tentative peek at Benton revealed that the lovestruck man was blind to it. Hope had reshaped his expression. He looked so sweet, so filled with anticipation and more handsome to Mindy than ever before.

Dragging her gaze to the JumboTron, Mindy accidentally knocked herself in the head with her big foam finger, then leaned into her hot dog, smearing ketchup on her cheek. She gaped at herself in the mirrorlike screen, her stunned, condiment-laden face blown up hundreds of times larger than normal for all to see. Then the shot widened to include Benton. Speechless, she turned to him. He offered a loving grin as he lifted one thumb to wipe away the gooey red smudge.

Thirty thousand people waited for her to give him an answer. In fact, a low, rolling cheer had risen from the crowd, and she slowly began to realize it was all for her, for them. It seemed as if the game was being held for a moment so Mindy, or Mandy, could give her answer to the man at her side while they all watched.

And that answer was simple.

She couldn't humiliate Benton in front of a stadium full of people.

She couldn't break his heart in front of them, either.

She dropped her hot dog and threw her arms around him, big foam finger and all.

The crowd went wild.

A FEW MINUTES later, after a barrage of congratulations and hearty pats on the back from strangers, Benton leaned toward her and spoke in his sexy, I-want-to-be-alone-with-you voice. "Let's get out of here." Mindy couldn't help recalling that those words had started all this, that night on the dance floor when he'd invited her into his bed. But no, *he* hadn't started this. *She* had. She was a slimeball. And she'd taken things too far. She had to fix them, once and for all.

Despite her efforts, this wasn't going to end the way she'd wanted it to. Benton wasn't going to decide he didn't want her. She was going to have to break his heart and make him hate her.

The situation became worse with the realization that had hit her in the surreal moment she'd flung her arms around him, accepting his proposal without saying yes. The fact was, if Benton knew the truth and was proposing to her, she'd have said yes then, too. A real yes.

But that didn't matter. Nothing seemed to matter now except the inevitable. She had to do the one thing she'd been determined not to since this charade had started, the very thing Jane had urged her to do—she had to tell him the truth.

"Where'd you park?" Benton asked as they left the stadium hand in hand.

They'd planned for him to pick her up at home, but

Mindy had called him saying she'd have to drive separately and meet him at the game. A client had contacted her, desperate for last-minute pre-date counseling and, in spite of appearances, Mindy *was* still Mindy; she still put her clients' needs first. Well, her clients other than Benton. To him, she'd claimed a work emergency at the office. Her unsuspecting lover had been the totally understanding, conscientious businessman he was. And Mindy had thought it a fortuitous twist of fate, giving him less time alone with her to pop the question.

"I got lucky and found street parking," she told him, pointing in the direction of her car and picking up her pace. She didn't look at him as they walked, couldn't look at him. She felt as if the last moments of her life were ticking away. She wasn't going to die when she told Benton the truth, but she knew something inside her would cease to exist when her real identity came out. It had to do with self-respect and dignity, but also with hope…and love. She supposed that until this moment, in some secret little compartment deep within her heart, she had believed this might somehow magically work itself out. But now she knew it wasn't so.

"I'm really sorry we drove separately," he said cheerfully from behind her.

She walked briskly, dragging him along, suddenly anxious to reach her car, then get this horrible event over with.

"I hate to leave you," he went on. "Tell you what, let's take your car, go someplace and celebrate, then come back for mine later. How about it?"

Oh God. He caressed her hand with his thumb in that loving way that always melted her, and for an instant, she considered *not* telling him, continuing the lie. *Just for a little while longer,* she promised herself.

But no, that was insane. This had to end now. There was no other choice.

When Mindy led Benton around a corner to her car, parked on a narrow side street, she turned to lean against it, then steeled herself. *Do this. You have to. Do it quick. Do it now.* So she didn't hesitate, and she spoke directly, almost sternly. "Benton, I have something to tell you."

He stepped close to her, extracting the big foam finger from her grip. She didn't realize she'd been digging her nails into it, clutching it like a lifeline. He laid it on the car's hood, then took both her hands in his. "What is it, darling?"

Darling? He was calling her *darling* now?

But then, he thought they were engaged. He thought they were getting *married.* Her heart shriveled in her chest.

Her next words were so painful she couldn't look into his eyes. She lowered her gaze, to his chest, then to his crotch—oh, *that* was a bad idea—and finally to his knees. Yes, knees were okay; knees were safe. "Benton, I'm...I'm afraid I can't marry you."

"Why's that?" he asked. "Because you're really Mindy?"

9

MINDY jerked her gaze to his eyes as shock crashed through her like a tidal wave. If she hadn't been leaning against her car's fender, the words would've knocked her down.

"Wh-wh-what did you just say?"

To her astonishment, Benton wore a smug, satisfied little smile, pretty much the last thing she'd expected upon turning down his marriage proposal. "I asked if you'd changed your mind because you're really Mindy. After all, going so far as getting married would make things a little messy for you, wouldn't it? Signing a false name to the marriage license would be illegal, and of course it would be difficult to explain why your sister wasn't at the wedding. But then again, you'd just tell me you were feeling ill and that it must mean Mindy was home sick in bed and you were just taking on her pain the way twins do. Isn't that right?"

The most shocking part of Benton's diatribe was the look of amusement that graced his face from start to finish. Mindy could barely process what was happening. She felt light-headed, faint, sick—and she wasn't pretending this time. "But, but, but…how?"

He tilted his head, the pleased-with-himself expression still firmly in place. "Your explanation about the bruises was weak, and besides, I saw that cute little birthmark on the inside of your knee on *both* of you.

And as far as your mysterious illness goes, you started out strong but lacked follow-through. The most telling element of all, though, was the hair.''

''The hair?'' She reached up to touch it almost protectively. She feared he was going to rip off her Mandy wig, and for some reason, even now, she couldn't bear the idea of being de-blonded that way.

''The little strands of red that peek out over your ear. I saw them after you danced out of your dress in my bedroom.'' Mindy cringed. ''And I caught a glimpse the other night when you were pretending to be sick, too.''

''I...I see.'' Her voice left her so feebly she barely heard it. Somewhere along the way, Benton had dropped her hands—or maybe she'd pulled them away, who could be sure?—and she began wringing them compulsively. They felt so empty.

''I have only one question, Mindy.'' His smile faded.

''Oh?'' She could hardly complain about one little question, all things considered, but knowing what he would probably ask made her less than enthusiastic about answering.

''Why did you do it? Why did you pretend to be someone you weren't?''

Yep, that was the question she'd feared. But Jane's voice echoed in her head. *Tell the truth.* At this point, Mindy saw no other path but honesty; besides, she couldn't have concocted another lie if her life had depended on it. And she had to get it all out in one shot or she'd never get through it. As before, she was unable to meet his eyes, even as she reached up and numbly drew the blond wig from her head.

''It started when you came into my shop with your

list of requirements for a wife. I thought they were rigid and outdated and I didn't even want to take you on as a client, but when you paid me the jacked-up fee I asked, I had no choice. And when your dates with Kathy and Anita failed so miserably, I didn't want to sacrifice another good client to you. So I decided to go myself, thinking that by the end of the evening you'd find me totally unsuitable, too, and that would be that. I'd have fulfilled my three-date obligation to you, and we'd never see each other again. But instead, no matter what I did, you still liked me. I kept trying to make you change your mind, but nothing I did worked.''

Benton stood before her, dumbstruck. A minute ago, when he'd been telling her he knew the truth, he'd felt almost gleeful to finally have it out in the open. He hadn't been able to keep quiet long enough to let her admit it—the urge to burst her delicate bubble had come over him with overwhelming force—but he'd still felt victorious. All that had been left was to hear her explanation, then tell her that no matter *who* she was, he was in love with her. That had been the plan.

Benton thought he'd have felt less humiliated if she'd turned him down on the JumboTron, if she'd gone shrieking from the stands in front of all those people.

He couldn't believe he'd misunderstood the situation so drastically. She hadn't wanted him at all; she'd been fulfilling an obligation. It had all been pretend, from her sweet, sophisticated side to her wild, adventurous side. From the long talks they'd shared to all the times they'd made love. A sharp pain seared his chest and made him dizzy. He'd been such a fool.

''Oh,'' he finally said. His mouth felt a little numb;

his voice was too quiet. "I thought you just wanted to be with me and didn't want to tell me. I thought I…brought out other sides of you, brought out the Mandy in you. Seems I misunderstood."

With that, he turned and walked away. He had nothing else to say. Everything was painfully clear.

"Benton, wait."

But he didn't wait. He put one foot firmly in front of the other as he moved up the sidewalk, turning the corner, leaving her behind. Leaving Mindy. Or Mandy. Whoever the hell she was. Forever.

ON SATURDAY NIGHT, Benton called Phil and Mike and invited them to a small, quiet pub not far from his home. He thought the outing would cheer him up, but instead, it only brought him lower. In addition to being happily married, Mike had two young sons, and Phil's wife had just given birth to a baby girl six months ago. Benton had known that when he invited them, of course, but hadn't anticipated an evening of hearing about how wonderful family life was.

"Kids," he muttered to his friends late in the evening when the alcohol had taken over. "I'm never gonna have kids." Then he turned to Mike, suddenly hopeful, raising his eyebrows. "Maybe I'll leave my house and money to your kids. Think they'd like that?"

Both guys lifted their gazes curiously, but Benton barely noticed, reaching to the bar for drink number…who knew?

"That's, uh, generous," Mike replied, looking perplexed, "but don't you think you're jumping the gun a little?"

"Or," Phil added, "at the very least, don't you

think you should leave something to your nieces and nephews?''

Benton waved a hand through the air. ''Ah, what's it matter? I'll just be lonely, eccentric Uncle Benton to all of 'em anyway. The old guy who gets passed around to a different house on every holiday out of pity. The one who walks around his big empty mansion muttering to himself all day.''

''Looks like you're already well on your way to that last part,'' Mike said with a slap on the back.

Phil lowered his voice, getting serious. ''What's wrong?''

Benton signaled to the bartender for another vodka and didn't answer. ''Women,'' he muttered instead. ''You can't trust 'em.''

''This is interesting,'' Phil said, leaning closer. ''Tell us more.''

''Yeah, you sly dog. What don't we know?''

But Benton wasn't really listening, too busy feeling sorry for himself. ''They're deceptive,'' he murmured. ''First they're redheads, then they're blondes, then they turn back into redheads again.''

''Huh?'' Mike asked, understandably confused.

Phil sighed. ''Okay, this is getting more weird than interesting.''

''And their names,'' Benton continued. ''They change their names when you're not paying attention.''

Phil and Mike exchanged glances and Benton saw Mike twirl his finger next to his head, making the universal sign for nutjob.

''Uh, buddy,'' Phil said, lowering a hand to Benton's shoulder. ''Afraid you're not making much sense tonight.''

"I'm not making much sense?" Benton bellowed, far beyond caring about a two-way conversation. "She's the one who didn't make sense."

Mike cast Phil a knowing look. "He's obviously had too much. We'd better drive him home."

And they did, Phil driving Benton in his Mercedes, Mike following in his own car.

On Sunday, Benton slept most of the day, tired and defeated, visions of blond wigs and tight, sparkly dresses dancing in his head.

He knew he'd have to call his friends and explain that he wasn't turning into a raging alcoholic as soon as he felt up to explaining what had really been wrong. But he wasn't used to failing at things, relationships or otherwise, so accounting for his current heartbreak to old pals wasn't high on his list of fun things to do.

And he'd definitely have to cancel the party they were planning for his birthday, too. Phil had called him last week, saying they wanted to throw a bash for his upcoming thirty-fifth. "If we can find a cake big enough to hold all those candles," Phil had said. Benton had laughed because he'd been happy then; he'd been seeing Mindy and thinking life was good. He'd offhandedly mentioned the party to her, hoping she'd accompany him and meet his friends. As Mindy or Mandy—he hadn't cared much at the time.

Now he wanted nothing to do with a party. For Benton, turning thirty-five with no prospects for a wife or a family was nothing to celebrate.

He kept reliving the moment Mindy had told him the truth. He'd been so sure, so arrogantly positive, that she'd masqueraded as Mandy because she wanted to be with him. It had never occurred to him there might be some other reason, let alone an embarrassing, patronizing one. The whole situation made him feel one step closer to becoming old, eccentric Uncle Benton, the mutterer. Had he actually bequeathed all his possessions to Mike and Phil's kids the previous night? Another good reason to make that phone call.

That afternoon, he showered and dragged himself to the fitness center he didn't visit as often as he should. He thought he might take a run around the track, lift some weights, work through his frustrations with physical exertion. But his efforts proved weak, his energy zapped by the rejection that kept roaring through him. He'd known Mindy was a force to be reckoned with, but he'd never thought about how that force would affect him if he found out she didn't really care for him.

The worst part, he realized as he gave up on the free weights he couldn't lift, was that he'd truly wanted to marry her, pretenses be damned. He hadn't quite known how much until she'd thrown her arms around him to the cheers of thousands of baseball fans, crushing that foam finger against his head, but then it had hit him hard. He'd found more excitement and joy with her than he'd believed a relationship could bring him. He'd been so mired in his work and ambitions for the past few years that he'd forgotten there was more to life. He'd decided he wanted a wife because he needed a companion, someone to have children with and grow old beside, but being with Mindy had shown him he could have so much more. He could see her being all those things to him, but also a thousand other things he'd never even known he wanted.

Yet it was not to be.

Upon returning home, he found a message from Mindy on his answering machine.

"Benton, this is…Mindy."

She sounded confused over who she was and it almost amused him, but not quite. Hearing her voice was at once a balm but also like ripping a scab off a wound that had just begun to heal. Okay, so it hadn't really healed at all, but if nothing else, he'd at least started accepting that she was out of his life, that the plans he'd begun to make for the future were as pointless as all the goofy things he recalled sputtering at his friends in the bar.

"Please call me. There's so much more to say. I'm so sorry about yesterday. Forgive me?"

Forgive her?

For her pretense? Yes. For breaking his heart? No.

BY THE TIME Benton came straggling into the office the next morning, he was disgusted with himself. For one thing, he was late again. For another, he didn't like the way he was handling this. He decided he could excuse himself for one misspent weekend, but he needed to snap out of it. He had a company to run. People who depended on him. Clients, employees. His father, who had built Maxwell Group from the ground up, had entrusted it to him.

"Late again," Claudia chided as he rushed off the elevator.

Her voice made his head hurt. So far this morning, *everything* made his head hurt. "Won't happen again," he reported as if she were his superior, and without waiting for a response, he headed down the hall to the meeting he knew he was missing.

As he burst through the door, every pair of eyes in the room, including Miss Binks's, found his. "At last," Percy Callendar said with a broad smile, "our fearless leader."

That hurt his head, too. He spoke quietly. "Perhaps not so fearless today, Percy."

When a noticeable pall fell over the entire table, Benton realized what he'd just done, the side of him he'd unthinkingly revealed. Clearly, a weak Benton frightened and worried them nearly as much as it did him.

"What is it, Benton? I mean, Mr. Maxwell." Miss Binks's eyelashes fluttered nervously as she addressed him.

Thinking quickly, he clutched his stomach. Mindy wasn't the only one who could put on a good act. "Just a bit of flu or something."

"This time of year?"

He sighed. "Sometimes things bring you down when you least expect it."

"Perhaps you should see a doctor." Concern etched itself across her face.

"I'll be fine, Miss Binks."

"Well, then, shall we get started?" Percy asked. But Benton didn't miss the look of awareness—or was that amusement—dancing in Percy's eyes as they shifted between Benton and his assistant.

Nor did he miss the baleful expression on Malcolm Wainscott's face as he craned his head to moon adoringly at Miss Binks. Out of recently acquired habit, Benton took a stab at seeing if his attempt to connect them had accomplished anything. "Let's begin with Malcolm and Miss Binks. How are your portfolio status report meetings progressing?"

Malcolm peered earnestly at his boss. "I've been

meaning to thank you for trusting me with that responsibility, Mr. Maxwell.''

For giving me time with Miss Binks, he meant. "Don't mention it, Malcolm. You've earned it."

"And I, for one, think it's been very productive."

Malcolm's eagerness wrenched a small smile from Benton, his first in two days. Then Benton switched his gaze to his stalwart assistant. "Miss Binks? Are you in agreement?"

She hesitated, then dropped her gaze slightly. Uh-oh. This couldn't be good. Finally raising her eyes to Benton, she sighed. "It's nothing against Malcolm— he's a wonderful worker and quite informed—but I'm afraid I don't find this new arrangement productive. In fact, it's quite *counter*productive."

Stunned, Benton raised his eyebrows.

"When I examined the reports with you, Mr. Maxwell, it was an efficient one-step procedure. Now I meet with Malcolm, then I write a report *about* the report, forward it to you, remind you to read it and answer any questions you have. Surely you can see the wastefulness."

Benton tilted his head. He felt lousy for Malcolm, both personally and professionally. Miss Binks was making him sound like a thorn in her side and likely causing him to feel worse. "Well, Miss Binks, I'll take your concern under advisement and get back to you." He looked at the rest of the people at the table. "Let's move on. Percy, how are the budget adjustments coming?"

Everyone in the room seemed to breathe a small sigh of relief as Percy began stating his budget assessments in the long-winded manner Benton welcomed more today than ever before, since he really wasn't in the mood to lead the troops. As Percy droned on, Benton thought about Malcolm and Miss Binks. His assistant had made several things clear. The news of Benton's new relationship hadn't dimmed the torch she carried for him. She wanted nothing to do with Malcolm and remained as blind as ever to his affections. And sadly, what she'd said was true—Benton had taken a system that worked and made it inefficient, all in the name of love.

So what was the point? Why was Benton trying so hard to bring them together when, deep inside, he knew the effort was doomed to fail?

And why had he let himself start believing in something so whimsical and romantic as love, anyway? When he'd met Mindy, he hadn't even been sure it existed. Now he knew it was real, but he wished he didn't. He wished he'd left well enough alone and dealt with finding a wife by himself.

Damn, he needed to shake off this depression, forget about his ill-fated attempt at love and start acting like himself again. And he shouldn't delay one more hour.

Benton Maxwell III didn't let emotions rule him. Oh sure, they might play a part in his life—he was only human—but the man he'd been before his misguided visit to Mates By Mindy knew how to keep his feelings in their proper place.

And Benton Maxwell III didn't make a fool of himself, either.

Well, not more than once, anyway. The little redhead might have him down, but he wasn't out of the game entirely.

This whole mess had started because he wanted a wife. He'd thought it would be nice to find love in the same place, but that had turned out to be a more complicated endeavor than he'd expected. Things were simpler when Benton didn't let sappy, idealistic nonsense cloud his judgment.

As far as Miss Binks and Malcolm were concerned, bringing them together had clearly been a lost cause from the beginning. He couldn't force something that wasn't there.

Yet he *could* accept circumstances as they were and make the most of them. And he could look a gift horse in the mouth one too many times. Benton wasn't going to do that anymore.

When the meeting concluded, he began doling out assignments to each person at the table, speaking with vigor, outlining goals, and as they all sat up a bit straighter to firmly meet his gaze, it was clear they knew the old Benton was back. As he finished with each employee, he excused them and moved to the next.

"Malcolm," he said, upon working his way around to the young man, "Miss Binks is right—I've created unnecessary work for her by asking you to review the status reports, so we'll scrap that idea for now. But come to my office at three o'clock this afternoon and we'll discuss other ways to expand your responsibilities."

Benton ignored the disappointment in Malcolm's eyes as he slowly pushed back his chair and exited the room, then he flicked his gaze to Miss Binks, the last remaining staff member.

"Miss Binks, are you free for lunch today?"

She looked stunned, understandably. The two of them rarely shared a meal outside the occasional group gathering. "Is there some urgent business matter to discuss?"

"Urgent, yes. Business, no." He could learn to appreciate Miss Binks—Candace, he should start calling her Candace—for what she had to offer. "It's about the relationship I mentioned to you last week."

"Oh?"

Benton saw no reason to mince words. "We've parted ways. I think getting out of the office and talking to someone will be just the thing to get her out of my system."

"ICE CREAM?" Jane asked gently as she and Mindy settled on a bench in Hyde Park Square on their lunch break. "I'll buy."

Mindy clamped her fists on the wooden seat on either side of her, eyes downcast. "That's sweet, Jane, but no thanks."

Jane raised her eyebrows hopefully and spoke as if addressing a toddler. "Mint chocolate chip, your favorite. Ooh, yummy."

Mindy shook her head and injected great drama into her words. "I can never eat mint chocolate chip ice cream again. It reminds me too much of him."

Jane smirked lightly. "No offense, Min, but you enjoyed hundreds of ice-cream cones *before* Benton. Why not eat up and let it remind you of *those* times? Better yet, why not let it remind you of that first day you met him and didn't like him, the day you nearly dropped it on his shoes! That was funny, wasn't it? Let's just pretend you *still* don't like him. How about it?"

Jane smiled hopefully, nodding enthusiastically at her suggestion, yet Mindy frowned. "Jane, I love him."

Jane frowned, too. "That's a bad attitude."

"Huh?"

"Remember the old Mindy, the love-isn't-for-me-I-just-like-creating-it-for-others Mindy? I say you bring her back. She was fun. And she got into a *lot* less trouble. She was right—who needs a man?" Jane dragged a dismissing hand through the air. "Not Mindy. Mindy's perfectly happy with her friends, her cat, her business. Mindy's one cool, confident chick who does *not* need a silly man messing up her life."

Mindy shook her head emphatically. "No, *you* were right, Jane. I *do* need a man. It's just as you said—I need him for companionship and fun and sex. And love. Maybe I hadn't quite realized it, hadn't quite admitted it to myself, but I fell in love with Benton, and it was the happiest time of my life."

"When you weren't miserable."

Mindy shrugged. "Well, yeah. But the rest of the time, when I forgot about being a crazed, lying lunatic on the loose, things were…*dreamy.*"

"All right, Patty Duke, back to earth. I know you're hurting right now, I know it feels like a huge chunk of you was ripped from your body and mauled before your very eyes, I know you think you'll never be happy again, but you will. How do I know this? Because I had my heart broken once upon a time, too, and I thought I'd never recover. But then Larry came into my life, and look at me now. I'm as happy as a frazzled, middle-aged housewife can be!" She smiled, and Mindy tried to smile back, appreciative of Jane's friendship.

But it was too soon to feel happy again, and maybe it would *always* be too soon. Maybe Jane was wrong. Maybe that big mauled chunk of her would always be missing. Love, it turned out, was powerful stuff, more so than she ever could have imagined without experiencing it firsthand. She'd never known an emotion could lift her to such heights of elation, then send her plummeting to such a low, painful place.

"I should close the shop."

"If you want to go home," Jane said, "I can stay until five."

Mindy shook her head. "No, I meant, I should close the shop *down*. For good. I have no business handing out instructions on people's love lives. And since I can't be disbarred for my disgraceful actions, I should do the responsible thing myself. Shut it all down. Close it up. Let people find each other the way they have for centuries, by chance."

Next to her, Jane released a long, drawn-out, put-upon sigh. "Mindy, Mindy, Mindy. Why, my friend, did you open this shop in the first place?"

Mindy considered the question and thought it was a good one. "Well, I suppose it didn't make much sense, in a way, did it? I'm the product of divorced parents, and until just a couple of weeks ago, I never believed I'd find love myself. But even though I've had reason to doubt love, you know I've believed in it anyway, believed it was real and that it mattered. Even if it wasn't for me. Plus, as you know, I have that knack for finding people who go together."

"That reminds me, Stacy Hennessey called to thank you for helping her out on Saturday. Her date with Greg went great, they really hit it off, and they're seeing each other again tonight. I could practically see her glowing through the phone lines."

Mindy smiled, pleased as ever to hear one of her clients had had a happy encounter because of her matchmaking skills. The moment Greg had come into the shop last week, she'd just *known* he was the guy she'd been waiting to match with quiet Stacy.

Then she remembered everything she'd been saying about why she'd opened Mates By Mindy and gave Jane a point-taken look. "Fine, you're right, I won't close the shop. But I really do feel rotten about Benton. And not just because I love him, but because I did a horrible thing to him after he trusted me with his love life. He even paid me for it, too. At the time, I thought he deserved it, but I was so wrong, Jane."

"Well, maybe you'd feel better if you returned Benton's money."

Mindy rolled her eyes. "Dr. Jane, back on the air."

Jane shrugged. "Just a thought. Forget I said anything."

Yet Mindy let out a long, conceding sigh. "Cut him a check after lunch, and I'll write a note to go with it."

A WEEK LATER, Mindy still hadn't shaken off her depression. She'd thought when Benton got her check, along with her sincere letter of apology, maybe she'd hear from him. She hadn't. Apparently, he'd moved on with his life. At least one of them had.

She sat on her couch, watching the *Casablanca* video she'd rented, nibbling on what remained of the mint chocolate chip ice cream he'd brought to her house. Okay, so she'd been wrong when she'd told Jane she could never eat it again—she had a real weakness for mint chocolate chip. And an even bigger weakness for Benton, it seemed, since she couldn't erase the memories of him from her mind.

She kept hugging her big foam finger, remembering when she was his. She thought longingly of the French maid costume she'd never get to wear for him, of all the cars they'd never steal together, of all the restaurants she'd never get to embarrass him in.

When The End flashed in black-and-white across the screen, she flipped off the TV, ditched the empty ice-cream tub in the garbage can and looked for Venus, who seemed to be avoiding her. The cat could probably sense her despair; either that, or she'd gotten tired of Mindy's constant hugging. It was when the cat had started going AWOL a few days ago that the big foam finger had taken her place in Mindy's needy arms. Finally locating Venus, Mindy picked her up and carried her to the bedroom, thinking about how Benton had changed his cat-hating ways for her once upon a time.

Lowering the cat to the bed, she spied her half-sewn Cher dress tossed in a pile of costume rubble—she hadn't had the heart to work on it since the breakup. Then she spotted a certain blond wig and thought about how she had changed when wearing it, how it had somehow energized and empowered her to be a slightly different, edgier, wilder woman. The mere memories conjured up a little of that energy inside her—the first burst of anything positive she'd felt in days.

But then she remembered everything that had happened to destroy that power and energy, and she let it depress her all over again.

She couldn't go on like this. Jane kept telling her so, and she knew it, too. Even her cat had turned on her.

She'd screwed up her life by letting Benton Maxwell fall in love with her, but she'd screwed it up much worse by letting him fall *out* of love with her.

Mindy picked up the blond wig, studied it, then

turned toward the mirror, but she didn't put the wig on. Instead, she looked at her reflection and asked herself a question.

What would Mandy do?

10

"JANE, I'm a nervous wreck!"

"Here, try this on. It'll look good with those black jeans you bought." Jane shoved a clingy top of cobalt blue in Mindy's direction.

"Ooh, you're right."

They'd decided to meet downtown at the Tower Place Mall to take Mindy's mind off what she planned to do tonight. The only problem was, every time she got nervous, she bought something. They both toted shopping bags in each hand, and all of them belonged to Mindy. If things went well this evening, she'd have tons of new clothes to wear on future dates with Benton. And if not, well, she'd be well-dressed and alone. Which was better than being poorly dressed and alone, she decided. At a moment like this, she had to hang on to any positive thoughts that came her way.

Because tonight's endeavor was very risky and might well blow up in her face.

Benton had mentioned a couple of weeks ago that his thirty-fifth birthday was coming up and that two friends were throwing him a party at O'Reilly's, an old downtown pub. "Second Saturday in June," he'd told her.

Well, today was the second Saturday in June. When she'd called O'Reilly's to make sure the party was still on—without identifying herself, of course—the guy who'd answered the phone had said the festivities started at eight but the serious fun began a little later…whatever that meant.

So Mindy had chosen to make a bold move, a totally Mandy move. She was attending Benton's party tonight, and she intended to tell him she loved him and wanted to marry him, too. She was going to go for it, throw caution to the wind and just do it! Mandy would.

Hence the nervousness currently eating her alive.

And since she was going as herself, not her evil twin, and since Benton had never seen the real her other than when she was working, what she chose to wear seemed important. It would be her personal statement about who she *really* was. That was how she and Jane had justified the spree, deciding Mindy needed some new clothes.

She exited the dressing room a moment later in the blue top and black jeans, one hand on her hip as she sashayed across an imaginary fashion-show runway. Jane waited until Mindy pivoted to face her before speaking. "This is good." She nodded and pointed, directing her finger from Mindy's shoulders all the way to her ankles. "This is very good. In fact, this is tonight's outfit."

"You think?" Mindy thought so, too, but wanted to hear Jane's reasoning.

Jane kept nodding. "It says confident but not brash. It says stylish but not overdressed. Most importantly, it says, 'I didn't labor over this outfit. It's just what I happened to pull out of my closet this morning.' It's perfect."

"All right then. *Sold,* to the panicky redhead in the corner."

Just as Mindy was about to slip back into the dressing room, Jane gasped. "Oh look! A whole rack of discount bikinis!" Mindy turned to see Jane holding up two small scraps of gold and brown snakeskin print.

Mindy shook her head. "I don't need a new suit. I have that black one-piece I bought last year." Jane, Mindy had discovered, was great at finding things she thought Mindy should spend money on.

"One-piece, schmun-piece—you need a fun piece. A fun two-piece, that is." Jane jiggled the hanger, making the bikini dance.

"I'm not that big of a pool girl. I freckle." Mindy rolled her eyes. "Besides, where on earth would I wear that?"

"Well, if things don't work out with Benton, you could take a trip. To the beach. Where they have cute lifeguards. You could fake a drowning."

"Jane, I've had enough faking to last me a lifetime." She put her hands on her hips. "And are you saying you don't think things will go well tonight? You don't think I should do it?"

Jane shook her head. "I'm not saying that at all. The way I see it, you have nothing to lose."

"Thanks for reminding me."

"That's not what I meant. But if I had your body and could flaunt it in this—" she wiggled the snakeskin again "—for the low, low price of nineteen ninety-five, it's an opportunity I wouldn't pass up."

"Fine," Mindy said, snatching the suit from Jane's fingertips. The bikini was the last thing she needed, but then again, she now possessed several shopping bags full of things she didn't need. Besides, maybe Jane was right, even if she *had* tried to squirm out of what she'd said. Things might not go as well as Mindy expected. Perhaps she should plan for the worst and surround herself with new things to wear while she sat at home crying on her annoyed cat.

Or maybe, she thought as she tried on the bikini, she shouldn't let Jane's doubts dampen her hopes. She had to be self-assured to pull this off. She had to be Mandy…without quite being Mandy.

Peering at herself in the mirror, Mindy discovered Jane was right—she looked *hot* in python!—so she added the swimsuit to her pile of impending purchases with the idea that Benton would like the way she looked in it, as well. It was no French maid outfit, but it was a very Mandy sort of purchase, and the decision to go for it was just the thing to pump Mindy up for tonight's daring venture.

MINDY ARRIVED at the bar a little later than planned, but thankfully, her watch indicated the party hadn't yet started and she still had plenty of time to prepare. She'd wanted to make sure she found the place okay and snag a parking spot nearby, as O'Reilly's location fell in the gray area of what was safe at night. She needed to go in, find the bathroom and change into her new outfit.

Unfortunately, she and Jane had shopped much later than they'd intended, only to discover when they were leaving the mall that Jane had locked her keys in her car. By the time Larry had shown up with an extra set, Mindy didn't have enough time to go home and get ready. But that was okay, she'd assured Jane. Ever since the purchase of the bikini, Mindy had felt more confident about the evening, so getting dressed at the bar was no big deal.

As she parked half a block away, a vision of tonight

implanted itself in her brain. Benton would walk in, spot her across the room and everyone else would cease to exist. They'd run into each other's arms, and Mindy would proclaim her love to a grateful and affectionate Benton.

She knew that in reality, he'd likely walk into a crowded bar where everyone would leap up and shout, "Happy Birthday!" and it would take him a while to even notice her. But the vision gave her the composure she needed as she strolled through the door, shopping bag in hand.

The old-fashioned tavern with its dark wood and brass decor was mostly empty. Two old guys nursed beers and chomped on peanuts at the bar while arguing with a husky, bearded bartender over who would win the World Series, and two younger, more clean-cut guys hung a computer-generated banner with Happy 35th, Old Man! stretched across it.

Old man, ha! she wanted to tell them. Could *they* do it three times in a row? She strongly doubted it.

"Looks like I'm in the right place," she said, more to herself than anyone else, but the taller blond man looked up with a smile.

"Oh good, you're here!"

"The cake's in back." The dark-haired guy, who sported a loud Hawaiian shirt, pointed over his shoulder through a doorway.

Mindy blinked. They were expecting her? And while it was no surprise to have a cake at a birthday party, why were they telling her about it? "Um, okay."

"I'm Phil, by the way," the blond guy said, "and this is Mike."

Mike nodded, and she nodded back. "Mindy," she

said uncertainly. "Is the, uh, ladies' room back there, too?" She motioned to the open door behind Mike.

He nodded again.

"Great." She held up her shopping bag. "I…need to change."

Both men smiled as if she'd told them a dirty joke, and she disappeared into the bathroom before trying to interpret their actions. Had Benton mentioned her, hoping she might come? But how would they know her on sight?

Well, it didn't matter. Maybe they'd had a few beers already. Dismissing their weirdness, Mindy changed into her new jeans, cute black heels and her slinky blue sleeveless top. After running her fingers through her hair for a nice mussed look, she freshened her makeup and made her way to the bar.

She'd settled on a stool and ordered a drink when someone tapped her on the shoulder. She turned to find Phil looking puzzled. "*That's* what you're wearing?"

She glanced down. Frankly, she thought she looked pretty good. Not that it was any of his business. She knew he was Benton's friend, but she'd had about enough of him and his party-shirted pal. "Yes, this is what I'm wearing. What's it to you?"

Phil's eyebrows shot up. "Well, I didn't pay two hundred and fifty dollars to watch you pop out of a cake in a pair of jeans. Sorry to be blunt, but you're gonna have to take off a little more."

Mindy's jaw dropped. "Pop out of a cake?" And then she understood. They'd hired a stripper and they thought Mindy was her. For a fraction of a second, she wanted to break into laughter, relieved to have solved the mystery and more amused than she could fathom to know they'd mistaken *her* for an exotic dancer.

But then shocking inspiration struck. What if she *were* the stripper?

What if she pulled Mandy out of retirement one last time to show Benton how much she loved him and that she'd do anything it took to express it? After all, she'd stripped for him once before, so it almost seemed apropos. Okay, so it also seemed crazy, but wasn't crazy behavior the very thing that had brought them together in the first place?

"Uh, well, yes, of course, I'll be wearing less when I pop out of the cake." She shook her head, as if she'd been confused for a moment but now everything was coming clear. "I just didn't know we were using a cake tonight, that's all. And I wanted to have a drink before I changed."

Both men looked baffled, and Mike the Hawaiian Shirt Man spoke. "So you just changed clothes to have a drink before you go change again?"

Mindy blinked. Oh dear. Think fast. "It's…a ritual." She nodded as she spoke, as if her words made perfect sense. "I change clothes several times before I strip to get me in the mood to take things off."

How stupid. They'd never buy it.

But both men shrugged, and Mindy breathed a sigh of relief. Men were easy when it came to women who were willing to shed their clothing.

"So of course I'll be taking off more for the…event. I have—" she glanced toward the shopping bag at her side and remembered "—a bikini. A bikini is good enough, isn't it?"

The two guys looked at each other, considering. "I was kind of hoping for lingerie," Mike said.

"But yeah, sure, a bikini's fine," Phil concluded.

Mindy knit her eyebrows. "Just one question. How

many people will be here for this?" *If he says fifty, I'm bolting.* "You see, I'm sort of new at the job and I still get a little nervous."

Phil gave a genuinely kind smile. "Don't worry, it'll be a small get-together, just a handful of guys."

Mike's expression was just as sympathetic and made her think more of them both. "*Nice* guys," he added.

Mindy smiled in reply. "Okay, that sounds doable."

Just then the bar door opened, and a voluptuous brunette walked in with a huge, scary guy who looked like a bodyguard behind her. She wore a trench coat.

Mindy swung her gaze to Mike and Phil. "Will you two excuse me for a moment? A couple of people I work with have just arrived, and I should see why they're here."

"Sure," Phil said. "Take your time. The party doesn't start for a while."

Mindy felt light-headed as she left the bar stool, but this was no time to start thinking about what she'd put into play, so she barreled ahead, briskly approaching the woman in the coat. "I bet you're the stripper," she said with a smile.

The woman nodded. "Where should I get ready?"

Mindy bit her lip and offered a desperate prayer that this would all work out. "Slight change of plans," she said. "Seems the guys accidentally hired two strippers for tonight, and they really only need one. But if you'll just tell me how much you're owed, I'll write you a check, and your work here is done."

The brunette exchanged surprised looks with her behemoth bodyguard, then turned to Mindy. "Get paid for nothing? Works for me." She and Mindy settled up for the evening, and Mindy watched blankly as the two departed.

As the door shut behind them, however, she realized there was no backing out, and a bit of nervousness began to set in. Time for a Mandy pep talk.

She'd come here to make up with Benton, hadn't she, and what better way to do it? She could sit on his lap and sing "Happy Birthday," and he'd think it was terribly sexy. And she had singing experience from Jane's party. Drat, if only she had her Marilyn dress. But as suggestive as the dress was, it probably wasn't skimpy enough for leaping out of a cake, so she knew fate had placed that new bikini in her hands—or on her body—for a reason. And once she and Benton became reunited, no one would even notice she wasn't taking anything else off. So this would be fine, just fine.

When Mindy returned to her stool, Phil and Mike were still there. "Any problem?" Apparently, they'd watched the whole exchange with the *real* stripper.

"No," Mindy assured him. "Just a mix-up—they came to the wrong place. But I gave them the correct address, and all's well."

"So this bikini," Phil said, raising his eyebrows as he turned the subject to the matter at hand, "what's it like?"

"It's a gold snakeskin print."

Mike grinned.

Phil smiled, too. "Well, it's probably time to get you out of sight in case our guest of honor arrives early." He ushered her off the stool and toward the back room, Mike following with her shopping bag in hand.

They escorted her into an office, currently home to an enormous white-plastic layer cake, and Mike lowered her bag into a chair. "You've still got plenty of time to get ready, though, so no rush."

Mindy swallowed. "That's good. I can…practice my moves a little." Starting by making some up.

"There's a mirror behind this door." Phil pointed. "And we'll be back to wheel you out in the cake when it's time."

Once Mindy was alone, she turned toward the big, silly-looking cake. A part of her *still* couldn't believe what she'd so haphazardly set in motion here.

Popping out of a cake, she reasoned, wasn't really similar to stripping, it was more of an old-fashioned burlesquelike act, an outdated, quaint, slightly humorous custom not really designed to titillate. Right?

She swallowed hard, hoping she was indeed correct about that, because dancing for Benton in his bedroom was one thing, but dancing for a bunch of men—or even a few men—in a bar was quite another. Yet this was for Benton, she reminded herself. All to show him she cared for him, *loved* him.

And maybe that was why she'd decided to do something this utterly crazy. Because Benton really *did* bring out the Mandy in her, just as he'd said before he walked away from her. She hoped her decision to pop out of his birthday cake would show him just how much he had changed her.

She'd come here to be bold, hadn't she? She'd come to show Benton—and maybe herself—that Mandy wasn't just an act, that Mandy was a real, true part of her.

As Mindy dug through her bag and extracted the little bikini, she decided she couldn't think of a better way to prove it to both of them. In the end, her plan would come off without a hitch, and they'd have a great story to tell their grandchildren.

Well, once their grandchildren were over twenty-one.

BENTON LOOKED around the bar, decorated with balloons and a banner reminding him he was getting old. He knew Phil and Mike meant well and were only joking, but his birthday still forced him to recall his regrets and recent failures.

He really *should've* canceled this party, but every time he'd tried during his recent phone conversation with Phil, his friend had interrupted him. Phil had started saying how they needed to spend more time together and not let life get in the way. Benton could tell he and Mike were concerned about him after his night of drunkenness. He could've explained that it was a needless worry, that he was back on track, his old self again, but it had seemed too complicated to go into. He hadn't been ready to enlighten either of them about Mindy. And he would've felt like an ass to call off the party knowing how much his friends wanted to have it.

Not that Benton was letting his emotions rule him. As he'd promised himself, he'd readopted the habit of keeping them in their proper place. Appreciating your friends, that was a proper place. Letting yourself get wrapped up in a woman? Benton had determined it wasn't for him.

Oh damn, a pile of gifts was stacked on the bar. He'd told Mike and Phil no presents. If the banner was any indication, he had nothing to look forward to but a bunch of ''Over the Hill'' boxer shorts and bogus bottles of Viagra. And, of course, he'd probably discover that Miss Binks had gotten his name engraved on something gold.

"Hey, buddy, how's it goin'?" Mike slapped an arm around Benton's shoulder. He was either drunk or still worried about Benton.

"What's with the shirt?" Benton pointed to the Hawaiian print, not Mike's usual fare, even if he wasn't always as formal as Benton.

Mike shrugged. "Carrie found it on sale somewhere and thinks I look cute in it. She thought it would be festive for tonight, so I figured, why not?"

Yeah, Benton knew how a woman could alter the way you lived your life. He didn't particularly like being reminded of it, or knowing his friend had fallen prey, as well, so he decided he needed a drink. "I'm going to get a glass of wine."

Mike laughed. "No wine tonight, buddy. They don't even serve it here. It's beer or hard liquor. But hey, after what happened the last time we saw you, I'd suggest sticking with beer. Or maybe Kool-Aid."

Mike winked, and Benton nodded, hardly in a position to argue the point.

He spoke to some other old friends at the bar, then took a sip of the beer someone had shoved into his hand, forced to remember he'd recently drunk beer with Mindy at the baseball game.

A hand landed on Benton's shoulder and he turned to find Phil, who gave him a hug. Clearly, being a family man was affecting Phil, turning him into a "sensitive guy." Benton had put all that emotional baggage in the closet where it belonged and he intended to keep it there, but it would be easier if everyone else would do it his way. "Take a look around, and if everybody's here, we'll get started with the evening's *entertainment*."

Benton drew back slightly. "There's entertainment?" From Phil's inflection, he got the idea it was of the feminine nature.

"Oh *yeah*." Suddenly Mr. Family Man seemed overly enthusiastic about a show Benton strongly suspected wasn't for family viewing.

Shaking off his surprise, Benton scanned the bar. Several guys from his college days had dropped in, as well as a few other friends he'd met since. But he didn't see… "The guys from my company you invited aren't here yet, so you might want to hold off a little while. And…I invited someone on my own who hasn't arrived, either." He didn't really care if any of them showed up, but hey, if there was entertainment, may as well wait. Poor Malcolm Wainscott probably needed such a diversion. And it would likely provide Percy with a handful of humorous remarks to pass around the office come Monday morning.

Not that Benton was particularly thrilled about the idea of some Nurse Goodbody climbing all over him, especially in front of his employees, which was bound to happen since he was the birthday boy. But he was gliding through life these days without much concern for anything but keeping himself in that unemotional place that let him function without the presence of a certain redhead. Whatever happened happened. No big deal.

WHEN MIKE AND PHIL returned to the office, Mindy was crouching inside the cake in her bikini and heels. She'd been practicing her exit. And she'd decided without doubt she could do this! She could be Mandy for Benton.

"Ready?" Mike asked, peering down at her.

"As I'll ever be," she murmured.

Phil gave her an encouraging wink, then closed the white lid on her cake.

As the big fake cake was being wheeled out of the office and down the hall toward the barroom, Mindy looked at her scrunched-up self and realized, for the first time, that she was truly about to pop out of a cake wearing a skimpy bikini in a roomful of strange men!

What have I done?

She'd made a huge mistake, that was what! What on earth had she been thinking?

As panic set in, Mindy poked her head out of the cake, flipping the lid open. She had to get out of there.

"Not quite yet," Mike said, gently pushing her head down and shutting her in the cake again.

Then it was too late. Mike announced, "Gentlemen, a little gift for Benton's birthday," and Mindy sensed herself being rolled through the doorway and into the bar. A few masculine cheers and whistles filtered through the phony confection, and Mindy felt completely trapped.

Where was Mandy? "Deserter," Mindy murmured under her breath. Apparently, Mindy had finally found the one thing even Mandy wouldn't do!

The first notes of some sensual-sounding song began to play. It wasn't helping.

But she was stuck, whether she liked it or not, since she doubted the cake had an escape hatch. So she mustered up her courage and lectured herself. *You have to do what you planned, what you practiced. There's no way out of it.*

"Uh, cake girl," Phil called a few seconds later when she hadn't appeared. He rapped lightly on the lid. "We're ready for you."

Just do it. For Benton. He'll love it! He'll love you!

Taking a deep breath and summoning all her nerve, Mindy burst through the top of the cake, arms poised above her head as if to say, Ta-da! She spotted Benton sitting directly in front of her among ten or fifteen other nameless, faceless spectators in time to watch his mouth drop open.

"Surprise!" she shouted. "I'll marry you!"

That was when she noticed the petite, sophisticated blonde hanging on his arm.

11

OH, DEAR GOD—Benton had a date! A date who was clinging to him as if she owned him, for heaven's sake! She was clearly everything Benton had ever wanted in a woman, certainly everything he'd asked Mindy to find for him. Worse, she was everything Mindy wasn't.

At the same time, Mindy and the woman said, "Who's she?"

Someone turned off the music, and silence fell over the scene.

Mindy had never seen Benton look more flabbergasted, which was really saying something, considering all the stuff Mandy had pulled when they were together. Slowly, he cleared his throat and spoke awkwardly. "This is Candace Binks, my associate and date for the evening. And this is Mindy…or is that Mandy?" He gave her a pointed look, which, amazingly, was the first thing to make her blush tonight.

Mindy knew in that heart-stopping moment she'd made a more horrible blunder than she ever could have realized when she'd been stuck in the cake. Benton had moved on…with Miss Blond Sophistication, who sat glaring at her. It felt as if Mindy's every hope since the minute she'd fallen for him were caving in on her.

She also knew that as hideous and humiliating as it was, she had it coming, every bit of it.

But she didn't have to stand around and take it. She had to get out of that room, away from the whole bar, fast.

Mindy climbed awkwardly, hurriedly, from the cake, aware of the countless frozen stares directed her way. She stumbled to the floor, barely able to keep her shoes on as she let go of the fake icing.

Then she caught her balance and went darting across the bar toward the door, all the while praying Benton hadn't seen the tears that had begun rolling down her cheeks.

"MINDY!" Pushing to his feet, Benton turned in time to the see the door close behind her.

"Benton?" Miss Binks—he couldn't really think of her as Candace no matter how hard he tried—popped up beside him. "Was that—was that—"

Poor Miss Binks. Benton knew he'd erred in trying to date the woman. Despite his efforts, everything they did together was forced and stiff and awkward, and the saddest part was that she hadn't seemed to notice. He'd made a terrible mistake by trying to connect with someone he had no romantic feelings for and a worse mistake by bringing her here tonight. His entertainment was Mindy? He still couldn't believe it. He turned to his assistant. "Yes, Miss Binks, that was the woman I was recently involved with."

"And she's a *stripper?*" Miss Binks looked horrified.

Benton hadn't the time to explain, especially since he had no idea how Mindy had ended up bursting out of that cake. "Evidently. But the bigger issue is—" he looked her squarely in the eye "—I'm a terrible person. I've led you on and used you when I knew in my heart I still cared for her. I'm sorry, but I have to go after her.''

With that, he turned her to face young Malcolm Wainscott who, as usual, gaped sympathetically in her direction. As if reading Benton's mind, Malcolm started toward her. Benton would make a couple out of them yet.

Leaving the matter in Malcolm's hands, Benton raced toward the door, pausing long enough to shoot Mike and Phil a warning glare. ''And you two, when I get back—''

Phil threw up his hands helplessly. ''Hey, we didn't know you knew the stripper, Mr. Casanova.''

''She's not a stripper,'' Benton said, adding under his breath, ''or not before tonight, anyway.''

As O'Reilly's door shut behind him, Benton searched up and down the city sidewalk, but he saw no sign of Mindy. Damn it, he'd tarried too long. Then it occurred to him that she should be easy to spot. He approached a well-dressed couple strolling toward him. ''Have you seen a girl in a bikini and high heels?''

The man pointed over his shoulder. ''She took a left through the crosswalk onto Vine Street. But you'd better hurry. She was really moving.''

MINDY HAD no idea where she was running to or why. She'd passed her car eons ago, realizing her purse and keys remained in the bar, the one place on the earth she'd rather be even less than sprinting up the street in a bikini.

At every turn, people stared, horns honked, catcalls echoed around her. She looked like a stripper on the run. She *was* a stripper on the run. And she was scared and alone and wanted nothing more than to go back in time and do this evening differently. If she had the chance, she'd be smart and stay home tonight, forget about being Mandy and forget about getting Benton back, because she knew it was impossible. Mindy's heart crumbled a little more each time she remembered seeing him with that woman. They were probably planning their wedding right this very minute.

"Woo-hoo! Hey, baby, where ya goin' so fast?"

A flashy car full of college-age boys went honking past, the inhabitants leaning out to leer at her. Mindy picked up her pace. Maybe she could get to the Main Street entertainment district and beg someone for enough change to call Jane. Of course, that meant a lot more woo-hoos and the accompanying potential danger, but she didn't think she had any choice at this point.

"Well, hello there."

Mindy jogged past the middle-aged man without acknowledging him, as if she were just out for a run. But her feet were killing her, and it was a long way to the Main Street bars.

"Mindy!" a voice called behind her. "Mindy, wait!"

She gasped, stopped, looked over her shoulder. It was Benton! He'd followed her!

But she was crying, and he had that little blond toothpick to love now. She turned and resumed running, unable to face him.

"Mindy, honey! Stop! Wait!"

It was so tempting—he was calling her honey again. But that meant nothing. He felt sorry for her, frightened someone would attack her. She harbored the same fear, of course, but that was beside the point at the moment. She jogged on.

Until she turned a dark corner, coming face-to-face with three less-than-reputable-looking young men, downright scary, in fact. One had a scar on his cheek, and another had clearly spent most of his life at a tattoo parlor. She pulled up short. "Oh!"

The scraggly guys all stopped what they were doing to look her up and down, and the one with the greasiest hair flashed a wide grin. "How much, sweetheart?"

"How much?" Then she understood; they thought she was a prostitute. Sadly, she couldn't blame them. "Oh I'm not, not…" Mindy started backing up, but as the snickering guys began to walk toward her, she had the ominous feeling she wasn't moving fast enough and that she might have landed herself in serious trouble.

"Mindy." Benton's strong voice hit her like the warm glow of a lighthouse in a storm. She peeked over her shoulder and flinched at the reassuring sight of him, all broad chest and wide shoulders.

Greasy Hair stepped forward. "Hey, buddy, we found her first."

"The lady's with me," Benton said in a way that left little room for doubt. Throwing his sports jacket over her shoulders, he pulled her around the corner.

Neither of them spoke as he led her across the street to an empty bench next to a bus stop, a place that felt quiet and much safer than where they'd just been. Finally, as they settled next to each other, he looked into her eyes, then reached out to wrap her in a firm, relief-filled embrace. "Are you *crazy?*"

She pulled back enough to look up at him, feeling

more than a little sheepish. "Yeah, I think so. If not, I'm getting very close."

Benton sighed, releasing his hold on her. He looked so tired, and Mindy feared much of that was her fault. He dropped his gaze to his feet, then raised it. "Honey, just tell me one thing. What on earth were you doing in that cake?"

Mindy bit her lip. This was her chance to say everything she wanted to, only it took a little more courage knowing Benton had already found another woman.

"Well, the cake was a last-minute decision, but...I came to your party tonight to tell you how sorry I am for my deception and to explain what I didn't get to say after the ball game. Which is that I didn't keep seeing you just to fulfill my obligation to you. I did it because I cared about you. And I guess I'd also like you to know I'm not really as crazy as I probably appeared on many occasions, but that the situation just spiraled out of control no matter how I tried to fix it. I'm usually quite ethical—I've never even stolen a piece of gum." She stared at her hands, which she wrung in her lap, and spoke faster. "But I understand why you're angry and can't forgive me. I've done nothing worthy of forgiveness. And even though you've found someone else, I just need to tell you one last thing, Benton."

"What's that?" he said softly.

"I love you."

Benton stayed quiet for a moment, then let out a long, heavy *whoosh* of breath, looking uncharacteristically harried. He ran one hand through his hair. "Really? You love me?"

Mindy sighed, still not quite able to look him in the

eye after such a confession. "Believe it or not, I wouldn't lie about something like that. But I'm glad you've found someone more like you were looking for, someone who fits your list, since I'm hardly what you want in a woman anyway."

"You little nut," he said.

That made her look at him.

To her surprise, he was smiling. "Honey, don't you know you're *exactly* what I want?"

"Huh?"

"Maybe it didn't start out that way, but you've *shown* me what I want, practically *slapped* me in the face with it."

Mindy cringed lightly.

Yet Benton only laughed. "No, I'm glad. I never would have believed it otherwise. And ever since we broke up, I've been trying to go back, trying to be the guy I used to be before you came along, but I'm just not happy. Not without you. And I know precisely what I need to do about it."

With that, Benton left the bench and dropped to one knee on the dimly lit sidewalk, the summer night hanging warm and dark around them. He peered intently into Mindy's eyes as he took her hand. "Ms. Mindy McCrae, will you marry me?"

Mindy sucked in her breath, trying to absorb what was happening. It seemed unreal. "But what about Candace Finks, or Plinks, or whatever her name is?"

He shook his head. "She doesn't matter to me, Mindy. I left her to come after you, and I have a feeling that right now she's hooking up with someone who can make her much happier than I ever could."

"Still," Mindy argued, "are you sure about this? Are you sure you want to marry a woman who lies, and falls off her heels in nice restaurants, and frequents sex shops, and pops out of cakes in bikinis? And I'm not even blond. Think about this, Benton. You're a prominent businessman. You have a reputation.''

Benton shrugged, smiling at her. ''So now I'll have a *new* reputation. I'll be known as the guy with the wildest, sexiest, most fun wife in town.''

Mindy still couldn't believe it. Blood pounded in her ears, her heart beat like a bongo drum in her chest, and if she wasn't mistaken, all her dreams were about to come true. But this time she had to make completely certain everything was out in the open between her and Benton; she wasn't letting any more secrets stand between them, on purpose or otherwise. She planted her hands on his shoulders as he continued kneeling before her. ''Okay, just a couple more things before I say yes.''

He laughed. ''Name 'em.''

''You have to understand that I'm not normally like Mandy was, but you were right—you do bring out the wild woman in me, so, well…I'm trying to tell you that I'm a mixed bag, I'm everything you've seen in Mindy, and to my own surprise, I'm everything you saw in Mandy, too.''

Benton lifted one hand to cup her cheek. ''I understand that perfectly. And I love both of you equally.''

Oh wow—he loved her! He really loved her! Hearing the words leave his lips so easily, as if it were meant to be, made her heart swell.

''And you have to dress up as Sonny Bono this Halloween.''

''What?'' Naturally, that one took him a little aback.

''You see, I always go to Jane's Halloween party as some flamboyant woman like Madonna or Marilyn

Monroe, and this year I'm going as Cher. So...it'll be the perfect way to initiate you into true Mindyhood!''

He let out another laugh, shaking his head lightly. ''Don't you think I'm a little tall to be Sonny?''

She smiled into his beautiful blue eyes. ''Don't you get it? That's the best part! It's hysterical.''

''All right, Mindy, for you, I'll be Sonny.'' His voice sounded sweetly conceding. ''Now, once and for all, will you marry me?''

Without further delay, Mindy threw her arms around Benton's neck, and this time, she didn't neglect to whisper one pertinent word in his ear. ''Yes. Yes, yes, yes!'' It seemed worth repeating.

A moment later, Benton pulled back to gaze at her. ''And not only is my wife-to-be fun, she runs a highly lucrative business with a success rate of...what? Ninety-six percent now?''

Mindy giggled at the realization. ''This proves it. I really *can* find a match for *anyone*.''

''I was that tough?''

''Yes, you were.'' She smiled. ''But I was actually talking about me.''

We've been making you laugh for years!

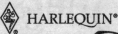 **HARLEQUIN®**

Duets™

**Join the fun in May 2003
and celebrate Duets #100!
This smile-inducing series,
featuring gifted writers and
stories ranging from amusing to zany,
is a hundred volumes old.**

This special anniversary volume offers two terrific
tales by a duo of Duets' acclaimed authors.
You won't want to miss...

Jennifer Drew's You'll Be Mine in 99

and

The 100-Year Itch by Holly Jacobs

With two volumes offering two special stories every
month, Duets always delivers a sharp slice of the lighter
side of life and *especially* romance. Look for us today!

Happy Birthday, Duets!

Visit us at www.eHarlequin.com

HD100TH

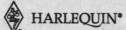

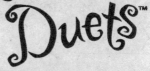

TWO ROMANTIC COMEDIES IN ONE FUN VOLUME!

Don't miss double the laughs in

Once Smitten
and
Twice Shy

From acclaimed Duets author
Darlene Gardner

Once Smitten—that's Zoe O'Neill and Jack Carter, all right! It's a case of "the one who got away" and Zoe's out to make amends!

In *Twice Shy,* Zoe's two best friends, Amy Donatelli and Matt Burke, are alone together for the first time and each realizes they're "the one who never left!"

Any way you slice it, these two tales serve up a big dish of romance, with lots of humor on the side!

Volume #101
Coming in June 2003

Available at your favorite retail outlet.

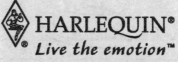

HARLEQUIN®
® *Live the emotion*™

Visit us at www.eHarlequin.com

HDDD99DG

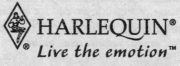

Two women in jeopardy...
Two shattering secrets...
Two dramatic stories...

VEILS OF DECEIT

USA TODAY bestselling author

JASMINE CRESSWELL

B.J. DANIELS

A riveting volume of scandalous secrets, political intrigue and
unforgettable passion that you will not want to miss!

*Look for VEILS OF DECEIT in April 2003
at your favorite retail outlet.*

HARLEQUIN®
Makes any time special ®

Visit us at www.eHarlequin.com

PHVOD

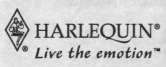

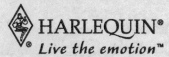

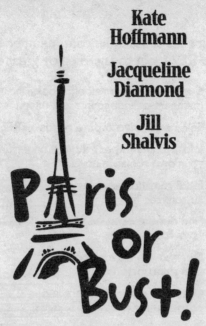